MIDWIFE'S CHRISTMAS PROPOSAL

BY
FIONA McARTHUR

MILLS &
BOON®

Published in Great Britain 2014
by Mills & Boon, an imprint of Harlequin (UK) Limited,
Eton House, 18-24 Paradise Road, Richmond, Surrey, TW9 1SR

© 2014 Fiona McArthur

ISBN: 978-0-263-90805-3

Harlequin (UK) Limited's policy is to use papers that are natural,
renewable and recyclable products and made from wood grown in
sustainable forests. The logging and manufacturing processes conform
to the legal environmental regulations of the country of origin.

Printed and bound in Spain
by Blackprint CPI, Barcelona

Dear Reader

I've loved Simon Campbell since he was a twenty-year-old on his first visit to Lyrebird Lake. That was about ten years ago in real time.

Simon has always made me smile, and has made me want to write his story for years. Readers have asked for him, and he's been in the back of my mind, but I just couldn't find the right woman for him—and he deserved the right woman.

Simon even visited in a couple of the Lyrebird Lake stories—a fleeting visit…just enough to remind me how much I cared about him, how much potential I always felt he had as a hero for the right woman. In the meantime he cared for his sisters, grew in his work, but always something was missing.

And then along came Tara… Tara who was so externally tough, so inwardly fragile, so able to be incredibly giving but so unskilled at relationships because she'd never had the chance. Tara who had missed out on so much in her childhood that only someone like Simon could hope to even the scales. Simon and the magic of Lyrebird Lake.

I've so enjoyed sharing with Tara and Simon in their journey to falling in love. I've loved the whole Christmas setting. I've loved revisiting the lyrebird dance. And I've absolutely *loved* setting a little of Maeve and Rayne's story amidst it all for the next book. I hope you do too.

Happy Christmas!

Fi xx

Dedication

To my son Scott, who gifted me my first parachute jump and the pictures that went with it. And to the experience that I knew I would put into this book.

And to Lawrence, my chute buddy from Coffs Skydivers, who made it such fun that I was never, ever scared.

Mother to five sons, **Fiona McArthur** is an Australian midwife who loves to write. Mills & Boon® Medical Romance™ gives Fiona the scope to write about all the wonderful aspects of adventure, romance, medicine and midwifery that she feels so passionate about—as well as an excuse to travel! Now that her boys are older, Fiona and her husband, Ian, are off to meet new people, see new places, and have wonderful adventures. Fiona's website is at www.fionamcarthurauthor.com

CHAPTER ONE

Simon looked away from the road as he drove and across to his sister. Saw the tiny furrow in her brow even while she was sleeping. His eyes returned to the car in front. So she was still angry with him. Where had he gone wrong? All he'd ever wanted to do was protect his family. Protect Maeve from making the same mistakes their mother had made.

Maybe he felt more responsible than other siblings because the day he'd found out he was only a half-brother to Maeve and the girls had been devastating and he did wonder if he'd over-compensated.

But he was concerned about Maeve. About the way she'd been taken for a ride and she still couldn't see it. If Simon was honest with himself, he was just as hurt because he'd thought Rayne was his friend and he'd been suckered in as well. His sister's predicament had been all his fault.

Simon could feel his knuckles tighten on the wheel and he consciously relaxed them. He needed a holiday, and Maeve needed somewhere safe away from the baby's father if he ever came back, so maybe Lyrebird Lake was a good choice, like Maeve said.

And it was Christmas.

Two hours later they drove into the driveway of the Manse Medical Centre, Lyrebird Lake. The long day drive north from Sydney had been accomplished with little traffic issues or conversation. The last hour since they'd turned away from the coast had been unusually relaxing as they'd passed green valleys and bovine pedestrians. It was good to be here finally.

Simon felt that warmth of homecoming he'd forgotten about in the rush and bustle of his busy life—almost like he could feel one of Louisa's enthusiastically warm hugs gearing up—as he slowed the car.

The engine purred to a stop and Maeve woke. She smiled sleepily, then remembered they were at odds with each other, and the smile fell away.

He watched her twist awkwardly in her seat as she took in the dry grass and huge gum trees 'I've heard such a lot about this place over the years. Thanks for bringing me, Simon.'

The tension in his shoulders lessened. At least she was talking to him again. He should never have mentioned his reservations about her idea of giving birth at Lyrebird Lake. That had been his obstetrician's point of view. Life had compartments, or should have, and he usually kept everything separate and in control.

Look what had happened when Maeve had lost control.

Simon's eyes travelled over the familiar sights—the hospital and birth centre across the road from Louisa's house, the sleepy town just down the road, and the sparkling harp-shaped lake to the left behind the trees.

Unexpectedly, considering the mood he'd been in when he'd started out for here against his will, he couldn't do anything but smile as he eased his car under the carport at the side of the house.

'Curious.' Simon admired the old but beautifully restored Harley-Davidson tucked into a corner and then shrugged. He couldn't imagine Louisa on it but there were always interesting people staying at the manse.

It didn't seem ten years since he'd first come here with his new-found dad, Angus, but this big sprawling house Angus had brought him to all those years ago looked just the same. He'd arrived expecting awkwardness with his fledgling relationship with his birth father, and awkwardness staying with strangers in this small country town. But there hadn't been any.

He glanced at Maeve. 'Louisa will have heard us arrive.'

'Louisa used to be the housekeeper before she married your grandfather? Right?'

'Yep. They married late in life before he passed away. I stay with her when I come at Christmas.'

Simon climbed out quickly so he could open her door, but of course, Maeve was too darned independent. By the time they reached the path out front Louisa stood at the top of the steps, wiping her hands on her apron, and beamed one of Lyrebird Lake's most welcoming smiles.

Simon put his bag down and leapt up the two stairs to envelop the little woman in a hug. She felt just as roundly welcoming as he remembered. 'It's so good to see you, Louisa.'

'And you too, Simon. I swear you're even taller than last year.'

He had to smile at that as he stepped back. 'Surely I've reached an age where I can't keep growing.' He looked back at his sister, standing patiently at the bottom of the steps. 'Though with your cooking there is a possibility I could grow while I'm here.'

He offered a steadying hand but Maeve declined, made her way determinedly balancing her taut belly out front, as she climbed to the top of the stairs, so he guessed he wasn't totally forgiven.

He missed the easy camaraderie they used to have and hoped, perhaps a little optimistically, that Lyrebird Lake might restore that rapport as well. He guessed he had been out of line in some of the things he'd said about her choice in men and choice in birthing place.

'This is my youngest sister, Maeve. Maeve, this is my grandmother, Louisa.'

Louisa blushed with pleasure. 'You always were a sweetheart.' She winked at Maeve. 'Grandmother-in-law but very happy to pretend to be a real one.'

Maeve held out her hand. 'It's nice to finally meet you. Simon's told us a lot about you and everyone here. He says you're a wonderful cook.'

He saw Louisa's kind eyes brush warmly over Maeve and Simon relaxed even further. Of course Louisa would make them both feel wanted. 'Boys need their food.' He smiled to himself because he wasn't sure how he qualified for boy when he'd left thirty behind.

Louisa went on, 'You're very welcome here, dear,' as she glanced at Maeve's obvious tummy. 'It will be lovely to have a baby back in the house again, even if only for a wee while.'

Simon squeezed her plump shoulder. 'Dad and Mia not here?'

'They're coming over for dinner tonight. They thought it would be less overwhelming for Maeve if she had a chance to settle in first.'

She turned to Maeve. 'And we'll take it gradually to meet everyone else. There's a huge circle of family and friends who will want to catch up with Simon and meet you.'

Simon went back to pick up their bags and followed Louisa and Maeve into the house. The scent of cedar oil on the furniture made his nose twitch with memories—overlaid with the drifting promise of fresh-cut flowers and, of course, the tantalising aroma of Louisa's hot pumpkin scones.

His shoulders sagged as his tension lessened with each step he made into the house. He should have come here earlier. Leaving it until now had been crazy but his last two breech women had come in right at the last minute and he hadn't wanted to leave them uncertain about who would be there for them.

But enough. He needed to let go of work for a while and just chill, a whole month to Christmas and his first real break in years—and maybe the strain wasn't all on Maeve's side because he'd been holding on too tight for a while now.

This was what this place was good for. Finding the peace you were supposed to find as Christmas approached.

Behind a bedroom door in the same house Tara Dutton heard the car arrive and when, minutes later, footsteps sounded down the hall she rolled over in bed, yawned and squinted at the clock.

Two o'clock in the afternoon. She'd had six hours sleep, which was pretty good. Her mouth curved as she rolled back onto her back and stretched.

Last night's sharing of such a long, slow, peaceful labour and in the end a beautiful birth just as the sun had risen made everything shiny new. Babies definitely liked that time just before morning. Man, she loved this job.

She wriggled her toes and then sat up to swing her legs out of bed. Heard calm voices. Relief expanded, which was crazy when she didn't know them—but they were here safely. It would be Angus's son, Simon, and his sister. They arrived today and she admitted to a very healthy curiosity about the man everyone obviously adored, and even more so for his sister.

Simon's arrival had been the main topic of conversation for the last few days but Tara was more interested in Maeve.

Twenty-five, pregnant and a newly qualified midwife. Two out of three things Tara had been before she'd come here. Pregnancy wasn't on her agenda.

But that was okay. She breathed deeply and vowed again not to let the unchangeable past steal her present, and thankfully the calm she found so much easier to find in Lyrebird Lake settled over her like the soft quilt on her bed.

Clutching her bundle of fresh clothes, she opened the door to the hallway a crack to check the coast was clear, then scooted up the polished wooden floor to the bathroom and slipped inside.

Simon heard the bedroom door open from the kitchen and leaned back precariously in his chair until the two front legs were off the floor, and craned his neck to see who was in the hall. He glimpsed the back of a small, pertly bottomed woman in men's boxer shorts, one tiny red rose tattooed on her shoulder exposed by the black singlet as she disappeared into the bathroom.

His mouth curved as the years dropped away. He remembered arriving here with his father and their first sight of the woman who would later become his darling stepmother.

See! Always someone interesting staying in this place, he thought to himself again with a smile, and eased the front legs of the chair back on the floor.

When Tara stepped out of the bathroom thirty minutes later she felt nothing like the crumpled sleepyhead she'd been when she'd slipped in.

Her glance in the mirror over the claw-foot bath had reassured her. Blonde hair spikily fresh from the shower and her eyes confident and ready to meet the new guy and his intriguing sister.

Tara had experienced a lot of heartache and struggle in her life and it had made her wary of meeting new people. But the shadows of her past had made her who she was today—her T-shirt said it all: 'Woman With Attitude'.

As she walked back towards her room she passed the open door of one of the guest rooms. She couldn't help but have a tiny peek inside.

Simon's bag lay open on the bed, and she blinked at the neatly folded clothes in piles lined up in a row as she drew level, unlike her own 'bomb-hit' room, and she vowed she'd keep her door shut until he left.

Simon came into view, busily unpacking, and must have become aware of the eyes on him from the doorway. He glanced up, smiled, and she faltered. Man, that was some smile, like a warm breeze had blown down the hall and into her face, and Tara nearly tripped on the towel that slipped unexpectedly from her fingers.

'Hi, there. You must be Tara.'

She bent quickly to retrieve the towel. 'And you're Simon.' Tara moistened her lips. Louisa had said he was a bit of hunk like his dad but she'd put that down as favouritism for a relative. She certainly hadn't expected the fantasy that suddenly swirled in her head. Something like inviting him in two doors down for some seriously red-hot tumbling, but, *mamma mia,* he had a wicked bedroom grin.

Whoa, there, libido, where did you spring from? More to the point, where have you been?

Then he stepped closer and held out his hand and she forgot to think, just responded, and his fingers closed around hers, cool and surprisingly comforting, as he leaned forward with grace and unselfconscious warmth so that she couldn't be offended as he unexpectedly kissed her cheek.

'It's very nice to meet you.'

A cheek-kisser? Her brain clicked in. And nice to meet you, too, mister. There was nothing gushing or sleazy about the way he'd done the deed but she still wasn't quite sure how he managed to get away with it.

It was as if his whole persona screamed gentleman and usually the goody-two-shoes type turned her off. Though she was trying to change her tastes from bad boys to normal men after the last fiasco.

This guy made her think of one of those lifesavers

on the beach at Bondi—tall, upstanding, with genuine love of humanity, careful of other people's safety but perfectly happy to risk their own lives to save yours. She blinked. And rumour said that apparently this guy wasn't even shackled to some discerning woman.

She was not bowled over! Not at all! She liked Angus for his solid dependability but this Simon beat his father hands down on the warmth stakes, that was all.

He was still waiting for her to answer him. Question? 'Nice to meet you, too.' What else could she say except something to get her out of his doorway? 'I'd better leave you to unpack.'

He didn't look like he wanted her to leave but she forced her feet to move. By the time she made it back to her bedroom her neck was hot with embarrassment. With great restraint she closed her door gently and with a sigh leant against it.

Talk about vibration. So much vibration it was lucky they hadn't spontaneously combusted. Holey dooley, she was in trouble if they were both going to live in this house for the next few weeks and react like that. Or maybe it was one-sided and he was totally oblivious to her. She smiled at her feet. Somehow she doubted it.

Simon watched her go. Couldn't help himself, really. Not a beauty in the stereotypical sense, her face was too angled for that, but she was a sassy, sexy little thing, and she had a definite pert little wiggle when she walked. She reminded him a bit of Maeve's girlfriends with that bolshie, I'm-my-own-woman persona that young females seemed to have nowadays.

Lord, he sounded like an old man but, seriously, this generation made him smile. But, then, didn't all women make him smile? Which might be why he hadn't seemed to find himself tied to just one. Problem with growing up with four sisters? Or problem with him and commitment?

Not that he didn't plan to have a family, settle down and be the best dad and husband he could be, but pledging to stay with one woman had been a tad difficult when he really didn't believe the odds of finding his other half.

Maybe he would end up in Lyrebird Lake at some stage, though after this last horror year he couldn't see himself taking the holistic approach to birth that was the norm here.

He turned back to the unpacking. Lined up the paired socks in the drawer and placed his folded jocks beside them. His last girlfriend had said his fussiness drove her mad and he was tempted to mess the line up a little but couldn't do it.

His sisters had always thought it hilarious that he liked things tidy. Having lived briefly with all of them as adults at one time or another, being the only sibling with stable housing, it wasn't such a bad thing. They were absolute disasters at order.

But he wouldn't change any of them. After his mother and stepfather had moved to America someone had needed to be able to put their hands on a spare house key to help out the current family member in crisis. And mild, acquired OCD wasn't a bad thing to have if you were a big brother—or a doctor. None of his patients had complained he was too careful.

He wondered what traits young Tara had acquired from her life and then shook his head. He didn't want to know. Lyrebird Lake was the last place to come for a fling because everyone would know before you'd even kissed her. A little startled at how easily he could picture that scenario, he brushed it away.

This was the place you brought one woman and settled down for good and he wasn't sure he believed in that for himself.

Five minutes later Tara had herself together enough to venture out to the kitchen, where Louisa had set out a salad for post-night-duty lunch.

The older lady hummed as she worked and the smile when she looked up to see Tara shone even brighter than normal.

'Have you met him?' No doubt at all whom she meant and Louisa wobbled with pride.

Tara had to smile. 'In the hallway.'

'Isn't he gorgeous?'

Tara picked up a carrot stick and took a bite. Chewed and swallowed—not just the carrot but the tiny voluptuous shiver as well. Back under control. 'He's very handsome. But no ideas, Louisa. He's an up-and-coming consultant here for a couple of weeks. And he's far too nice for me.'

'Silly girl. Of course he's not, he's just what you need.' She turned and started humming again and Tara had to smile as she glanced out the window to the veranda looking over the lake. She wasn't sure what that meant but she couldn't get offended by Louisa's mutterings—wouldn't do her any good if she did.

Tara had never had the kind of hugging acceptance she'd found in the small semi-rural community and sometimes she had to remind herself it might even be okay to learn to care for these people.

Then reality would resurface and she knew it would be just like the past—something would happen, she'd have to leave under a cloud and she'd be forgotten.

But she'd always have her work now wherever she went, she reminded herself, the first stability she'd known since the orphanage, and attainment had been such a golden rush as she'd passed her last exam, and that was priceless.

While socially she might be a bit stunted, okay, she granted more than a little stunted, but the work side of her life here couldn't be more satisfying with the midwifery-led birth centre.

She could finally do what she loved and, man, how she loved doing it. Loved the immersion in a woman's world of childbirth, the total connection as she supported a woman through her most powerful time, and then the exclusion when that woman departed for home.

Just like a foster-family and she was good at saying goodbye. Except unlike where she'd done her training in the city, you bumped into the women again in Lyrebird Lake, and she wasn't quite used to that but it wasn't as bad as she'd thought it would be.

Technically she was autonomous in that she had her own women to care for, under the aegis of Montana, the most senior midwife, and they case-conferenced once a week so everyone knew what was going on. She was an integral part of the team of midwives and doctors who worked in the adjoining hospital as well on quiet days, and they were always happy to be back-up for any obstetric hiccough. So she felt supported in her role and that she contributed. It was a heady feeling and she still couldn't believe her luck.

Incredibly, everyone seemed as eager to learn new trends as she was, and everyone researched changes in medical practice and then helped others to learn too. There was also enough going on in the other half of the hospital to stay updated on the medical side. This place was a utopia for a fledgling midwife who planned to make her career her life.

In the six months she'd been here her professional confidence had grown along with her belief in women and her own attending skills.

The motto of the lake, 'Listen to women,' had been gently but firmly reinforced. Very different from her training hospital's unwritten motto of 'We know best for all women.'

She wondered what the gorgeous Simon's philosophy was but coming from a busy practice working out of a major city hospital she had a fair suspicion.

Steady footsteps approached down the hallway and the object of her thoughts strolled into the room—which inexplicably seemed to shrink until he owned the majority of it—and she found herself basking in the warmth of his smile again.

Another unexpected flow of heat to the cheeks. Man, she'd never been a blusher. Thankfully, he turned the charm onto Louisa and Tara wilted back into her chair with relief.

She heard him say, 'I might go for a wander along the lake, Louisa, and relax after the drive.' He eased his neck as if it was kinked. 'Maeve's putting her feet up for an hour before this evening.'

Tara saw Louisa's eyes glint with determination and not being known for subtlety, Tara's stomach tightened, but it was too late. 'Why don't you join him, Tara? You always say it's good to walk after a night shift.'

CHAPTER TWO

Now, THAT WAS sink-into-the-floor-worthy. Tara could have glared at Louisa except the older lady didn't have a mean bone in her soft little body. Instead she shook her head. 'No. No. Simon will want to reacquaint himself. He doesn't need me to hold his hand.'

'I won't hold your hand if you don't want me to,' he was teasing, but this time there was no hiding the connection and she closed her eyes.

When she opened them he was smiling quizzically at her, and grudgingly she accepted that as a recipient it didn't feel as bad as it could have.

'I don't bite,' he said. 'I'd like the company but only if you want to.'

Growth experience. He thinks you're a socially adept woman. That would be a first. She could do this. The guy worked with women all the time. Practise at least on a man who was skilled at putting women at ease. Made sense. 'Fine. I can't feel more embarrassed.' She glanced at Louisa, who apparently didn't bat an eyelid at putting her in the hot seat and was humming happily, satisfied two of her chickens were getting along.

She could almost smile at that. Tara picked up the sunglasses she'd left beside the window because she still suffered from that night-duty glare aversion that too little sleep left you with. Simon held the door open for her—something that happened a lot in the quaintness around here. A few months ago she would have been surprised but today she just murmured, 'Thank you,' and passed in front of him.

They'd turned out of the driveway before he spoke and surprisingly the silence wasn't awkward. Thank goodness someone else didn't mind peace and quiet. Years of keeping her own counsel had taught her the value of quiet time—but quiet time in the company of others was an added bonus she could savour. She didn't think she'd met anyone she felt so in tune with so quickly. Though the air might be peaceful, it still vibrated between them.

Stop worrying, she admonished herself, a habit she'd picked up in the orphanage and on foster-parent weekends. Just let it be.

She looked ahead to where the path curled around the edge of the lake like a pale ribbon under the overhanging trees, and the water shimmered through the foliage like diamonds of blue glass in the ripples.

This place soothed her soul more than she could have ever imagined it would. Until unexpectedly a creature rustled in the undergrowth and her step faltered as it swished away from them into the safety of the water's edge. Typical, she thought, there's always a snake in the grass.

She shuddered. Snakes were the only creatures she disliked but that was probably because someone had put one in her bed once. 'Hope that wasn't something that can bite.'

Simon glanced after the noise. 'No. Doubt it. Might even have been a lyrebird.' He grinned. 'Have they told you about the legend of the lyrebird?' There was definitely humour in his deep voice. The man had a very easy soothing bass and she found herself listening more to the melody of the words than the content. Tried harder for the words.

'Nope. You mean as in why they call the place Lyrebird Lake?' She shrugged. 'Not really into legends.' Or fairy-tales. Or dreams of gorgeous men falling in love with her and carrying her off. Pshaw. Rubbish.

'Ah. A disbeliever.' He nodded his head sagely and she had to smile at his old-fashioned quaintness. 'So you wouldn't believe that in times of stress or, even more excitingly, when you meet your true love, a real live lyrebird appears and dances for you.'

Now she knew he was laughing at her. She rolled her eyes. 'Well, I haven't seen one and I've been here six months.'

'Me either. And I've been coming here off and on for ten years.' The smile was back in his voice. 'But my father and Mia have.'

This time her brows rose and she had no doubt her healthy dollop of scepticism was obvious. 'Really.'

His eyes crinkled. 'And Montana and Andy. And Misty and Ben.'

'You're kidding me.' These were sane, empowering people she'd looked up to. Consultants and midwives. Icons of the hospital. Or maybe he was pulling her leg. 'Don't believe you.'

'Nope. All true.' His eyes were dancing but she could see he was telling the truth as he believed it.

Then he'd been conned. 'How many times has this happened?'

He shrugged. 'Don't know. You'd have to ask.'

Brother. 'I will.' She shook her head. He'd probably just made it all up. Men did say weird things to impress women. Though he didn't seem like one of those guys, but, then again, her sleaze detection system had never worked well. 'What else don't I know about this place?'

He glanced around. 'Well, half of that hill behind the lake…' he pointed across the water '…is full of disused gold mines and labyrinths of old tunnels crisscross underneath our feet.'

She looked down at the path and grimaced. Imagined falling through into an underground cavern. She'd always had claustrophobia—or had since one particular foster-sibling had locked her in a cupboard. Now, that wasn't a pleasant thought. 'Thanks for that. How to ruin a walk.'

'Well, not really under our feet. That might be

stretching it a bit far. But certainly all around the hillside and a long way this way.'

'Okay.' She shook off the past and thought rationally about it. 'I guess half our hospital's business comes from the mines out of town so it makes sense we'd have some here.' She glanced at him as they walked at a steady pace around the lake. Maybe she could start fossicking for gold after work—above ground, of course—and make her fortune to pay off the debts Mick had left her with. 'Have you been in them?'

He laughed. Even looked a little pink-cheeked. 'Once. To my embarrassment.' Shook his head at himself. 'I can't believe I brought this up.' He glanced at Tara ruefully and sighed. 'I had to ring Mia to get my dad to rescue me.'

She looked across at him and grinned. Good to see other people did dumb things. 'Ouch.'

'Not one of my more glorious moments.'

She looked at him, loose-limbed, strongly muscled with that chiselled jaw and lurking smile. A man very sure of his world and his place in it. She wished. Shook her head. 'I'm sure you have enough glorious moments.'

The quizzical look was back but all he said was, 'Yep. Hundreds.'

She had to laugh at that. 'I'm still waiting for mine.'

'My turn not to believe you.' So he'd noticed her scepticism. He tilted his head and studied her with leisurely thoroughness. 'Do you enjoy your work?'

'Love it.'

'Then I'll bet you have lots of successes too.'

She thought about earlier that morning and smiled. 'I do get to share other women's glorious moments.' Changed the subject. 'Mia says you're running a breech clinic at Sydney Central?'

'Yep. Was converted by an amazing guy I worked with when I was a registrar. Had the motto "Don't interfere". Said most women had the ground work for a normal breech birth.'

She couldn't agree more but her training hospital hadn't subscribed to that theory. The only babies allowed to be born in the breech position were the ones who came in off the street ready to push their own way out. She'd never been lucky enough to be on duty for that. 'I've watched a lot of breech births on videos but I haven't seen one in real life.'

'You will. Hopefully trends are changing with new research. Women are demanding a chance at least. Maybe one of your glorious moments is coming up. You obviously love midwifery.'

'I was always going to be a nurse, because my mother was a nurse, even though I don't remember much about her, but then one of my friends lost a baby and I decided I'd be a midwife. It was a good decision.'

'I think it's a fabulous decision. Some of my best friends are midwives.' He returned to their previous conversation. 'But I can't believe there isn't more to your life than your job.'

'You're right.' She thought of her arrival here six months ago. 'I love my bike.'

'Ah. So the black monster is yours?'

'Yep. The sum total of my possessions.'

'University can be expensive.'

She'd only just started paying that back. It was the bills Mick had run up all over town that crippled her. More fool her for having the lease and the accounts in her name. They'd both been in the orphanage together and when she'd met him again she'd been blinded to his bitter and dangerous side because, mistakenly, she'd thought she'd found family.

But her dream of everything being fair and equal had been torn into a pile of overdue notices. 'Druggie boyfriends can be expensive too.' Unintentionally the words came out on a sigh. What the heck was she doing?

'Nasty. Had one of those, did you.'

She turned her face and grimaced at the lake so he couldn't see. She was tempted to say 'Dozens' but it wasn't true. It had taken her too long to actually trust someone that first time. 'Hmm. I'm a little too used to people letting me down. Don't usually bore people with it.'

'Don't imagine you bore people at all.'

She could hear the smile in his voice and some of the annoyance with herself seeped away then surged again, even though it was unreasonably back towards Simon. What would he know about where she'd been? What she'd been through?

Then, thankfully, the calmness she'd been practising for the last six months since she'd met these people whispered sense in her ear and she let the destructive thoughts go. Sent the whole mess that was her past life out over the rippled water of the lake and concentrated on the breath she eased out.

She had no idea where the conversational ball lay as she returned to the moment but let that worry go too. Took another breath and let her shoulders drop.

'That's some control you have there, missy.'

She blinked at Simon and focussed on him. On his calm grey eyes mainly and the warmth of empathy— not ridicule, as she'd expected, but admiration and understanding.

'I'm practising positive mindfulness and self-control.' She didn't usually tell people that either.

He nodded as if he knew what it was, probably didn't, then he surprised her with his own disclosure. 'I'm not good at it. But if it makes you feel any better I have hang-ups too. Luckily I have a very busy work life.'

She smiled at the statement. 'Funny how we can hide in that. I was studying like mad, paying bills for two in my time off, and he was gambling and doing drugs when I thought he was at uni.' She shrugged it away. 'Now I have a busy work life and a really big bike.'

'The bike's a worry.'

'The bike?' She shook her head and could almost feel the wind on her face and the vibration in her ears. 'Not if you have no ties. Always loved the spice of danger.

It would be different if I had someone who needed me.' There was a difference between someone needing you and someone using you. She'd agreed not to drag them both through the court system but she would only keep all the bills at the cost of his bike. Even though it had only been worth a quarter of the debts he'd run up, possession of the bike had restored some of her self-esteem. Mick hadn't been happy and sometimes she wondered if it really all was finished.

'Ah. So you admit that motorbikes are the toys of possibly "temporary" citizens?'

'Spoken like a true doctor.'

'Ask any paramedic. The stats are poor.'

She grinned at him—he had no idea. 'But the fun is proportional. I could take you for a ride one day.'

He raised his brows. 'I'd have to think about that.'

'Sure. No rush. You have time.' She couldn't imagine him ever saying yes. Which was a good thing because she suspected the experience of Simon's arms wrapped around her and his thighs hard up against her backside would make it very difficult to concentrate. Instead she looked up ahead. 'So how far are we walking? You'll be at your father's house soon.'

He glanced up in surprise. Looked around. 'You're right. I guess he'll be at work anyway.'

'Mia will be home. She was on duty the night before me.'

'I'd forgotten you were up all night.' His glance brushed warmly over her and surprisingly she didn't feel body-conscious. It wasn't that kind of look. 'You do it well. I always look like a dishrag for the next few days.'

She nodded wisely. 'That would be the age factor.'

It was his turn to blink then grin, and she was glad he had a sense of humour. Nice change. Not sure why she'd tried to alienate him, unless she'd wanted him to turn away so she wouldn't have to.

'*Touché*, young woman.' He looked ahead to the house they were approaching. 'Let's go and see my gorgeous step-mama and my second family of sisters. This old man needs a cold drink.'

CHAPTER THREE

SIMON'S STEP-MAMA, NOT all that much older than Simon, greeted them with open arms, her red curls bouncing as she rushed out to hug him. Her eyes sparkled as she stared up at Simon fondly, and Tara was pretty sure nobody had ever looked at her like that.

Two copper-curled miniature Mias tumbled out of the door, one more demurely because she was eleven, and the other squealing because she was eight, but in the end both threw themselves at Simon, who scooped them up one in each hand and spun them around as he hugged them. 'How are my little sisters today?'

Tara unobtrusively admired the stretch of material over his upper arms as with impressive ease he twirled the girls like feathers. He might be way out of her league but this Simon Campbell was certainly delicious eye candy. She could deal with just looking in. She did that all the time.

He kissed them both on the cheek and they giggled as he put them down.

'It feels like ages since we saw you, Simon.' The elder girl, Layla, pouted.

'Eleven months. Christmas.' He put them at arm's length and looked them over, nodded, satisfied they looked well, before he turned back and studied Mia again. 'And how is my gorgeous step-mama?'

'All the better for seeing you.' They embraced again and the genuine warmth overflowed to where Tara was standing. 'Once a year is not enough.'

Touchy-feely family or what! Tara pushed away the tiny stab of jealousy. So what if Simon had this whole network of adoring relatives and she didn't.

Simon grinned and stepped back so that Mia turned to Tara and leaned in for a hug. Tara tried, she really did, to hug back. She seemed to be getting better at it. 'Tara. Great to see you, too.' Mia nodded her head at Simon. 'So you two have met.'

Simon grinned. 'In the hallway. Made me think of you and Dad. Then Louisa nagged Tara into accompanying me on my walk.'

'Poor Tara.' Mia grinned and looked at her. 'Met in the hallway, did you? I hope you had clothes on, Tara. I was in a towel when I met his father and sparks flew even on the first day.'

Tara had to laugh. 'In that case I'm glad to say I was dressed. And had six hours' sleep under my belt.'

Mia's eyes sharpened. 'That's right. You were on night duty last night. How was Julie's labour? What time was her baby born?'

'Quarter to five this morning, on the dot. Sunrise.'

Mia shook her head with a smile. 'Babies seem to love sunrise.'

'I was just thinking that.' Tara soaked up the warmth she was getting used to from these people and then blinked as Mia spun on her heel. 'Come in. What was I thinking?' She waved a hand. 'Have a cold drink. Angus will be jealous I got to see you first, Simon.'

'But not surprised.'

Mia laughed. Then she sobered as she remembered. 'Anyway, how are you? You look tired. And how is Maeve?'

'I'm fine. Maeve's pregnancy has four weeks to go and the baby's father is still in a US penitentiary. I hope.'

'I'm sorry you've all had that worry. What did your mother say? It must be hard for her to be living so far away in Boston when her daughter is pregnant.'

'There's not a lot she can do. Maeve refuses to have her baby in America and Dad's unwell and Mum can't leave.'

'Then Maeve is lucky she has you.'

He shrugged. 'My youngest sister has me stumped the way she is at the moment. I can't say anything right. I'm worried about her.'

Tara wasn't quite sure if she was supposed to hear all this or whether she should drift away and look out the window over the lake or something, but she guessed everyone else would know the ins and out of it. She'd find out eventually.

Mia was talking and walking until she opened the fridge. 'So you could've brought her here earlier, even if you couldn't get away. She could have stayed here or with Louisa. You know how Louisa loves to have people under her roof. And Tara's there.' She turned to Tara and drew her back into the circle.

'Isn't that right, Tara?'

'I've never felt more welcome in my life,' she said quietly, and hoped the others missed the pathetic neediness in the statement.

Thankfully they must have because Simon went on as if all was normal. 'Well, now that I'm here I'm hoping I can manage a few weeks of relaxation till she settles in. Though I may have to do a quick trip back and forth in the middle. It depends when my next two private women go into labour, but they're not due till after the new year.'

Mia closed the refrigerator and returned with two tall glasses of home-made lemonade. 'So how are your training sessions going? Have you managed to inspire a few more docs to think breech birth without Caesarean can be a normal thing?'

He took the glass. 'Thanks. 'I'm trying. My registrar's great.' He took a sip and closed his eyes in delight. 'Seriously, Mia, you could retire on this stuff.'

She actually looked horrified. 'Retire? Who wants to retire?'

'Sometimes I think I do,' Simon said half-jokingly, and Mia raised her brows.

The concern was clear in her voice. 'You sound like your father when I first met him. You do need a break. Watch out or Angus will be nagging you to move here and set up practice.'

'Haven't completed the research I want to do. A few years yet.'

A vision of Simon with a wife and kids popped unexpectedly into Tara's mind. Made it a bit of a shame she didn't stay in places too long, then she realised where her thoughts were heading. That way lay disappointment. Didn't she ever learn? She'd rather think about Maeve. 'So has Maeve joined any parenting classes?'

Simon shook his head and his concern was visible. 'Wouldn't go to classes in Sydney.'

Tara shrugged. 'I don't think that's too weird. She's a midwife. She knows the mechanics. And sometimes women don't want to think about labour until right at the end. Or be involved in the couples classes without a partner. I get that.'

She could feel Mia's eyes on them and obviously she wanted to say something. Tara waited. Mia was very cool and worth listening to.

'Why don't you ask her if she'd like to be on your caseload, Tara? I think a younger midwife would help when she's feeling a bit lost and lonely.'

Tara could feel her chest squeeze with the sudden shock of surprise. That was pretty big of Mia to trust a family member to her. Her eyes stung and she looked away. Nobody had ever treated her as she was treated here. Or trusted her. She just hoped she didn't let them down. 'You know I'd love to. But I guess it depends who she wants.'

Simon looked at Mia too. He felt the shock and turned to look at his stepmother. He wasn't sure what he thought about that and saw Mia nod reassuringly. Someone else looking after Maeve, not Mia? He looked at the bolshie but sincere young woman beside him. Was she experienced enough? What if something went wrong?

Then saw the flare of empathy for his sister in Tara's face and allowed the reluctant acceptance that Mia could be right. Maeve wanted to run the show. Wanted to listen to her body without interference, if he'd listened at all to the arguments they'd had over the last couple of weeks, and he had no doubt young Tara was holistic enough for his sister to be able to do that.

Normally he would be right there with a woman, cheering her on, but he was having serious personal issues doing that with the sister he had felt most protective of all his life. Not that he'd actually be there, of course. But he was darned sure he'd be outside the door, pacing.

So maybe Mia was right. It could be harder for Maeve to relax with the connection so strong between her brother and his stepmother.

He found the words out in the air in front of him before he realised. 'We'll see what she says.'

He reassured himself that if Mia didn't have faith in

Tara, she wouldn't have suggested it. And despite the mixed feelings he was starting to have about this intriguing young woman he really did feel a natural confidence in her passion for her work.

He'd seen it before. How Lyrebird Lake could bring out the best in all of them. Maybe he had lost that since he'd been so immersed in the high-tech, high-risk arena of obstetrics he studied now.

He'd even seen it with his own father. From hotshot international evacuation medic to relaxed country GP.

Maeve and Tara did have a lot in common and would get on well, the dry voice in his head agreed—all the way to dropkicking past boyfriends!

No. It would be good. This was all going to turn out even better than he'd hoped.

CHAPTER FOUR

THE DINNER PARTY was a reasonable success. Maeve smiled and said the right things but still kept her distance and seemed a little flat to Simon. His stepmother was her own gorgeous self and treated both young women as if they were long-term friends of hers, and his father said very little but smiled every time his eyes rested on his wife or daughters.

Louisa was in her element because she loved dinner parties and seeing the family together. She was always happiest when children were around.

And young Tara, dressed in skin-tight, very stressed jeans that showed glimpses of skin beneath the ragged material moulded to her lush little body, drew his eyes like a magnet every time she walked past to the fridge on some errand for Louisa.

His father came to stand beside him. 'Mia says you seem to get on well with Tara.'

'She's easy to get along with.'

Tara laughed at something Louisa whispered as she walked past again with a platter of fruit for dessert and both men sneaked a glance.

Angus looked away first. 'I think our Tara's had an interesting life. She's a tough little cookie, on the outside at least.'

Simon glanced at his father's face. 'Lots of people have tough lives.'

'Guess so.' Angus took a sip of his beer. 'What happened to Julia?'

'Didn't work out. Said I didn't pay her enough attention. Let my work come between us.'

'Did you?'

'Maybe.' Simon thought about it. 'Definitely. Spent a lot of time apologising for leaving and heading into work. Started to enjoy work more than home and she found another guy.'

'Took me a while to find Mia. It will happen to you one day and you'll recognise it.'

They both looked at Angus's wife. 'If I find a woman like Mia I'll be very happy.'

'Would you settle here?'

'So this is a job interview?'

'Cheeky blighter. Would you?'

'Not yet. But in the future I'm not ruling it out.'

Angus nodded then added innocently, 'Can you do three days for me, starting Monday?'

Simon laughed. 'I knew this was leading somewhere. Why?'

'Seeing as you're here, and Mia's had a big birthday last week, I thought I might take her up to Brisbane to do Christmas shopping. She loves it. Take her and the girls for a mini-holiday.'

Simon laughed. 'Can't see you shopping with Christmas music in the background.'

He grimaced. 'It's only a couple of days. I'm going to sit back and watch my women. Need more of that when you get to my age.'

'Poor old man.'

'Absolutely. So, will you?'

Simon had done the occasional shift in the small hospital over the last few years when one of the senior partners had had to go away, and he'd enjoyed most of the small-town country feel of it. Angus knew that. 'Sure. Why not? Andy will be point me in the right direction if needed. Haven't done much general medicine for a few years, though.'

'You've got a young brain. You'll manage. And it's almost December. Louisa wants the decorations up.'

Simon laughed. 'Thanks. And no doubt you'll bring her back something new I'll have to assemble.'

Tara walked past again and Simon's eyes followed. Angus bit his lip and smiled into his drink.

The next morning Tara heard Simon go out not long after daylight. It would be pleasantly cool before the heat of the day, she thought as she pulled her sheet up, the blanket having been discarded on the floor, and she wondered drowsily where he was going.

And then, as her fantasies drifted, wondered what

he was wearing, wondered if he wore his collar open so she'd see his lovely strong neck and chest. Funny, that—she'd never had a throat fetish before.

She grinned to herself and snuggled down further. Nice make-believe. And Mia was amazing. They all were, and yesterday, as far as Tara was concerned, had been an intriguing insight into the Campbell family and Simon in particular.

Watching the dynamics between Simon and his father had been fascinating. She certainly looked at Angus differently after some of the exploits Mia had mentioned. Who would have known?

She'd never seen such equal footing between father and son but, then, her experience was limited to snatches of dysfunctional family life. Maybe it was because Simon had made it to twenty before he'd even met his biological father. Angus was certainly proud of him and the feeling looked to be mutual. And both of them obviously adored Mia and the girls.

She'd have felt a bit like the Little Match Girl looking in the Christmas window if it hadn't been for Maeve, who, despite looking like she'd just stepped out of a fashion magazine, had looked more lost than she had. Why was that?

Maeve was who she should be concentrating her thoughts on. Especially if she agreed to join Tara's caseload.

An hour later she wandered down to the kitchen and Maeve, immaculate in designer maternity wear and perfectly made up, was there, picking at a piece of toast as if she wanted to eat it one crumb at a time. Perhaps her pregnancy hormones still gave her nausea in the mornings. Tara had seen lots of women like that well into their last trimester of pregnancy.

'Morning, all.' Friendly but not too pushy, she included Maeve and Louisa in her smile as she sat down. Louisa liked to fuss and judging by the tension in the room Maeve didn't appreciate it.

'Hello, dear.' Louisa cast her a relieved glance. 'What are you doing today?'

'Have a young mums' class this afternoon but happy to do whatever if you need something, Louisa.'

'No. I'm off to bingo with a friend down at the hall and I wondered if you and Maeve could fix your own lunches.'

'No problem.' She smiled at the younger woman. 'We'll manage, won't we, Maeve?'

The girl barely looked up. 'Of course.'

'Still nauseous?' Tara could see she looked a little pale around the cheeks.

Maeve grimaced. 'Getting worse, not better. And I'm starting to get this insane itch that's driving me mad.'

Tara frowned. A tiny alarm pinged in her brain with the symptoms but she let it lie for a moment. 'Not fun. What have you tried?'

'Pretty well everything.' She shrugged. 'Pressure-point armbands. Ginger. Sips of cold water. Sips of hot water for nausea.' She absently scratched her belly through her shirt. 'And just calamine for the itch but

I only put it on the places you can't see. I never liked pink as a kid and it's too embarrassing to be painted pink all over.'

Tara laughed. 'That's the thing with midwives. We know all the things we tell other women and it sucks when it doesn't work.'

'Embarrassing really.' The young woman looked a little less tense now that Tara had acknowledged Maeve knew her stuff.

'I imagine being pregnant would expand your thirst for remedies?'

Maeve rolled her eyes and even smiled. 'You have no idea. I've read everything I can find on common complaints of pregnancy.'

'I'll have to get you to brush me up on them later.'

Tara was glad to hear that Maeve really did have a sense of humour. 'Makes you wonder what the women thought when it didn't work for them either.' They smiled at each other.

Maeve nodded. 'I'll clarify next time. Works *most* of the time.'

'Have you had a chance to sit down with someone and talk about the actual plans you have for labour?'

It was a reasonable question, considering she'd just moved to a new centre for care, but Tara felt the walls go up from across the table.

Maeve shot her a glance. 'You mean antenatal classes? Simon been talking to you?'

'I'm guessing Simon talks to everyone.' A little bit

ambiguous. 'But Mia asked, yes. I usually run a younger mums' class this week and I thought seeing as you were a midwife you might be interested in helping me—from a pregnant woman's perspective. But, then, you might prefer the idea of just a chat, and I'd be happy to do that if you did want one if you're not already teed up with someone else?'

'Sorry. I'm just a bit narky lately. Everything is a mess.'

Life. Didn't she know it could do that! 'Oh, yeah. It gets like that sometimes. I'm an expert at it. Plus your itch and nausea would impact on anyone's day, let alone someone carrying a watermelon everywhere.'

Maeve did laugh then. 'Feels like it. And it feels like this pregnancy is never going to end, but I'm going to be patient and not let anyone push me into something I don't want.'

'Good on you. Who were you thinking of seeing here?'

Maeve shrugged. 'Don't know. As long as it's low key I don't care. I saw the doctor Simon teed me up with a few times but last month he started talking about induction of labour and possible epidurals and maybe even Caesareans. I couldn't believe it, so I told Simon I was out of there. He wouldn't hear of a home birth and we compromised on Lyrebird Lake Birth Centre.'

'And the father of the child?'

Maeve looked away. 'Conspicuous by his absence. And I don't want to look back on this birth and regret

it. I'm already regretting enough about this pregnancy.
I need to have some control and I wasn't going to get it
at Simon's hospital.'

Tara was a hundred per cent agreeable to that. 'Go,
you, for standing up for yourself and your baby.' Tara
wondered if she could offer without putting too much
pressure on her.

'There's three doctors here who do antenatal care,
and four midwives. If you think you'd be happy on a
midwifery programme, you just need to pick someone.
I've two women due in the next fortnight but apart from
home visits I'm free to take on new women. You could
meet the other midwives tomorrow but keep it in mind.
You're probably due for tests around now anyway.'

Maeve looked across and smiled with a shyness Tara
guessed was way out of character. 'Actually, that would
be great.'

'You sure?'

Maeve looked relieved. 'Very. And we can talk about
the labour then too.'

'Fine. We'll wander down to the clinic after morning tea, check you and baby out, and get all the papers
sorted with the stuff you brought. If you change your
mind after I've nosed my way through your medical
and social history I can hand you on to someone else.'

'Lord. Social history. And isn't all that a disaster?
Sometimes I feel like I'll never get sorted. I never used
to be like this.'

'Sympathy.' Tara smiled in complete agreement. 'I

was pretty lost before I came here. The good news is that you're female so you'll still come out on top.'

Maeve blinked and then smiled. 'Okay, then. Must remember that for my clever brother.'

'He seems nice.'

'Too nice.' Both girls looked at each other, were obviously thinking of their previous boyfriends who had been anything but, and laughed. Ten seconds later they heard footsteps leaping up the back stairs and Simon appeared behind the back porch screen door. Of course both of them struggled to control their mirth.

'What's so funny?' The door shut quietly behind him and he looked from one to the other, brows raised, fine sweat across his brow. Obviously he'd been running.

'Nothing.' In unison.

He shook his head at them. 'Okay. Girl talk. You want to go for a swim, Maeve?'

Tara saw her face change. Become shuttered. 'No, thanks. I'm catching up on my emails.'

'Tara?'

She could just imagine Simon in swimmers. Wouldn't she just. 'No, thanks.'

'You sure?'

Maeve chimed in. 'Go. It's your day off. We can do that other thing when you come back. There's hours before then.'

Tara didn't understand the wall Maeve had erected between herself and her brother. If she had a brother like Simon she'd be all over him, but there was probably

stuff she didn't know. 'Fine. Thanks. I love to swim.'
She looked at him. Saw him glance at his watch. 'I'm
guessing you want to go now?'

Simon nodded and he seemed happy enough that
she'd agreed to come. She'd hate to think all these people were forcing her on him but what the heck. She'd
enjoy it while it lasted.

'Five minutes enough time? Out the front?' he said.
'I'll be there.'

Simon watched Tara towel her shoulders vigorously
and then rub shapely calves and stand on one leg and
dry her toes.

He suffered a brief adolescent urge to metamorphose
into her towel. Apart from her delightful breasts her
body was firm and supple and he suspected she would
feel incredibly sleek and smooth in his arms.

The swim had proved to a little more bracing than
they'd both expected and he saw her shiver. He guessed
she'd had a cold start. 'Sorry. I was hot from my run so
it feels good to me.'

She shrugged. 'Hey, it's summer in Queensland. I
can swim all year round.' The idea was sound but the
rows of goose-bumps covering both arms and her delightful thighs made Simon want to bring her in close
and warm her against his chest.

Or maybe it wasn't the goose-bumps he wanted to
warm against him. It had been a while since the last
time he'd noticed so much about a woman. Passing

glances, inner appreciation, sure, but this little fire-brand had him constantly ready without any effort on her part. Danger. Alert.

Thankfully she remained oblivious to his shift in thoughts. That was a good thing.

He could see her mind was still on the swim. 'And Lyrebird Lake's too far south for crocodiles.'

Crocodiles. Now, there's a thought. He'd bet she wasn't afraid of any animal. 'Not sure why but I get the feeling it would take more than a crocodile to scare you off something you wanted to do.'

She grinned at him and that was an added bonus. Her whole face lit up and warmed him more than any towel could. 'Thank you, kind sir. I'll take that as a compliment.'

'It was.' And a bit of a surprise. He didn't usually go for the daredevil type. 'So you have an interesting bucket list?'

'I've always wanted to go skydiving. Birthday present for myself next week.'

Of course she was. 'Seriously?'

'Yep.' Her eyes shone at the thought.

Well it was the last thing he wanted to do. 'Birthday wish I wouldn't be keen on.'

She shook her head and her spiky hair flicked drop-lets around like a little sparkler. 'They say you're never the same after you do it. All to do with my belief to live life so I know that I've been here before I leave this earth.' She looked so intense when she said that.

There was something incredibly gloomy about such a vibrant young woman contemplating her mortality that chilled him.

'You planning to leave this world?'

She shrugged. 'Not planning to, but anything can happen. My dad and mum died when I was six. That's why I'm always glad when people driving arrive safely. I was made a ward of the state. I grew up in an orphanage.'

'I'm sorry about your parents.' Hard reality to face at that age. At any age. 'What about her mother? Your grandmother?'

'Died in childbirth. No siblings.' No expression. No plea for sympathy. And he was guessing not much childhood—which explained a lot. But there was a wall that said as good as a raised hand, 'Don't give me any sympathy.'

'Nasty family history.' Understatement. He seriously wasn't being flippant. It was a shocker and he could see how that could be a trigger for more risky, adventurous behaviour. 'My life is boring in comparison.'

'Tell me about boring.'

He shrugged. 'Nothing to tell except my mother didn't tell my biological father she was pregnant, a minor glitch I didn't find out about till after I grew up. That was as adventurous as I got.'

'That's adventurous. Especially searching him out as an adult.' There was wistfulness in her eyes when she said that and he knew she wished she had someone to search out. He'd never actually looked at it like that.

'So, anyway, maybe I should be up for exciting escapades.' His voice trailed off as she pulled her T-shirt over her head and it stuck, alluringly, in a few damp places.

He closed his mouth and glanced away. Regathered his thoughts with some difficulty. 'One day I will try being adventurous for a change.'

She looked him up and down and he sucked in his belly. Not that he was ashamed of his six pack, and not quite sure why he should even think about it because he wasn't usually a vain man, but he had no control over the reflex. She just did that to him.

'You could jump with me on Tuesday if you like.'

He knew the horror showed on his face.

To make it worse, then she laughed at him. And not even with him. Not sure he liked that either.

Tough. He wasn't jumping. 'How about I come and be ground support? Hold a glass of champagne for you.'

He could see she liked the idea of that and he felt he'd redeemed himself somewhat. 'Thank you. That'd be very cool.'

'Okay. We'll talk about it later when I get the picture out of my mind of you stepping out of a perfectly good plane.' They picked up the towels and walked back towards the path.

'So what were you and Maeve talking about doing later?'

'Antenatal clinic. I offered and she's accepted to go

on my caseload.' She sounded a little hesitant and he guessed it could be confronting to take on the sister of the consultant. He needed Maeve to see someone and he didn't have much chance of her listening to him at the moment.

'That's great. Really. I think you guys will have a great rapport.'

She flashed a grateful glance at him. 'Thanks, Simon. I'm looking forward to it. I'll take good care of her.'

CHAPTER FIVE

THE ANTENATAL CLINIC opened at eleven a.m. seven days a week. That way the morning midwife had discharged any women and babies who were due to go home. Plus the ward was often less busy so the women booking in could look around. Except when there was a woman in labour.

Tara had ten women on her caseload at the moment in various stages of pregnancy and two who had already delivered on the six-week postnatal check programme.

The first visit at least would be held at the clinic but most visits she would do at the woman's home. All the midwives took turns to carry the maternity phone in case one of the other midwives needed help in the birthing suite or two women went into labour at once on the same midwife's caseload.

Maeve looked very interested in the running of the unit, judging by the way her head never stopped swivelling, and Tara smiled quietly to herself. She'd bet there'd be some thought about staying on after Maeve's baby was born.

Even during the antenatal check Maeve was asking questions about the way they ran the caseloads, and the girls were firm friends by the time the official paperwork was completed.

Tara sat back. 'Okay. So your blood pressure is slightly elevated and your baby is a little under the normal size for thirty-six weeks but all of those things could be normal. It's nothing startling but we've done a couple of extra blood tests to rule out anything we need to watch for.'

'You thinking my blood pressure could go up more? So watch out for toxaemia?'

'We'll both have a good look at the results. At the moment you feel well in yourself, and baby is moving nicely, but I wonder about the nausea and the itch.' She looked at her. 'Don't you?'

'Yeah.' Maeve sighed. 'Of course I'm thinking it could need watching. That's why I'm glad we sorted out the caseload. In case Simon decided I was high risk and whisked me back to Sydney.'

'If you got a lot worse we are a low-risk unit. But being thirty-six weeks helps so we don't have to deal with a premature baby if things did escalate.'

'Don't tell Simon.'

Tara had wondered if this would come. 'If Simon asks, I'm not going to lie.'

'And if he doesn't ask, don't tell him.'

'As long as the tests come back normal, there's nothing to talk about. Sure.'

'You wiggling out of that?'

'You asking me for the impossible?' Tara countered, and she saw the realisation in Maeve's eyes that she wasn't a pushover. She couldn't be.

Maeve stood up and so did Tara. It was going to go one way or the other.

'Fine.' Maeve shook her head. 'Sorry. I don't know why Simon makes me so wild. He hasn't done anything wrong. I guess it's because I feel like I let him down when I made the choices I did.'

'Choices are there to be made and who knows what the end result will be? But, boy, do I know that feeling.' She handed Maeve her antenatal card. 'I'm trying to learn that blame and guilt are useless emotions. So is resentment. It's helped me. Hard to do but letting all that go has really made me start each day fresh.'

Maeve patted her stomach. 'A bit hard when the reminder is poking out in front.'

'Nah. Perfect time to be fresh with a new baby. I'll be there for your birth, Louisa will spoil you rotten, and Simon will be a doting uncle.' She looked at Maeve. 'You say the baby's father is out of the picture. Do you think he'll try to find you when he gets out?'

'I don't think so. As I said before, a crazy, stupid, one-night stand with one of Simon's old friends, a hunk I've always fancied, but he didn't think to tell me he was going to prison. He hasn't answered one of my letters. Or Simon's attempts to talk to him. So that just makes me feel even more stupid.'

'Nope. Silly would be if you were waiting for him with open arms and no explanations.' Maeve made no move to go now they were finished and Tara glanced at her watch.

'If you want to come and help me with the young mums' class, it starts around one p.m. In the mothers' tearoom behind the desk.' Tara pointed.

'Thanks. I'll think about it. I might go for a walk now after sitting for so long.'

'Sure. Or have lunch and come back. I'll go home soon and grab a bite.' One of the midwives signalled to Tara as they walked out the door and Maeve shooed her towards the midwife.

'I'll go for a walk and come back.'

Tara arrived back at the manse half an hour later and Simon was in the kitchen, making coffee. He'd been waiting for them to return and, to him, it seemed like they'd been gone for hours. Maybe Maeve did have something wrong. Maybe his niggling worries did have some foundation. By the time Tara arrived, minus Maeve, he could barely contain his concern.

He forced himself not to pounce on her and gestured to the pot. 'You want one?'

'Love one, thanks. Black.'

'No sugar.'

'How did you know?'

He had to smile at that. He'd asked Louisa yesterday. 'So how did the antenatal visit go?'

'Fine.'

'So everything's fine?'

'I could tell you but then I'd have to kill you.'

'Come on. Reassure me.'

'Sure. We did bloods for thirty-six weeks and baby is moving well.' She rolled her eyes. 'Nothing else to tell until the blood results came back or we'd be speculating.'

'Speculating about what?'

'Nothing yet.' She was squirming and he wanted to know why, though it warred with his sense of fair play, but then there was big brother mode.

He saw the way Tara straightened her back and he felt a pang of guilt. She shouldn't have had to gird her loins against him.

She sized him up. 'You know, you're the one who said we should have a great rapport, and I'm just wondering how you think that will be built if I run to you with results and private information. I'm assuming you don't discuss your pregnant ladies with their relatives?'

He paused. Looked at her. 'No. You're right. I take that on board.' In fact, he was ashamed of himself for leaning on her but the niggling unease about his sister's health was also a concern. 'But if you're keeping something from me about my baby sister, I won't be happy.'

He couldn't seem to stop himself.

Tara was up for the challenge. 'Thanks for that. Didn't pick you for a bully. Silly me.'

True, and he didn't know what had come over him.

Simon reached out, wanted to touch her briefly on her shoulder, but pulled back. 'Tara, I'm sorry. I have no right to harass you. Please accept my apology.'

Her phone rang and she glanced at the number. 'Now I know why you drive your sister mad. Good intentions and apologies. Would make anyone feel bad. But I'm not going there.' She answered the phone. Listened and then said, 'Okay.'

She glanced at Simon with a bland smile. 'No problems. Gotta go.' Pulled open the fridge and grabbed an apple before she sailed out the door. 'See you later.'

Simon watched her walk away and he knew he'd been in the wrong—but she still hadn't given him answers.

The problem was that the last few days he'd been aware that something was not quite right about Maeve. He hated it had been a month since she'd last been seen, and he couldn't put his finger on the symptoms. But pressuring Tara was unlike him.

He guessed on Monday he'd be in a position to access his sister's blood pathology files when he went to work but he'd try not to look. It wasn't his practice to second-guess a colleague and he shouldn't start now. But it would be challenging not to peek.

CHAPTER SIX

MONDAY MORNING SAW Tara scooting around the ward, tidying up after their last discharged mother and baby. The first thing she'd done was check Maeve's results and thankfully they were totally normal so it was fine she hadn't mentioned anything to Simon.

As she worked she was thinking at least if Simon asked she could say everything was fine. Funny how she wasn't looking forward to the next time she saw him in one way and in the other she looked forward to just 'seeing him'.

Before she could think too much of it a car screeched to a stop out front and a harried-looking man she hadn't seen before leapt from the driver's side before Tara could open the passenger door.

'Her waters broke. She's pushing.'

Tara sent a reassuring nod towards the strained face of the woman seated awkwardly in the front seat, and wished this had happened earlier at handover so at least there would be two midwives there for the birth. Judging by the concentration that had settled over the woman's face and the tiny outward breaths she was making, that wasn't going to happen.

The man said, 'It's breech and they said Susan had to have a Caesarean birth in Brisbane.'

Tara doubted a Caesarean would be possible in the minutes they had left. 'Okay. I'll grab a wheelchair while you stand Susan up and we'll get inside at least.'

She was thinking breech, Simon, handy, and before she spun the strategically placed wheelchair out the door she pressed the little green button they used for paging help so that someone from the other side of the hospital could lend her a hand, even if it was only to phone the midwife and doctor on call.

'It's okay, Susan.' She spoke in a slow, calm voice, because people arriving at the last minute in labour wasn't that unusual, and she smiled again as she eased the woman into the chair and began pushing swiftly towards the door. 'You'll be fine. Help's coming, and we've had breech babies here before.' Not in her time but she'd heard the stories and Susan's belly didn't look full term so baby might be a little early as well. All good things for a breech delivery.

The stress on the husband's face eased a little and Tara shared additional comfort. 'The more worried Susan is, the more painful the contractions feel. That seems a shame so if everyone takes a deep breath and just accepts that baby is going to do this his or her way, we'll work it out.'

'Thank God, someone with sense.' The muttered

comment from the woman who hadn't previously spoken startled Tara, and she had to bite her lip to stop a laugh, but then Susan was hit by another contraction and became far too busy to add further pithy comments.

The sound of footsteps meant help was almost here and by the time Tara had Susan standing up from the chair beside the bed Simon appeared at the doorway.

From worrying about when she saw him next to relief at his appearance. Another miracle. 'Simon. Great. This is Susan, who's just arrived. Waters have broken and she wants to push her breech baby out very soon.'

Susan glared at him and said, 'I'm not lying down to have this.'

'Sounds good.' Simon crossed the room quietly and shook the harried man's hand. 'Simon Campbell. Obstetrician.'

'Pete Wells, and my wife, Susan.'

Simon turned to Susan and touched her shoulder briefly while he glanced at her tight belly and then her face. 'Hi, Susan. First baby?' The woman nodded.

'And what date is your baby due?'

'Four weeks.'

'And breech, you think?'

'Was yesterday at ultrasound. We were on our way to Brisbane.'

'Unless you've noticed lots of movements since then, your baby probably still is breech.' He glanced at Tara. 'What's the plan?'

'The plan was a Caesarean in Brisbane, but Susan

wants to stand up for a vaginal birth. So I thought that seeing you're here you could check and see where she's up to, and baby will tell us what to do. Unfortunately, Susan has to lie down for a part of that.'

Simon grinned at her. 'Interesting take. And I concur with it all.' He looked at Susan. 'You fine with those plans?'

'Perfect. As long as you are quick. I never wanted the Caesarean.'

'Ah,' said Simon, as Tara helped Susan undress and reluctantly lie down for the examination. 'A rebel.' Simon quickly but thoroughly palpated Susan's belly, stepped aside so Tara could also confirm the position of the baby, and then washed his hands and pulled on the sterile gloves. 'Baby taking after the mum? I'll be as quick as I can so you can stand up again.'

One minute later it was confirmed. 'Yep, breech. In perfect position. And ready to come.' He nodded at Tara. 'Best get another person here for baby and we can send them away if we don't need them.'

Tara crossed to the phone and called the switchboard then dragged a sheet-covered mat to the side of the bed in case Susan wanted to kneel down at some stage, and prepared her equipment. She'd never opened up sterile packs or drawn up needles so fast and excitement bubbled inside her. She was going to see her first breech birth.

Then Simon made it even more exciting. He spoke to the couple. 'I guess I should tell you that my specialty is promoting vaginal breech births at the Central Women's Hospital in Sydney, and if you don't mind I'd like to talk Tara through this birth so she can practise her own breech deliveries.'

He looked at Susan and then Pete. 'Is that all right with you?' Susan ignored Simon but nodded at Tara while she pushed, and Pete reluctantly agreed. Tara slid the little ultrasound Doppler over Susan's belly and they all heard the cloppety-clop of the baby's heartbeat. Susan's shoulders sagged with relief and she bore down with a long outward breath now she knew her baby was fine.

Simon went on. 'If baby decides to do anything tricky, I'll take over.'

Pete still didn't look happy but Tara was beginning to think poor Pete didn't handle stress well. 'We'll have to take your word for it,' he said.

'I guess that's all you can do.' Simon smiled sympathetically as he pulled a chair across and sat down beside Tara, who was perched on a little wheeled stool, leaning towards Susan. 'Though I could give you my card and my phone to ring the Sydney ward but you might miss the birth.'

Because it was coming. A little pale crescent of buttock appeared as Susan breathed out and Tara felt the increase in her own heartbeat. OMG. She was going to cradle her first breech in a totally natural, peaceful environment and she didn't even have to feel terrified because Simon was right there beside her and she felt anything but.

'So Tara isn't going to touch the baby at all until the last moment. Your baby is nice and relaxed at the moment and we don't want to scare it by putting a cold hand on him or her unexpectedly. The heart rate is great and Tara will listen after every contraction to Susan's tummy.' Simon spoke in a very quiet conversational tone and Tara listened and obeyed every word without feeling like he was saying she didn't know what to do. It was obviously a skill he'd mastered.

Simon went on. 'Breech babies have the same mechanisms as head-first babies and once the hips are through it pretty well means everything is going to fit because the hips are roughly the same size as the shoulders.'

Tara hadn't realised that. Now they could see the little swollen scrotum and penis and Pete gasped and grinned when he realised what it was. Tara couldn't believe how fast everything was happening.

'You're doing beautifully, Susan,' she whispered. 'You're amazing. Not long now.'

'Okay.' Susan sounded strained but not frightened and Tara could feel the swell of emotion she felt at every birth at the miracles women could perform. It was all happening like clockwork. The pointy bottom seemed to be curving out sideways before it stopped and swivelled and Tara looked at Simon to ask if she should flick the leg out but he just smiled and shook his head.

The buttocks came down a little further and the foot

lifted and sprang free. The other soon followed until baby was standing on tiptoe on the mat as his mother followed her instincts and crouched. Now the whole belly of the baby and the stretched umbilical cord could be seen.

'This is where we make sure the baby doesn't decided to spin the wrong way, but most of the time they drive better than we do.' Sure enough, the baby's body straightened, the stretched little chest lengthened, until there was just the top part of the baby inside.

'I can't stand it,' muttered Pete, as he twisted his fingers together, and Tara cast him a sympathetic look.

'I want to kneel,' Susan panted, and Tara cast a look at Simon.

'Just hang on for one sec, Susan. I'll move out of the way. You're almost there.' Tara pushed the chair away and knelt beside Susan as she turned sideways and with her reduced height the baby settled into a strange sitting position but with the movement the head slowly appeared, the little face flopped forward as the baby was born and Tara reached out and caught him before he fell forward onto his tummy.

'Well done,' Simon murmured with a definite thread of exultation in his voice. Tara felt a rush of emotion stinging her eyes as she dried the little body until the newborn screwed up his face and roared his displeasure.

She could see Simon's satisfaction in her management and she'd never felt so proud in her life. There was time for one brief glance of shared excitement and then it was back to the job.

'I'm just going to pop baby through your legs and you can see what you've had, Susan.' There was a flurry of limbs and cord and then Susan had her baby in her arms as she knelt upright. The face she turned to the three of them was exultant with fierce pride and joy. 'A boy. My vaginal breech birth boy. I knew I could do that.'

'Magnificently.' Simon shook his head with a twinkle in his eye that said he'd never grow tired of these moments, and Tara felt like she wouldn't want to sleep for a week she was on such a high.

Pete was in shock, and a little on the pale side as he flopped back into a chair Simon pushed up to him, while Susan was helped back up onto the bed by Tara. The new mum lay back with a satisfied smile and baby was just plain curious about the world and maybe even a little hungry.

They thanked the other doctor who had quietly arrived as unneeded back-up and he left. A few minutes later, after checking that all was well with Susan and the baby, Simon left too.

Tara leant against the doorpost, keeping watch that all was well now that she'd backed out of the circle of mother, father and child, and just soaked in the magic.

She couldn't believe it. Couldn't believe the experience that Simon had given her. Not just with his innate love of teaching and promoting breech birth to his less-experienced colleagues, but the ambience and peaceful joy of the occasion, because everyone, including her, had felt safe, and imbued with the faith that they'd had everything needed for the occasion. Her glorious moment! Because Simon had been there.

She'd never experienced anything like it. How could one man make that difference? It was a gift she hugged to herself.

Two hours later Susan was tucked up into bed for a well-earned rest but her eyes were wide and alert, baby Blake was tucked up in his little cot sound asleep beside his mother, and Pete snored gently in the big chair beside the window.

Susan and Tara looked at each other and smiled.

'I wish I could sleep,' Susan said dryly.

'It's the adrenalin from the birth,' Tara said quietly. 'Your instinct is to stay alert so you can snatch up your baby and run. You'll slowly calm down and drift off to sleep soon.'

'Thanks, Tara,' Susan said sincerely. 'From the first minute I saw you I knew everything was going to be fine.'

Tara had too. But Simon had ensured it really had gone well. He'd been amazing and she'd tell him so. 'I'm so glad. And thank you.' They grinned at each other as Tara gently shut the door to keep out the noises that might wake them.

CHAPTER SEVEN

SIMON DROPPED IN before the afternoon midwife arrived
to see how Susan was faring.

'She's great. Talking about going home tomorrow.
You going in to see her? Baby is awake and Pete's gone
home.'

Tara was at the desk, completing Susan's patient
notes. She went to stand and he put his hand up. 'Stay
there. I'm just saying hello and I'll pop out to see you
when I've finished.'

Tara nodded and carried on, wanting to have it all
completed before the end of her shift. There was a
mountain of paperwork when a baby was born, let alone
when the woman arrived not expecting to have her baby
with them, and she was transferring all the information
they'd had faxed after the event from Brisbane.

But she still had to thank Simon and she didn't want
him to leave without having the chance.

When Simon reappeared he had Blake with him.
'Susan's gone to the loo and Blake was complaining.'
He carried the baby like a little football tucked onto his

hip and his large hand cradling the baby's head with relaxed confidence. There was something incredibly attractive about a man comfortable with small babies and Tara hugged the picture to herself. Not that she was doing anything with it—just enjoying it.

Simon bounced the little baby bundle gently, feeling his weight. 'He's heavy.'

'Seven pounds on the dot.'

'Impressive for a breech.' He smiled at her. 'So were you.'

Tara could feel the heat in her cheeks. She hadn't been the amazing one. He'd instilled confidence in all of them, even the nervous Pete, so what was it about this guy that made her blush like a schoolgirl? Seeing that even when she'd been a schoolgirl she'd never blushed? 'I didn't do anything except put my hands out at the end, but I really appreciated the chance to be hands on, hands off. Thank you. And Susan was amazing.'

'It's okay, Tara. You were good because you didn't do anything. You did so well.'

'I can see why it's hands off now.' She changed the subject. Had never had never been able to deal with compliments. Probably because she hadn't received that many in her life. She inclined her head towards Blake. 'You always been this good with babies?'

He grinned and she tried not to let the power of the smile affect her. Losing battle. 'I was a couple of years older than the eldest sister and Mum had three more pretty fast. So I guess I did get good with babies. I enjoyed helping with the girls and Mum was pretty busy by the time she had Maeve. I wasn't into dolls but it was always going to be obstetrics or paediatrics.'

He looked at Tara. Tried to see into her past. 'Were you a girly girl?'

Hadn't had the chance. 'What's a girly girl?'

'Dress-ups. A favourite doll?'

There had been a couple of shared toys she'd been allowed to play with but not her own. 'After my parents died I never owned a doll. So I guess not.'

His brows drew together but thankfully he changed the subject. 'What time do you finish?'

'Three-thirty.'

'Fancy another swim?'

Simon studied the strong features of the woman across from him. He became more intrigued the more he saw her. His four sisters had all been spoilt by everyone, including himself, and secure in their knowledge of their own attraction. Even Maeve in her current circumstances dressed and acted like the confident woman she was.

But Tara favoured the unisex look of jeans and T-shirts and now he knew that at work, despite the choices of the rest of the staff, she even favoured shapeless scrubs.

But in her plain black one-piece swimsuit she couldn't hide the fact she was all woman. A delightfully shapely woman with determination to the little chin and a wariness of being hurt that seemed to lurk at the back of her eyes.

An orphan. And a loner perhaps? 'Tell me about your childhood.'

'Why?'

'Because I'm interested.'

A wary glance and then she looked away. 'Nothing to tell.'

'Are you always this difficult when people want to get to know you?'

A clash of her eyes. 'Yes.'

'So did you always live in an orphanage or did you have foster-parents?'

'Both.'

He waited and she gave in with a sigh.

'I preferred the orphanage because at least I knew where I stood.'

He would have thought an orphanage would be way worse but he knew nothing. Hadn't ever thought about it. Didn't actually like to think about it when he looked at Tara. 'How so?'

'Being a foster-child is tricky. You know it's not permanent, so it's hard not to be defensive. If you let people get to you it hurts too much when you have to leave.'

He knew he should drop it, but he couldn't. 'Don't some foster-parents stay with the same children?'

Her face gave nothing away. 'I seemed to find the ones who shouldn't be foster-parents.'

He felt a shaft of sympathy for a little lost Tara.

Found himself wanting to shake those careless foster-parents. It must have shown on his face.

'Don't even think about feeling sorry for me, Simon.' There was a fierceness in her eyes that made him blink.

And apologise. 'Sorry. I think my sisters had it too much the other way with people looking after them. I've always been protective. If you ask Maeve, too protective, and I guess I got worse when the truth came out that I really only had half the right.' It wasn't something he usually burdened others with twice but maybe unintentionally he'd trodden on Tara's past hurts and felt he should expose his own.

Of course Tara pounced on the chance to change the subject and he guessed he couldn't blame her. Served him right.

'So how old were you when you found out you had another father?'

The way she said it, like he had been lucky, if you looked at it from her point of view when she didn't even have even one father and he had two. Even privately complained about it. Novel idea when he'd been a cranky little victim despite telling himself to get over it.

He brought himself back to the present. 'After my dad's first heart attack, that would be the man I thought was my real dad, I heard my mother question whether I should be told about Angus. Not a great way to find out. Nineteen and I hadn't been given the choice to know my real dad for the whole of my childhood. And to be still treated like a child.' He hadn't taken it well and had half blamed Angus as well for not knowing of his existence.

'So how'd you find him? Angus?' Tara had looked past that to the interesting bit. Maybe he should have done that too a long time ago. She made him feel petty and he didn't like it.

'It was more than ten years ago, but at the time it all seemed to move too slowly. Took six months. He was on some discreet medical assignment overseas and the government wouldn't let me contact him. Then he came to see me and brought me here to meet my grandfather. It must have been a family trait because he hadn't seen his own dad for twenty years.'

'Louisa's husband?'

'Yep. Apparently Angus and Grandfather Ned fought over my dad's relationship with my mother, and when they ran away together and it didn't work out, he never came back here.'

She didn't offer sympathy. Just an observation as she glanced around. 'It's a very healing place.'

'Well, Angus brought me here to get to know him. And this was where he met Mia.'

He wondered if that was why he hadn't been able to commit to a relationship in the past. To fully trust people because even his own parents had betrayed him. He shook his head. Didn't know where all that angst had come from, it certainly wasn't something he'd talked about before, and if he'd stirred this kind of feeling in Tara by asking about her past, he could see why she didn't want to talk about it. When he thought about her life he felt incredibly selfish and self-indulgent complaining about his own.

She'd said Lyrebird Lake was a healing place. Maybe it was. Did that mean his coming here with Maeve meant it was his turn to move on? He mused, 'I don't know if it's the place or the people, but whenever I visit it seems when I leave here I'm usually less stressed.'

She laughed and he enjoyed the sound. 'Even if you lose some of your holidays to fill in for your dad and unexpected breech deliveries.'

'They're the good bits.' And he realised it was true. He smiled at her. 'The really good bits.'

'Like today.' She smiled back and the way it changed her face made him think of a previous conversation. Tara's glorious moment. She certainly looked the part.

He caught her fingers. 'Today has had some very magical moments.'

He smoothed the towel out of her grip and let it fall and gathered up her other hand. He half expected her to pull away but she seemed bemused more than annoyed. He tugged her closer until their hips met. Liking the feel of a wet Lycra mermaid against his chest, unconsciously he leaned in and her curves fitted his like they were designed for each other. He looked down at her long, thin fingers in his bigger hands, stroked her palm and felt a shiver go through her.

'What are you doing?' she whispered.

He had to smile. 'Enjoying another magical moment.'

Looked down into her face and then there was no way he could stop himself bending his head and brushing her lips with his. Watched her eyelids flutter closed and the idea that this prickly, independent woman trusted him enough to close her eyes and allow him closer filled him with delight.

Lips like strawberry velvet. A shiver of electricity he couldn't deny. 'Mmm. You taste nice.'

Her turn to smile as she opened her eyes and ducked her head to hide her face but he couldn't have that. Wouldn't have that as he slid one finger under chin, savoured the confusion in her eyes and face and then leant in for a proper kiss. She was like falling into a dream, soft in all the right places, especially her lips.

As she began to kiss him back there wasn't much thinking in his mind after that but a whole lot of feeling was going on. Until abruptly she ended it.

Tara felt as if she was floating and then suddenly realised she was kissing the man everyone loved. Who did she think she was? She pulled away and turned her back on him. Picked up the towel she'd dropped. Didn't know what had happened—one minute they'd been flirting and teasing, probably to get away from the previous conversations, and then he'd confused the heck out of her with the way he'd looked at her—and that kiss!

She could still feel the crush against his solid expanse of damp chest and was surprisingly still dazed by a kiss that had gone from gorgeously warm and yummy to scorching hot in a nanosecond.

And she'd thought he was a little stand-offish! This wasn't going anywhere, except a one-night stand, maybe if she was lucky a one-month stand. Well, she'd been as bad as him. She sighed and turned back to him with a smile that she'd practised over the years that shielded her from the world.

'Guess we'd better get back.'

He narrowed his eyes and there was a pause when she thought he was going to get all deep and personal or apologise, but he didn't. Thank goodness.

She just wanted to finish drying off and walk back to the manse. Maintain the reality that she was playing with a toy that didn't belong to her and if she kept touching it she'd be in deep trouble.

Simon really wanted to hold her hand, it would have been…nice? But Tara had tucked her fingers up under her elbows in a keep-off gesture that he couldn't help reading. Maybe he had come on a bit strong but, lordy, when he'd kissed her the second time the heat between them had nearly singed his eyebrows off. The thought made him smile. And grimace because it obviously hadn't affected her the way it had affected him. Did she realise the power those lips of hers held?

When they arrived back at the manse the kitchen was in chaos. Simon figured out that Louisa had cajoled Maeve into helping her assemble the Christmas tree and mounds of tinsel and baubles lay scattered across the kitchen table and cheesy Christmas tunes were playing in the background.

The manse had a big old lounge room but he knew every year Louisa put the Christmas tree up in the kitchen because that was the place everyone seemed to gravitate to—and this year was no different.

Simon loved the informality of it, unlike his mother's colour-co-ordinated precision, and he enjoyed the bemused expression, mixed with a little embarrassment left over from their kiss, on Tara's face as she looked round at him.

'Excellent timing, Simon,' Louisa said, as she handed him an armful of tiny star-shaped bulbs on a wire and a huge black plastic bag. She gestured vaguely to the screen door and he inclined his head to Tara and opened the door for her. The long post and rail veranda looked over the street and then the lake.

'Outside is where it really happens.' Good to have something to fill the silence between them. Awkward-R-Us. He waved the roll of bulbs at Tara and set about repairing the damage he'd done by kissing her.

'This is the start of the outside contingent. My job is to help Dad put these up when I'm home.' He pulled a little stepladder along behind him until he reached the end of the veranda and climbed up. Started to hang the tiny lights as far as he could reach before he climbed down again.

Tara was still looking bewildered and maybe still a little preoccupied from their kiss at the lake. He was sorry she was feeling uncomfortable, but he knew for a fact he wasn't sorry he'd kissed her. He wanted to do it again. Instead he carried on the conversation because she sure wasn't helping. 'These go along the top wooden rail. You can see them from down the street. Looks very festive.'

'I imagine it does.' She closed her eyes and he realised she was doing one of those breathing things he'd seen her do before and when she opened her eyes she was the old Tara again.

She smiled, so she must be okay, and he felt inordinately relieved. 'I'm not experienced at decorations. Put a few up in the ward last year when I worked Christmas week. Santa Claus was a big hit with the mums and their new babies.'

Now, there was a fantasy. Maybe he could dress up as Mr Claus and she'd sit on his knee. Naughty Simon. 'Santa has potential for lots of things.' He could feel the smile in his voice and packed that little make-believe away for later. Then he realised that, of course, she'd missed out on family Christmas for most of her life too. Not a nice thought. 'I'm guessing he didn't visit the home?'

She looked at him with disgust. 'Don't go there, Simon. I'm fine. They looked after me and I was never hungry. Lots of kids can't say that.'

Okay, he knew that, but there was more to being cared for than food in your belly, he thought as he hung each loop of Christmas lights over the tiny hooks under the eaves, and winced again at how easy his own child-hood had been.

He glanced towards the kitchen, where his sister stood watching Louisa tweak the tree.

Maeve had been loved and cared for and told she was wonderful since the day she was born. A lot of the time by Simon because he'd thought the sun shone out of his youngest sibling. Though that wasn't doing him much good at the moment.

He remembered his father saying Tara was tough. He guessed she'd had to be. 'Okay. Moving on.' And he tried to. 'As you are inexperienced I will explain. You, Mrs Claus, have to hold the big ladder while I put the star up.'

'Louisa has a star?' The look she gave him made up for everything. She appreciated him backing off. Okay. He'd avoid the orphanage topic but he still planned to make this Christmas special.

'Yep. In the bag.'

Tara undid the string and peered in. 'A blue one. Looks three feet tall?'

He was going down the stairs to the lawn. 'Goes on the corner of the roof.' He pulled out a large metal lad-der from behind a water tank stand, and the long ladder reached all the way to the top of the roof.

Simon sneaked a look at her face, saw excitement growing as they put up the decorations, no matter how hard she tried to hide it.

She was loving this!

The thought made his heart feel warm and a feeling of delighted indulgence expanded in his gut. 'Louisa has everything Christmas. It started after she married Ned. Grandfather discovered she'd always wanted Christmas decorations and each year he bought something even more extravagant for her collection. She has a whole nativity scene with life-sized people for the front lawn, and all the animals move.'

'Now, that is seriously cool.' Tara's eyes shone as she looked at the ladder. Then she frowned as she looked back at him. 'If you can climb that and not worry, then parachuting would be a cinch.' She crossed over to him, carrying the star, and waited for him to put his foot on the bottom rung.

He looked at her but ignored the parachute comment. 'Hmm. The decorations are cool, but not when you have to assemble them and put them up, then pull them down every year. I could live without the ladder climb.' He grinned at her and knew she could tell he didn't mind. 'Dad usually does it but he asked me to start. Louisa likes it up before December and that's tomorrow.'

He sighed, glanced at the ladder and held out his hand. 'Better get it over and done with. At least there's clips up here for the star. It just snaps into a slot and the wiring is already in place. It will be exciting for the little girls when they come home.'

She grinned. 'You're a wonderful grandson. And brother.'

He edged up a step at a time. 'Don't think so. Sometimes I only see them once a year at Christmas.'

She raised her voice. 'They said you write to them.'

He stopped. Looked down at her. 'I send a pretty card or a funny postcard every now and then. They phone me on Sundays if I'm not working.'

She couldn't imagine what it would be like to have someone do that. Imagine if Simon did that for her? Her whole world would gain another dimension, and then she stopped herself. Smacked herself mentally. He was just a nice guy. A nice guy who seemed to like kissing her?

CHAPTER EIGHT

THE FOLLOWING SATURDAY was Tara's birthday. She hadn't mentioned it, so he hadn't, but he'd quietly arranged a cake at the place where they were going to breakfast after the jump.

He'd learnt something as a brother of four plus two sisters. Women loved surprises.

He didn't even know why he was looking forward to Tara's adventure when he hated the whole concept of risk, except now he wouldn't miss it because it involved Tara. He hoped he wasn't getting too caught up in the whole Tara fantasy. It wasn't like it was a date.

She'd started off quiet, and he'd wondered if she was sorry she'd asked him. In truth, the discussion had been before he'd kissed her, but then as they drew closer to the jump zone she became more animated.

He glanced across at her face, eyes shining, a huge grin on her face, and she squirmed in her seat like the kid she'd never had the chance to be. This was a whole new side to the woman he considered the most self-sufficient young woman he'd met, and he savoured her little bursts of conversation in a new way from his previous lady friends.

She had her own ideas, often contrary to his, on work, on politics, on sport even, but was always willing to listen to another point of view.

He'd rarely enjoyed a conversation so much. He could have driven all day with her beside him instead of doing what he'd come to do. Watch Tara jump out of a plane.

When they arrived Simon followed Tara from his car and almost had to run to keep up. Now, that was what he called eagerness to embrace the experience. He might even be starting to get her interest, even if he didn't share it.

He'd read the skydiving webpage when he hadn't been able to sleep last night. It had been intriguing with the way they mentioned 'changing your life with a jump', though he couldn't see how Tara's life needed changing in that way. She was the most centred person he knew to be around.

Apparently, sky-diving freed you of the minutiae of the everyday that could cloud the joys of living.

Okay, rave on, yet the expression had resonated with him and made him wonder with a startling moment of clarity if that was what he did.

He organised and pre-planned as much as he could, as if he could keep all the facets of his world—in his mind he could picture pregnant Maeve, so that included his sisters—in order and safe from the possibility of harm.

He glanced up as another plane droned overhead

into a scatter of puffy clouds in the blue sky. Safe from harm? Well, that went out the window with sky-diving. Literally.

Simon shrugged and guessed he could imagine the small stuff didn't matter when you were hurtling at two hundred kilometres an hour through those clouds before your parachute opened. If it opened. He shuddered and increased his pace.

Inside the flimsy building—how much money did they spend on this operation anyway, and just how safe were they?—Simon's gaze travelled around suspiciously until he realised what he was doing and pulled himself up. Tara would be saying he could draw bad luck with negative thoughts, and despite his scepticism he refocussed on the woman he'd brought here, and just looking at her made his mind settle.

She was grinning like there was no tomorrow. He jerked his thoughts away from that one as she beckoned him over.

'Simon?'

Her expression puzzled him—eager, mischievous, with just a touch of wariness. 'They could squeeze you in if you wanted to change your mind.'

'And you're telling me this because?'

Her eyes glowed with excitement and for a minute there he wanted to take her outside this building and back her up against a tree and kiss the living daylights out of her. Then she said, 'Why don't you jump with me? Do it spontaneously.'

He blinked. One pleasant picture replaced with another he didn't fancy. 'Like spontaneous combustion. One whoosh and I'm gone?' She was dreaming. 'Then who would do all the things I do?'

Her voice lowered and she came closer until suddenly there seemed only two of them in the room. 'Stop thinking about everyone else for a minute. Do it for yourself. Be irresponsible for once and find out what it feels like. Change your life.'

There's nothing wrong with my life, he thought, but he didn't say it. Just stared into those emerald-green eyes that burned with the passion of a zealot. The woman was mad. 'Nope. But thank you. You go ahead and have your instructions for insanity and I will arrange breakfast for afterwards when you land on the beach.'

'They say it's the closest you'll ever get to flying on your own.'

'I read that.' He'd actually done a bit of almost-flying when he'd kissed a certain someone the other day. He was barely listening as he soaked in her features. How could he have ever thought this woman was average?

She looked at him for a moment and then leant forward and kissed him quickly on the lips. 'Okay.'

Then she was gone, leaving an echo of her scent and the softness of her mouth that vibrated quietly in the back of his mind and all the way down to his toes. And a tiny insidious voice poked him with a thought. Imagine if it did change the way you lived. Not his work but his private life.

His lack of trust in relationships. The business of assembling scenarios so he could be sure he had all his bases covered. The worry about minutiae, like it said in the brochure. Possibly left over from the time he'd realised his own father had been totally unaware of him—when he should have checked if he had a son!

No way. He shut the thought down. Not today. But unconsciously, as he leant against the wall and watched her follow the instructions of Lawrence, her 'chute buddy' coach, he paid more attention as they prepared her for the way she left the aircraft and the way she had to bend her legs and point her toes as they landed.

He watched her tilt her head back, exposing her gorgeous tanned throat. Apparently that was so when you hurtled out of the plane your head didn't slam backwards and knock out the person who was going to pull the ripcord. Good choice. Tilt head. He could just imagine her. Wished he could see her do it. He grinned and looked away. No, he didn't. At least he was calmer than he'd thought he'd be, watching all this.

Simon glanced at the cost of the extravagant packages that could come with the jump and doubted she had enough for the whole experience to be filmed, captured in photographs as well and saved in a bound volume. He wandered discreetly over to the sales desk, enquired, and hoped like hell she wouldn't mind if he paid for the video/album package to arrive in the mail.

He ensured Lawrence switched on his high-definition camera. It was the next best thing to being a fly on the wall without having to actually be there. And she'd have a permanent memento of the event.

She hopefully wouldn't take it up full time if she loved it. Simon found himself smiling as he drifted back to the doorway, where he leaned while he waited for her to finish her induction.

Then it was time for her to go. Go as in jump.

Tara bounced across the room with her harness all strapped between her legs and over her shoulders. Plastic wind protection goggles sat on top of her head and she radiated suppressed excitement like a beacon in a storm.

The two other people in her group seemed to radiate less exuberant anticipation. Right there with you, buddy, Simon thought with some amusement, and appreciated again that Tara did bring a sparkle into his day. As long as she didn't want him to join her he was quite happy to stand on the sidelines and enjoy the show.

Tara barely felt her feet on the floor. She couldn't wait for that moment when they tumbled out. She glanced back at her older instructor who carried the chute that would float them to the ground again and wanted to hug herself with excitement. Or have Simon hug her.

She glanced at Simon, who watched her with a whimsical expression on his face. It was so cool he'd come with her. Even if he didn't want to jump, and it had been a pretty big spur-of-the-moment ask, he still looked fairly happy. She'd been a little afraid of that. That he'd radiate stress vibes and doomsday foreboding but he'd surprised her with how calmly he was taking it and how supportive he was.

She had an epiphany that maybe real men didn't have to do crazy things to be in tune with her. Look at her last man. He'd been crazy and had turned out to be a loser of the highest order so maybe the opposite worked.

She knew for a fact that Simon was far from a loser but she also knew she wasn't looking long term for someone like him. People like him spent their lives with prim and proper doctors' wives, not someone who wanted to seek thrills and drift from town to town like her. People like Simon hadn't been brought up in orphanages and foster-homes.

But you could kiss those people. The ones you weren't going to marry. It was a shame she'd enjoyed it so much because the idea of kissing Simon again intruded at the wrong times—like that mad moment when she'd asked him to jump and then kissed him.

But she wasn't worrying about that now and peered ahead to the tarmac where their little plane waited patiently for them. Excitement welled in her throat as they all paused at the gate and the actual jumpers farewelled their ground crew.

'Good luck. You look beautiful.' Simon's words took her by surprise and she could feel the smile as it surged from somewhere in her over-excited belly.

'Thank you. So do you.' She grinned at him and he leaned in and kissed her firmly on the lips so that she knew she'd been kissed. For the first time the ground felt a little firmer under her feet and the haze she'd been floating in sharpened to reality. Luckily, that made it even more exciting.

The next fifteen minutes was spent crammed into the plane as they climbed in a slow spiral up to fifteen thousand feet. She sat perched on the lap of her chute buddy and surprisingly time seemed to pass very quickly with the hills towards Lyrebird Lake in the distance and the white sand of the beach underneath them.

They were going to land on the beach below the lighthouse and apparently Simon would already be there with the ground crew waiting for them to land.

Her chute buddy was fun and kept saying how relaxed she looked. But this wasn't something she was afraid of.

Finally they reached fifteen thousand feet, the roller door slid back along the roof and the cold wind rushed in.

He'd told her it was one degree outside but it would only take thirty seconds to get back to warm air, but she doubted she'd have time to feel temperatures as they hurtled through the clouds.

The boy next to her, now securely strapped to his chute buddy, cast an imploring look at the safety of the plane and then, with one wild-eyed glance at the occupants, disappeared.

'Let's go, Tara,' Lawrence shouted in her ear, and he edged his bottom and Tara as well, balanced on his lap, towards the opening and swung both their legs out until their backs were to the plane. Below them the ocean and the beach curved below under the scattered clouds.

She pushed her head back into Lawrence's shoulder and then they were out. Wind rushed past their faces, she had a brief glimpse of the plane above them in the sky and then they were facing the ground with the wind rushing into her face and her hands clenched tightly on the chest straps.

Funnily, even in that moment, she could see Simon's face. She grinned at the image and stared out into the vacant air in front of her. 'Woo-hoo.'

Simon had watched the plane disappear into the clouds.

Fifteen minutes later he watched the blue parachute as it came into view, imagined the grin on her face, the joy in her eyes and found himself very keen to see her feet touch the ground. Though no doubt she'd be wanting the descent to last for ever.

At the last minute he pulled his phone from his pocket and videoed her landing. She waved as she sailed past, and he chuckled out loud. This had been fun and he'd been dreading it.

She landed smoothly on her bottom with her feet out in front of her, strapped like a little limpet to her chute buddy, and with a couple of snaps of the buckles she was free to stand and twirl around with excitement. He grinned as he watched her.

Later when he took her to the little restaurant on the river for a late breakfast she couldn't stop talking, re-living the experience, and he watched her shining eyes blink and frown and widen as she told the tale of her tumble from the aircraft, the whoosh of the parachute opening and the moment when she'd seen him watching her land.

Then he watched her eyes widen wistfully when a birthday cake was carried across the room and she glanced behind them to see where it was going. But his breath caught in his throat when he saw her eyes fill with tears when she realised it was hers. What was wrong? Had he done wrong?

He'd upset her and he didn't know why. 'It's yours. For you. Happy birthday, Tara.'

She just sat there staring at the lit candles as they burnt merrily. The candles started melting and began to dribble wax down onto the cake. Spluttered and dripped. Still she didn't blow them out.

'Blow them out.'

She looked at him. Her eyes still looked haunted. Then she whispered, 'Are you sure?'

'Quick.'

The waitress and chef who had followed the cake out were looking at each other, not sure what was going on, as they waited to sing like they did every time a cake was ordered.

Then she blinked, shook her head and blew them out. Almost defiantly. Certainly with ample power. To her horror, she even blew wax onto the tablecloth. Blushed and glanced at the waitress and her 'Sorry' was drowned out by the lusty singing of 'Happy Birthday'. Then she did cry.

The waitress and the chef bolted back to the kitchen and Simon handed her a napkin. Tara hid her face in it.

'Don't ever do that to me again.'

With startling clarity he suspected what was wrong. 'Have you ever blown candles out on a cake before, Tara?'

She glared at him. 'Not since I was six. As if you couldn't tell.'

'No cakes at the orphanage?'

'A hundred children would be a cake every three days. I didn't even know it was my birthday half the time. You couldn't know—I understand that—but it's never been a big day for me.'

He didn't want to think about a hundred kids without birthdays because it hurt all the way down to his toes. 'So why the parachute jump this year?'

She shrugged. 'Coincidence and maybe Lyrebird Lake warmth. They had a birthday party for Louisa and it was very cool. Started me thinking about a new life and a celebration that I had control of and wasn't using.'

'So a present?'

'Yep. That's my present to myself. I can't really afford it but...' she shook off the melancholy and gave

him a watery smile '…it was so worth it.' She straightened her shoulders. Smiled at him again, though still
a little misty-eyed. 'Thanks for the cake, Simon, and
sorry for the drama. It just took me by surprise. I blew
some candles out once and they weren't mine. Got in
all sorts of trouble so just had a bit of a time slip there.'

'Well that cake was a hundred per cent yours and
even the singing was good.'

She glanced towards the kitchen with a little embarrassment still on her face. 'Very good. They must
think I'm mad.'

'I'm sure they're thinking you must have a very good
reason for acting as you did. Or they think I upset you.'

Her first cake with candles? Damn it, he wished he
could turn up on her birthday and buy her a cake every
year until she was so blasé about it she didn't notice.
Then he listened to the wild thoughts in his head. How
had he got to this point?

Because seeing Tara every year for the rest of his life
didn't seem an unreasonable thing. But that was crazy.

After breakfast they went back to check out the
beach. Simon kept saying she'd eaten and she wasn't
allowed to swim for an hour but, seriously, she only
wanted to splash in the waves anyway.

They stripped down to swimsuits and she kicked a
skid of water his way.

After some serious splashing in his direction Simon
stopped watching her with a smile on his face and
started to chase her. She was pretty fast.

But he was faster. When he caught her and lifted her, spun her, held against his strong broad chest like a prize, it was as exciting as falling through the air this morning.

She'd always watched others do this, dreamt of doing it herself one day with some hero, and now here she was, with this gorgeous guy tossing her around like she was a lightweight as he shuffled on the sand and pretended to throw her into the water. She squeaked in mock terror, feeling like she was in a movie, a fabulous romantic movie, and while she knew it was just that, a fantasy that would stop when the hour or two was up, she was darned well going to enjoy every fabulous second of it.

Plus it was her birthday. She was the birthday girl and Simon would not let her forget it. That was very cool.

Then Simon walked purposefully forward through the knee-high waves until he sank into the surf with her still in his arms and the cold salt water foamed around them. She could feel the core of warmth where their skins still connected and she couldn't do anything except turn her face to him and lean in for a kiss. A salty, exuberant kiss that was her way of saying thank you.

He must have been waiting because his arms tightened even more firmly around her and the kiss spiralled into a hot, hungry, searing feast of strength and softness and sliding tongues that were as hot as the water was cold around them. She grabbed on tighter and jammed her breasts harder against his chest and they didn't come up for air until a bigger than normal wave smacked them in the head and they broke apart coughing and spluttering and finally laughing.

Phew. She'd needed that bucket of reality because she'd been getting swept away in the fantasy of it all.

She swam away from him, bobbed with the waves, their feet still touching the golden sand below their toes but rising up and down with the cool green waves as her heart rate slowly began to settle.

This had to be the best birthday ever.

CHAPTER NINE

BACK AT THE manse life carried on as usual. Maeve slowed down even more as her baby grew and weighed her down, but her nausea had eased, although her mood remained sombre. Tara suspected she held unrequited affection for the baby's father and wondered if maybe someone should try again to contact him by phone. But that was for Maeve and she had enough happening.

Last night another of Tara's caseload women had had her baby and Tara had been up most of the night, but when she'd woken after lunch she'd felt strangely unsettled so she'd come out to the manger on the front lawn to find her peace.

Everything was so…Christmassy. She felt like a minor character who'd forgotten her lines. Presents were appearing under the tree inside and she'd started to buy little gifts for everyone but lacked the experience to know how much to spend so had gone for quirky.

With combined family enthusiasm Louisa had managed to assemble her Christmas nativity scene on the front lawn. Tara had been surprised that the little straw-filled crib was empty despite the adoring looks and nods from the mechanical Mary, Joseph and the three wise men, until Simon had whispered that baby Jesus would arrive on Christmas morning.

There was something very centred about the anticipation of the baby that appealed to Tara. When she needed to get away to think she ended up on the garden seat that had a clear view of the people and animals in front of the manger. The whole concept of sharing their front lawn with the town took a bit of getting used to so she tried to come when it was deserted.

Those crazy manger animals nodded twenty-four seven and at night floodlights bathed the area.

During the day it wasn't unusual for children to drop by on the way home from school to check out the display and in the evenings families wandered down and oohed and ahhed and discussed what was new this year.

Angus and Mia had brought back an outdoor train set that ran on solar lights, and it chugged around the lighted Christmas tree on the lawn with pretend presents in the carriages behind. That one was a big hit with the little boys. Tara was secretly very impressed with it too.

Then she noticed Simon coming towards her with a determined stride and her pulse rate jumped at the grin he was sending her way. She'd been busy with her caseload women and hadn't seen him for more than a few minutes in the last few days since the parachute jump and beach. It was probably for the best because she was taking heed of her sensible side.

'There's a parcel for you, Tara.' He handed her a thick, flat package and she took it and turned it over in her hands but really she was absorbing the vibration between them as Simon sat down. There was a little gap between their bodies and the air seemed to be vibrating in the space. Very unsettling. He nudged her.

'Go on. Open it.'

Something was going on because there was definite mischief in his eyes as he waited for her to open the parcel.

She glanced down at the address. 'It's from the parachuting club.'

'Let me guess. You've become a life member.'

She had to laugh at that. 'Only if they want a resident midwife—but I don't imagine there's a lot of call for parachuting pregnant ladies.'

'Perhaps not.' He was still waiting for her to open it obviously.

'Aren't you going to leave me in peace?' She looked across and raised her eyes. 'Sticky beak?'

'Yep.'

She smiled and began to ease open the package, careful not to tear any of the envelope.

He huffed out his impatience. But he was pretending. 'Rip it!'

'No.' Shook her head. 'Envelopes can be re-used. And it's not like I get many parcels.'

He folded his arms and she could feel his eagerness. She began to suspect what it was. Oh, my. 'Did you buy me the package, Simon?'

She surprised a look of wariness on his face she hadn't expected. He didn't say anything, just waited for her to pull it out.

When she did she couldn't speak. It was a bound volume of at least a hundred photos from right at the beginning of her instruction session to the moment she actually launched into space and all the way down until they landed. And then she saw the DVD.

She'd seen the camera on Lawrence's arm but had assumed it was there for safety reasons and had been sort of aware they'd been filming some of the jump. Not the whole lot!

If she thought about it she'd guessed some people might change their mind and buy packages after the jump. She'd lusted after one but had decided it was an expense she hadn't needed.

And Simon had bought her the full extravaganza. How did she thank him for something so huge—it was too huge—but it wasn't the sort of gift you could give back and say, *You keep it*. He just kept taking her breath away.

His voice was worried when she didn't say anything. 'Hope that's okay? I know how independent you are. But I just thought everyone would like to see your adventure too—without having to jump,' he added hastily. 'I can afford it, you know.'

'I guess you can. And it was a lovely thing to do. Probably the loveliest thing anyone has done for me— except maybe the birthday cake the other day.' She leaned across and kissed his cheek but it was a dutiful kiss. 'But that's it. Don't start buying presents for me, Simon. I move a lot and can't build up possessions.' Or unreal expectations.

He shook his head. 'You don't *have* to move a lot.'

He just didn't get it. The world always moved you on when you started to love a place. 'Sure. Okay. And thank you.'

She could feel the tears pushing one way as she pushed them back the other but more than that she wanted to look at the pictures and re-immerse herself in the jump so she could forget the look in his eyes. The more she thought about it and the reason Simon had said he'd done it, the more touched she was.

She was an ungrateful wretch with no gift-receiving skills. Where the heck did you get those skills? She leant across and kissed him on the mouth this time. The anticipation was building. 'I'm sorry. Thank you. It is great.' She glanced at him under her brows. 'Wanna look with me?'

He seemed to deflate with relief and she realised he wasn't as calm as he looked. Maybe Simon was having a hard time dealing with the undercurrents between them too? An intriguing thought that could come back to haunt her.

He slid next to her until their thighs were touching, and she wondered what the passing manger lovers would think about Dr Campbell snuggling up to the midwife, but then she gave up and prepared to open the book. The relief in his face confirmed her suspicion. He'd been worried he'd upset her and she guessed she could get tetchy so he'd been brave to push ahead and buy it. The guy was certainly a keeper. Such a darned shame she couldn't.

Instead, she opened the album and the first picture captured the day. There she was, the plane disappearing above them, and an expression of sheer exhilaration on her face as they freefell into the clouds. She looked at Simon and there was a look of indulgence on his face that made her pause and then dismiss the ridiculous idea that he might care for her just a little more than she'd thought.

After a hilarious fifteen minutes sitting on the bench, poring over the album, they took the DVD into the house, where they dragged Louisa and Maeve into the lounge room to watch it on the old television.

During the ten-minute DVD Louisa gasped and covered her mouth and even Maeve laughed out loud and expressed her envy that Tara had done something she'd wanted to do. Then it was over and Louisa and Maeve went back to the kitchen and she had to go and check on one of her early labour mums.

'Thanks again, Simon.' She'd probably kissed him enough, she admitted with a definite tug of despondency as she turned away. 'I'd better get going on my home visit.'

Simon nodded and held the door for her and he didn't lean down enough for her to attempt any sort of cheek-kissing salutation like he did. But he did say, 'So when are you going to take me on your bike?'

That stopped her. She'd thought it unlikely this conversation would ever come up. And it wasn't like she could say no now. In fact, she owed him big time. 'Any time you're ready.'

He shrugged. 'I'm officially off call and ready when you are. Make a date and do your worst.'

She looked him over coolly but inside she was doing a little shaking and wondering if this would be a clever thing to do. Simon, pressed up against her, his arms holding on tight. Leaning into corners together. His strong thighs alongside her thighs. But there was barely a wobble in her voice when she answered, thank goodness. 'I don't have a worst. Where did you want to go?'

He shrugged. 'It doesn't really matter as long as I get to try the full experience.'

This was getting weirder. Whatever that meant. 'Fine. Then Saturday. We'll go up to the lookout, it's a nice drive through the forest and it's a great place to watch the sunset.'

'You're on.'

Almost enthusiastic. Her voice held a hint of indulgence. 'You'll be wanting to parachute next.'

'I haven't ruled it out in the far distant future.'

She looked at him and he was smiling but whether he was teasing or serious she couldn't work out. What she could read made her cheeks feel hot. She almost wished he didn't look at her like that because it was going to be incredibly hard some time in the definite future when the feeling it gave her was lost.

But then her sensible side, the one that said she would survive no matter what, decided that being with Simon was like parachuting—the rush was incredible but the reality was the ground waiting for you. But it didn't mean you shouldn't enjoy the ride. This would never last but it was wonderful while it did and from now on she was going to take what was on offer with open arms.

On Saturday Simon was waiting for her when she returned from an unscheduled home visit. One of her caseload ladies was having breastfeeding problems so Tara had sat with her for the last feed until mum and baby were back in sync.

She glanced at her watch. 'Do we still have time before sunset? Or do you want to wait until tomorrow afternoon?'

'I've been waiting all day to hang off the back of your bike.' The words were jaunty but the unease was not quite hidden on Simon's face and belied his statement as he picked up his backpack.

She had to smile at that. 'Liar.' She watched him slide his arms into the shoulder straps and hoist the pack onto his back in one adroitly muscular movement. Dragged her eyes away. 'What's in the bag?'

'Never you mind. You worry about me and I'll worry about the bag.'

Oh, she was worried about him all right. 'Sounds intriguing. You'll have to wait while I change.' She glanced at his long jeans and solid shoes and nodded approval. 'I don't ride in shorts either.'

'Tell me you come in leather.' A wicked wink suggested he was fantasising and hoping she'd come to the party.

'I can do.' She raised her brows suggestively, playing along with him, and couldn't believe how much fun this stuff was. 'But normally only for long trips.' She tossed over her shoulder, 'You'll just have to wait and see.'

Simon watched her scoot along the hallway and despite his misgivings about actually being a pillion passenger on a motorbike he had the feeling Tara would be worth waiting for. Ten agonising minutes later he wasn't disappointed. Sweet mother!

Tara's long sexy legs were encased in skin-tight, dull black leather trousers and high black boots. The material's softness curved around the cutest tight little butt, and his fingers curled in his pockets. Untucked, she wore a white shirt with a plunging neckline and a short, black, sleeveless leather vest was loosely laced over the top. Yep, that completed the outfit, and he had to jam his hands into his pockets. Now he really couldn't wait to get on her bike.

She looked like something out of a Hell's Angels fantasy world and he was glad they were going into the country and not on the main road. He was man enough to prefer to have her to himself like this and couldn't wait to have the excuse to hold her around her waist and snuggle up against her. Must have a latent dominatrix fantasy he hadn't known about and he grinned to himself as he followed her outside and around to the carport.

She pulled the cover off the bike and sat astride as she wiggled it backwards. No, she wouldn't let him help pull it out and face it the right way, so he did the next best thing and just stood there and enjoyed the show. He decided that Tara was a strong little thing, and the thought made him even hotter, in a non-weather-related way.

Tara set about checking everything was right and finally gave him the nod. She handed him her helmet and pulled her spare on.

'So have you ever been on a bike before?'

'No.'

'Okay. So hold on loosely around my waist, tighter on the corners. Sit up straight. Try and lean gently into the corners in the same direction as I do. If you find the corners too hard just don't lean the opposite way.'

'Yes, ma'am.'

'Good. Remember that. I'm the captain.'

The captain. He kept his tongue firmly between his teeth when he really wanted to say, *Aye, Aye,* and grin at her. Or kiss her. Definitely the last. He'd been waiting all day for this moment, the sliding on behind her thing, of course, not the actual motorbike thing, and as he climbed on and shifted in until his thighs were up against her leather-clad buttocks it was as exciting as he'd imagined. See. He could be adventurous.

Initially she took off slowly and rode along the back streets of the lake and Simon found that holding onto Tara while the big bike vibrated strongly beneath them was a very pleasant experience. He'd decided that worrying about accidents wouldn't help at all so tried conscientiously to focus on the other, more positive things.

Lots of delightful sensory input to distract him, especially the really tactile stuff, like Tara's waist was the perfect width beneath his hands, and he tried not to dwell on the fact if he reached up and spread his fingers he could span her rib cage and even brush the undersides of her breasts. Felt the uncomfortable tightness in his jeans and dragged his mind away from that scenario because it was just too uncomfortable.

Her buttocks pressed against him as they sped up an incline and if he tightened his arms his chest could stretch forward and lean into her back any time he chose.

'You okay?' She turned her head a little and he heard the words. She sounded strained but it was probably the wind snatching them away.

'Fine,' he shouted back. Conversation was impossible and he didn't even try. They'd picked up speed and were climbing a narrow tarred road that curved around the mountain towards the lookout. Heavy forest growth hid the thousands of cicadas that were humming as a quiet thrum under the rumble of the engine as they rode along, and every now and then a circling eagle would soar into view.

The wind rushed past and he enjoyed the sensation of the breeze along his arms. Even got some of the reasons Tara enjoyed the freedom of riding her bike so much.

They came to a long curve in the road and he'd learnt to lean the same way as she did and felt a little of the thrill of adrenalin she'd talked about. He could imagine it would be even better if he was the one steering and Tara was holding on—maybe something for the future to consider.

By the time they arrived Simon was so comfortable behind Tara he'd moved on to enjoying the view but couldn't help appreciate how comfortable and secure he felt in such a short time—testament to her skill and confidence. It still made him shake his head how she had so much control over the powerful bike considering it was bigger than she was for a start and had a whole lot more horsepower than she did.

He got off first and she propped it sideways on its stand. Flipped her helmet open to talk as she fiddled with the chin strap. 'Enjoy that?'

'Yes, thank you. I actually did. And I'm very impressed with your riding skill.' His helmet was off and he stepped forward to assist her. She let him, just—irritable little thing. She obviously didn't like asking for aid so it was nice she was learning to take some help from him.

The strap came undone and she lifted her helmet off. 'I gave you the easy one to undo.'

'Ah,' he teased. 'Of course. Thank you.' He looked around. They had the lookout to themselves. 'I came up here years ago but had forgotten how amazing the view is.'

They walked towards the grassy edge that disappeared into the valley below. There was a little secondary platform screened from the road and he jumped down to the next level and held out his hand. 'It's even nicer down here.' He couldn't help the satisfaction in his voice. This was an excellent place.

Hmm, Tara thought. Simon looked pretty darned hot down there. More than hot. And there was a little bit of heat singing her even up here.

A tall, tanned, smiling hunk of a man, one she admired privately and professionally, holding his hand out to invite her to join him. Though, having been sandwiched against him for the last thirty minutes, she wasn't sure that jumping into his arms would be safe at this minute.

Looked a bit of a set-up, Tara admitted with an inward jiggle of awareness, and couldn't help but remember what had happened after the lake, and definitely after the beach frolic, but she had way more clothes on this time. Note to self. Keep clothes on.

She shrugged mentally and took his hand as she landed beside him. Sucked in the fresh, cooler air and shaded her eyes to estimate how much longer they had to get back before dark.

'Probably two hours till sunset?' In the distance the lake sparkled in the afternoon sun, and the mountains behind which the sun would sink were already dusted with gold. Simon was also dusted with gold, everything felt golden, and she could feel the prickle of nervousness again. 'I like this road for a run on the bike. I've been here a few times.'

The air shimmered between them with a bigger thrum than three million cicadas and the awareness in the pit of her stomach growled like a nasty case of hunger pains. Maybe it *was* hunger pains. She glanced at his backpack as Simon put it down on the grass. 'So? What's in the backpack?'

'A picnic for the princess, of course. Louisa is renowned for her picnic hampers. And I'm not without a few surprises.'

Surprises. Yep, he liked surprises. The first time, with the birthday cake, she'd cried. She was not going to cry this time. 'Ooh. Picnic. Cool.'

'Prepare to be amazed.' He crouched down. Withdrew the tartan rug and spread it in the centre of the grassed area so they were facing the view. He patted the rug beside him. 'Come on. Down you come.' He undid the laces on his shoes and pulled them and his socks off.

She was distracted for a minute. He had very attractive feet. Long toes and very masculine-looking feet. He wiggled the toes and she caught his eye. He was grinning at her.

Maybe she could lose her own boots? She sat down, feeling a little heated, a little confined in her outfit, and before she realised what she was doing she'd removed her vest and was reaching down for her boots.

Simon was pretending not to look as he studied the hamper with only occasional sideways glances at her cleavage. Ogler. She laughed at herself. No use getting prudish about that. Why had she worn that shirt if she hadn't wanted him to appreciate? And she guessed she would have been miffed if he'd sat there and stared at the view and not her.

'Yep, that's more comfortable.' She stretched out her legs and leaned back, resting her weight on her hands.

'Non-alcoholic sparkling wine?' Simon held out a plastic champagne flute and Tara grinned.

'Classy.'

'Story of my life.'

'Not mine.'

'Some people are classy no matter what. You're one of them.'

Aw, he said the nicest things, and she could feel the prickle in her throat. Not crying. Ha, said a little voice, you said you weren't taking any of your clothes off either.

He leant over and dull-clunked their plastic flutes in a toast. 'To the classiest lady I know.'

'To the smoothest man around.' She took a sip and it wasn't bad for a soft drink.

He took a sip and then put his flute down on the lid from the container that held cheese, nuts, celery and carrot sticks, and in the middle was a big dollop of guacamole.

'You had that in the backpack?'

'I told you Louisa was the picnic queen. She has a whole set of bowls she uses for hampers.' He pulled out another that held marinated chicken wings.

By the time they'd picked and sighed over the food, laughed at how strangely hungry they were, and had eaten far too much whenever the conversation flagged, the sun hovered over the distant mountains like a gold penny about to drop.

Simon had packed the food back into the insulated backpack, Tara was gazing into the small pool of liquid in her glass, and the playful mood had deepened back into the awareness that had always been there but which now eddied between them like the afternoon breeze.

'It's been fun, Simon.'

'It has, Tara.' There was a tinge of amusement in his voice as he slid across next to her. When his hip touched hers he lay back on the rug, one hand behind his head and the other he used to catch her hand.

'Those clouds over there look like a castle with a dragon.'

She looked up, squinted and frowned. 'Where?'

'You'll have to lie down to see.'

'Ha.' But she lay down and he pointed and she could just see what he meant before the turbulence slowly rearranged the puffy paintwork in the sky into something else.

'I can see a dinosaur.'

'Where?'

'To the left of the dragon.' She lifted her hand and he followed where she pointed.

'That's not a dinosaur. More of an elephant.'

She giggled. 'That's not an elephant.'

He rolled onto his side and she could feel him watching her. So this is was what they meant when they said 'basking'. Tara felt herself 'basking' in Simon's appreciation and it was a feeling she'd never really experienced. Could certainly grow accustomed to it too if she had the unlikely chance of that.

He leant over and kissed the tip of her nose. It was unexpected and she sneezed.

Simon flopped back and laughed out loud. 'It's hard being a man, you know,' he complained. 'I have to make all the moves and then she sneezes.' He put his hand over his eyes. 'I had this fantasy that this incredibly sexy woman—dressed in black leather, mind you— would attack me and have her wicked way with me, or at least kiss me senseless.' He sighed again. 'But it hasn't happened.'

Tara rolled over to face him, with her arm tucked under her cheek. Then, with a 'nothing dared, nothing gained thought behind her eyes', she climbed on top of him until she had one leg on either side of his body and her weight resting on her hands. She leant in and kissed his lips, once—he tasted so good—twice—*mmm...yum*—and a slower third time that threatened to turn into something bigger until she sat up. Feeling pretty impressed with her own daring, actually. 'Consider yourself attacked.'

'Mmm.' His eyes had changed to sleepy sexy and his hands reached up and slowly pulled her face down to his. 'I could get used to this.'

The sun was setting. And she wanted nothing more than to lose herself with Simon in this private place above the world. But she wasn't quite sure this was the right time—goodness knew where that thought had come from. 'I think it wouldn't be as much fun in the dark.'

He smiled lazily and kissed her neck. 'You sure?'

'Mmm. Maybe it would be.' She had no doubt it would be. No, Tara. Stop it, the voice of reason nagged in her ear. 'But I don't make out on deserted roads with bikers.' She said it as a joke to lighten the moment, because Simon had been on his first bike ride now.

He pretended to be disappointed. He kissed her again. 'I should have known that about you.' He hadn't given up hope.

But then she thought of Mick. The picture of a dishevelled biker. And she guessed she had. But she'd never really seen that until the end. She'd seen the lost little boy from the orphanage. The brother of her best

little friend who had died so tragically young and someone who had needed her. She shuddered to think what
Simon would have thought of Mick.

Simon's face changed and obviously, unless he could
read her mind, he thought it was something else. 'You
okay? I didn't mean to upset you. Hell, Tara, I think
you're amazing. You blow me away and yet you make
me feel so amazingly good.'

He rolled her off him and sat up. Reached down and
pulled her up to sit next to him, tucking her into his side
with his arm around her shoulders. 'Not sure how you
do that but it's a great feeling. There's no pressure for
anything else.'

'Ditto.' This guy was too much. Too nice, too amazing—for her. He'd be gone in a couple of weeks and
she'd look back and wish she had made love with him. It
was a gift to be here with him, right at this moment, and
she was throwing it back because she was too scared
of the moment—or was she too scared of the emptiness later?

Simon was like the foster-home she knew she'd have
to leave. It really was better not to suffer the separation.
But it felt so good to be tucked into his side, his strong
arm around her shoulder. Close to him.

'You could still hold me, Simon.'

He cuddled her into him, gave the impression he
couldn't get close enough, then lifted her onto his lap.
'Can't think of anything I'd rather do.'

So they sat there. Tara was still on Simon's lap as

the sun set with a magnificent orange glow that turned to pink and purple in front of their eyes, reflecting off the lake, and she snuggled into his shoulder as peace seeped into her.

Then she heard the strangest thing. It sounded almost like her motorbike but distant. The throbbing roar of her Harley-Davidson. For a horrible moment she thought Mick had found her then remembered she had the bike.

Simon shifted her off his lap and stood up as she scrambled to her feet herself.

But when they looked her bike was there. Less than ten feet away from them and definitely still and quiet. Then the noise came again. The louder roar of the engine then the sound of a bike idling. It came from the bushes across the car park and Simon started to laugh.

'What was that?'

'If I'm not mistaken, that, dear Tara, was our lyrebird.'

'You're kidding me. How could a bird make that noise?'

'World's greatest mimickers. They can sound like babies, chainsaws...' he grinned '...and apparently Harley-Davidson motorbikes.' Simon slipped his hand into hers and pulled her into his embrace. Kissed her gently. 'I'll have to apologise to my dad. Lyrebirds make amazing noises. That's pretty special.'

Still distracted, she kissed him back but not with her full attention. 'Not possible.'

But the sound came again and closer to them. To the side there was a rustle of bushes, the crack of tiny twigs, and she twisted her head to see past Simon's shoulder and then she saw it. A small grey-brown bird the size of a chicken, his reddish-brown throat lifted as he gazed at her. But it was the two long feathers that hung each side of his tail that told her what it was.

She whispered. 'Simon. Turn slowly and look to your left.'

Simon turned his head and saw it. A slow smile curved his mouth. 'I told you!' He squeezed her. 'Our lyrebird.'

He'd said 'our' again. She hugged that defiantly to herself and ignored her voice of caution. 'Why doesn't it run away?'

He grinned cheekily. 'Well, it knows I don't want to move.' He squeezed her gently. Looked down into her face. 'I really don't want to.'

But the lyrebird could. He strutted across to a little mound of dirt about six feet from them and climbed to the top, where he spread his gorgeous tail. Swivelled his head to glance at them as if to tell them to pay attention, and the two long tail feathers spread like the outside edges of a fan and outlined the distinctive harp-shaped feathers in the centre that had given him his name. And then he began to prance.

Tara could feel the rush of goose-bumps that covered her arms. A shivering perception of something magical and mystical, totally surreal, and Simon's eyes never left the bird's dance until he felt her glance at him.

The lyrebird shook his tail at them once more in a grand finale and then sauntered off into the bushes.

They stood silently, watching the bush where it had disappeared, but it had gone. Job done. Simon looked amused and then strangely thoughtful. 'You know what this means?' Simon said quietly.

He watched her with an expression she didn't understand and she searched his face. Then remembered what he'd said weeks ago when he'd first arrived. But she wasn't saying that.

Simon sounded more spooked than excited. 'It's a sign.' He tilted his head. 'Which I didn't believe in before, I admit.' Then he shrugged and said lightly, as if sharing a joke, 'We must be meant for each other.'

She stared at him—couldn't believe that. More goose-bumps covered her arms at the thought. She and Simon? For ever? Nope. Couldn't happen. 'Or there's a gorgeous female lyrebird behind us that we can't see.'

He smiled but she had the feeling he was glad she'd poo-pooed it too. 'Could be that as well.'

Then he pulled her closer in his arms until they squeezed together and with the magic of the moment and the dusk slowly dimming into night, he kissed her and she kissed him back, and the magic settled over them like a gossamer cloud, but it wasn't quite the same, Simon wasn't quite the same, and when it was the moment that balanced between losing themselves or pulling back it was Simon who pulled back.

If she wasn't mistaken, there was look of poorly disguised anxiety on his face.

CHAPTER TEN

IN THE LAST glow of the dimming evening the motor-bike's engine thrummed beneath them and Simon held onto Tara on the way back to the lake. A single beam of light swept the roadside and the rest was darkness, a bit like the bottom of the deepening hole of dread inside him. That had been too close. He wasn't ready for that kind of commitment. Sharing a lyrebird was for those who knew what they were doing.

Thank goodness she'd had the presence of mind to see his sudden distance because suddenly he hadn't been sure he really wanted to step off the edge with Tara. When had it become more serious than he'd intended? Did she really feel the same and if she did could he trust himself to be everything she thought he was?

On the mountain, at the end, it had been Tara who had agreed they should go, agreed when Simon had said he was worried about hitting wildlife in the dark. But, despite the peculiar visions of lyrebirds scattering in the headlights, the real reason had been that he wasn't sure he was as heart-whole as he had been any more.

In fact, he'd had a sudden onset of the heebie-jeebies about just how deep he was getting in here, and none of this was in his plans—or his belief system.

And then Tara had agreed so easily that now, contrarily, he'd decided she didn't feel secure either.

But earlier, standing with her in his arms, losing himself in the generosity that was Tara, despite her fierce independence, he'd almost believed the sudden vision that he could hold this woman for the rest of his days.

But what if he broke her heart for ever if he had to move on?

Like his mum had moved on from his dad. Like Maeve's man, and his ex-friend, had moved on from them. The problem was that since the lyrebird, just an hour ago, Simon felt connected to Tara by a terrifying concept he hadn't expected but which was proving stronger than he had felt with anyone in his world. And he wasn't sure he liked it.

She made him feel larger than life, which he wasn't, exuberant when he hadn't thought he had an exuberant bone in his body. She made him want to experience the adventure of the world. And with Tara it would be an adventure. A quest towards the kind of life he had only dreamt of having for himself.

Except it wasn't him.

He wasn't quite sure who she was seeing in him but it wasn't Simon Campbell. He needed to get a little distance back while he worked through this.

Because he wasn't the adventurous, fun guy Tara

needed. She needed someone to jump out of planes with, fall head over heels in love with her, and be there for the next month, the next year, the next lifetime. He couldn't be sure he could sign up for that.

She deserved someone who would do that. So why did he have the feeling there was a great cloud of foreboding hanging over his head?

Next morning at breakfast Maeve wandered into the kitchen and ducked under a Christmas streamer before she sat down. 'What's wrong with Simon?' She absently scratched her tummy and inclined her head back towards the bathroom her brother had just disappeared into.

The door slammed and Tara winced. 'No idea. He's been acting strange since we came back from the picnic last night.' Maybe he was always like this and she'd been too blinded by his pretty face.

Or she'd said something that made him realise she was the last woman he wanted to get involved with. Suck it up, princess, you know this happens to you all the time. 'Is he usually moody?'

'Nope.' Maeve shook her head. 'He's the most even-tempered of all of us. The only time he gets techy is if he's worried about something big.'

Did she qualify for big? Did he think she was trying to trap him? Cringe. Cringe.

Lord, no. She'd never do that. She'd been told often enough by Matron to push herself out there and be a little more demanding but it just wasn't in her make-up. If the family hadn't seen how badly she'd wanted their life, she hadn't been about to tell them and get knocked back for her pains.

She guessed Simon was that all over again. 'He'll get over it.' And her. Already had, it seemed. It was probably all in her imagination anyway and he had just been amusing himself.

Well, problem was there was so much to admire about him, and he seemed to enjoy her company, plus he was a darned good kisser, and she'd practically thrown herself at him last night and he'd knocked her offer back, and that had left them in an awkward place, now that she thought about it. Thanks very much, Simon.

Time to change the subject. And the focus of her life. 'So how are you going, Maeve?'

Simon's sister shrugged. 'I'm fine. Feeling less nauseous and much heavier around the middle.' She sent Tara one of the most relaxed smiles Tara had seen from her. 'But I'd rather talk about you two.'

Darn! Lulled into a false sense of security. 'There's no "us two".'

Maeve raised her brows disbelievingly and Tara wanted to bury her head in her hands. Seriously. How many other people thought she'd fallen for Simon? Or he for her? Just because they'd hung out together a bit, and kissed a few times, that smug voice inside insisted.

Maeve wasn't having any of that apparently. 'Well, if there's not a "you two" he's been pretty hopeless at getting the message across. What with parachuting photo packages, and pestering you for a bike ride, and Louisa for a picnic hamper—and the rug!'

Lots of eyebrow waggling coming her way here and Tara could feel the heat creep up her cheeks. So this was what it was like to have a sister.

Obviously Maeve had no scruples in laying stuff out in front of her and teasing. Maybe she hadn't been so unlucky as an orphan to avoid this stuff. Apart from Mick's sister, she'd never really been one for girly relationships. Again the idea of becoming fond of someone when you never knew when they'd go away for a weekend and never come back. She'd decided a long time ago it was better to keep her distance.

But Maeve wasn't keeping her distance, neither had she finished. 'Seems a lot of effort for someone he doesn't care about.'

Tara had no idea how to deal with this. With her acquaintances she'd just tell them to shut up but you couldn't do that to Maeve—or she didn't think it would work anyway. 'Can we change the subject?'

'Not until I give you some advice.'

Oh, no. 'Do you have to? Please. I hate advice. Comes with having to sort yourself out all your life.' She said it but now she knew Maeve better she doubted anything would stop her when she was on a roll. She almost wished for the washed-out, droopy dandelion Maeve had been before she'd recovered her spirits.

She looked again at the new, brighter Maeve and she

knew she was happy her friend had found her equilib-
rium. Lyrebird Lake was doing its magic. So, no, she
didn't wish for droopy Maeve back.

Over the last few weeks, gradually they had become
friends, good friends, if she dared to say it. She and
Maeve had found lots to smile about. Lots to agree and
not agree about and quirky, girly conversations that
had often little to do with Simon. And, at Maeve's request, nothing at all to do with Rayne, the father of
Maeve's baby.

'Me? Not give advice?' Maeve laughed at her.

Tara sighed. 'But you're not having this all your own
way. I'll listen to you if you tell me what you're thinking about Rayne.'

Maeve blinked in shock and Tara grinned. 'And if I
have advice then you have to listen to me.'

Ha. Miss Bossy didn't like it so much in return. But
to give Maeve her due, she sat back with a grimace. 'I
was being pushy, wasn't I?' She shook her head and
smiled wryly. 'You haven't seen this side of me yet but
I'm not normally the pathetic wimp I've been since I
came here.'

She looked around and then back at Tara. 'You know
what? You're right. I do feel better since I came here.
This place really is as amazing as Simon says it is.'

Tara looked around with fresh eyes. Made herself
feel the moment. Smell the furniture polish. Taste the
freshly brewed tea from the pot that Louisa had made
before she'd gone out. Saw the little touches that spelt

people cared. A Christmas nativity scene tucked in behind the bread basket. The growing pile of gifts under the tree. The photo frames of family that Louisa polished with her silver cloth every morning. 'I think it's the people.'

And Tara didn't ever want to leave but she wasn't expecting the world to be that perfect. 'Yep. It's amazing. And it is good to see you firing on all cylinders—even if you are a bit scary sometimes.'

'Scary? Me? You should meet my oldest sister, Kate.' Then Maeve showed she at least was focussed. 'Seeing that you hate advice, I'll keep it simple—and let you in on a secret.'

She sat forward, ready to impart her wisdom, and Tara pulled a face as she waited. 'My sisters and I have decided Simon's been hiding from a real romantic relationship all his life—he's terrified the fairy-tale isn't real.'

'Um. I hate to tell you this, but it isn't,' Tara said, but Maeve ignored her.

'Whether that came from our mother and his dad not staying together or the fact that he never knew his dad, we don't know.'

She lowered her voice. 'What we do know is that the right woman can help him come out from the place he's been hiding all these years—but she has to get past the barriers.'

'Barriers?' Tara was lost. She had no idea what Maeve was talking about. She hadn't noticed any barriers.

'Not when-you-meet-him barriers. He's too good a people person for that. It's later. Whenever a woman is getting close, he'd discover some other place that needed him more than he needed her and bolt. She'd try and hold him, he'd spend less time with her, and then she'd give up and drop him. I've seen it time and again. But you're different.'

Her? Tara? Different? She couldn't help the tiny glow of warmth the words left in her chest. Then she thought it through and decided there was another reason she was different. Maybe because she didn't expect people to want to look long term with her?

'He's scared of long term, Tara.'

Well, there you go. Maybe she was the right girl for him after all. She forced a smile. 'I'm not presuming long-term.' Had lost that expectation years ago.

'Might be the way to getting it.' Maeve looked at her.

That didn't make sense. 'You mean, actually say, *Hi, Simon, I don't expect long term*?' The fantasy was tragically attractive—but it was fantasy. But that didn't mean one day it mightn't happen. Did it?

Maeve waggled her brows. 'And that just might be the way to break through the barriers.'

Nope. Tara didn't understand and she backed away from reading anything ridiculously ambitious into Maeve's comments. 'Okay. I've listened.' And you are scaring the socks off me at the thought of having any such conversation with Simon. Although if Simon was scared she would try to trap him, he did need to know that wasn't in her plans.

But he had changed after the lyrebird, true, and he'd practically said he remembered what seeing the bird dance meant. True love and all that stuff. For a guy who wasn't thinking long term she guessed that could be scary. She wasn't scared, just didn't believe the hogwash. All too confusing for a conversation.

'Your turn.' She sat forward. 'Tell me about the father of your child.' She really did want to know. She couldn't imagine anyone leaving Maeve. She was gorgeous and funny, and she was classy.

Maeve's shoulders drooped. Her confident persona disappeared into the dejected woman Tara had first met. There was an extended silence and Tara thought for a moment Maeve was going to renege. Then she sighed. 'I fell for Rayne like a ton of bricks.' She lifted her head, her eyes unexpectedly dreamy, and remembered. 'He's a head taller than me, shoulders like a front-row forward, and those eyes. Black pools of serious lust when he looked at me. Which he did from across the room.'

Tara had to grin. Descriptive. 'Crikey. I'm squirming on my seat over here. So what happened?'

She shrugged. 'We spent the night together—then he went to jail.'

Tara remembered Maeve saying he'd omitted to tell her he was going to jail. 'Was he wrongly convicted?'

Tears filled Maeve's eyes. She chewed her lip and

gathered her control. Then looked at Tara with a wry and watery smile. 'Thank you.'

Tara wasn't sure what was going on but she seriously wanted to get to the bottom of it. 'Did he tell you about it?'

Shook her head. 'Didn't have a chance. And since then he's refused to see or talk to me on the phone.'

That didn't make sense. 'So when did this happen?

Maeve patted her stomach. 'Eight months ago.'

O-o-o-kay. Tara suspected Simon might have reason to worry. 'And how long were you together before you fell pregnant?'

She sighed. 'One night. But I've always loved Rayne. He was the bad boy all the girls lusted after. I always thought the problem was more his mum than Rayne—she was a single mum and couldn't kick her drug addiction—but despite our mum's misgivings he and Simon were always friends.'

And now he'd got Simon's sister pregnant on the way to jail. Probably why Simon wanted to wring his neck.

Maeve was still talking. 'Simon and he were mates through med school and then Rayne went to California to do paediatrics. And he was supposed to come and work with Simon at his hospital this year.'

She shrugged. 'Something happened when he was over there, and apparently as soon as he hit Australia alarm bells went off. Simon picked him up from the airport, and neither of us knew that the police would come for him as soon as he was back in the country. It seems he suspected it was a possibility and didn't tell us.'

'Wow. Seems a strange way to act.'

'I'm pretty sure he planned to tell but Simon got called out to a patient before he could, I think.' Maeve shrugged.

'Problem was, I've fancied this guy since I carried a lunchbox to school, hadn't seen him for eight years, and that night Simon left.' She shrugged. 'I was feeling low after a break-up, here was this guy coming I'd had a crush on since puberty and it all just happened. Except Simon has never forgiven him—when, in fact, the guy had little choice because I practically seduced him.'

Her face went pink and Tara could see a heck of a lot had happened. Wow again.

'Obviously I've thought about that night and I think Rayne's natural resistance was lowered by the fact he might be in prison for the next ten years and I was throwing myself at him.'

'Imagine?' Tara looked at Maeve. Gorgeous, sexy, and, she was beginning to suspect, wilful and a little spoilt, but in a nice way. A way Tara could quite easily be envious of except she'd shaken that out of herself years ago as a destructive waste of wishful thinking.

'And then the next morning the police came and took him away. It was a shock because we'd slept together and he just walked away without looking back.'

Absently she stroked her belly. 'Simon was livid when he found out that Rayne had suspected they might come. But I think he'd come to explain and get advice from Simon, except it hadn't worked out. And then I complicated matters.'

Wow. Maeve had certainly complicated matters. It was like an end-of-season episode of a soap opera. Tara had major sympathy for Simon. But Maeve had problems too. And then there was the mysterious Rayne.

'Do you love him?'

She spread her hands. 'I've had all pregnancy to think about it. About the fact that he might not be the guy I think he is. Or if he was he might change a lot in prison. So when I see him again he might not be the hero that I always imagined him to be and I fell for the pretty face I'd always fancied and created the energy between us by wishful thinking.'

Tara agreed with her there. It all sounded explosively spontaneous. 'It's a possibility.'

'I know. I know. It was a whirlwind event that will affect the rest of my life. But really I don't know. He doesn't care enough to answer my calls. Or answer my letters. Or comment on the fact that I'm pregnant and soon to have his child. That hurts.'

Yep. That would hurt. 'That is hard.'

Maeve went on. 'When I found out I was pregnant I thought Simon was going to have a stroke. We had a huge fight. I said I was old enough to make my own mistakes and he said he could see that was true but not under his roof. Then he absolutely tore Rayne's actions to shreds when I knew it was mostly me. So we really haven't made up since then. But I still live under his roof so we've had sort of a cold truce for most of this year.'

She sighed again. 'I know I let him and my parents down. Crashed off my pedestal and that hurt too. But I swear, one look at Rayne, at his need for comfort, and I was a goner, and seeing how it turned out I can understand his reluctance to let me into his life now. I can regret the timing but if I'm ever going to have a child the fact that it's Rayne's is no real hardship.'

A can of worms getting wormier actually. 'I'm not sure I have advice for you. Except to say that guys in jail, even innocent ones, do change from the experience. I've known people who have. I'm not saying it won't work out between you, but he might be a harder, tougher man than the one who went in. If you do meet him again, which I guess you will if you're having his baby, make sure he is the man you love before you commit to anything. You have your baby to think of as well as yourself.'

Maeve looked back soberly. 'I guess it has been all about the baby and me. I do need reminding that Rayne is in a different world right now and that he's having it tough too. Thanks, Tara.'

Tara wasn't sure that was what she'd been trying to say. 'And thanks for your advice, though I can't see myself starting a conversation like that with Simon.' She smiled and stood up. 'As for your story, you make my life seem pretty boring.'

'Simon doesn't think you're boring.'

And here we begin the conversation again. Enough. 'The good news is I have to go and do some home visits so I'm going to leave you.' She carried her cup and saucer and cereal plate to the sink and rinsed them. 'Catch you later.'

As she walked towards her room she mulled over the conversation. No wonder Maeve had been low in spirits when she'd arrived. And it explained the tension between Simon and his sister.

It was understandable Simon felt betrayed by his friend and to a lesser degree by his sister. She'd actually love to hear Simon's side of the story but couldn't see how she could ask without betraying the confidence that Maeve had spoken to her about it all.

And that it all happened under his own roof wouldn't have helped his overactive protective bone.

Maeve had been very generous with her sharing and her advice and it had been nice to talk like that. Exchange banter with her friend. She was getting better at relationships with other people. Letting herself be more open and looking a little more below the surface to try to connect to other people instead of being too wary.

She'd never had a friend like Maeve before and hoped she'd helped her. Maeve had certainly given her something to think about with Simon. Maybe she could have real friendship relationships with women apart from being their midwife. Though she guessed she was Maeve's midwife as well.

She pulled on her jeans to ride the bike and slipped

into her boots. Organised her workbag on autopilot and mulled over Maeve's words. Shook her head. He wasn't scared. Simon didn't care enough.

When they'd been together at the lookout he'd been a gentleman and not raised her expectations. She supposed it was a good thing but she really would have liked to lose herself all the way in those gorgeous arms. And he'd been such a good kisser. She shook her head. Come on. He was way out of her league. Get with the programme.

CHAPTER ELEVEN

SIMON STOOD IN the shower and could feel the edges of panic clawing at him. And he couldn't ease away by running back to Sydney Central work like he usually did because Maeve was getting close to having her baby. He had to be around in case anything happened.

This was certainly the time he usually left a relationship—way past it, in fact, as far as rapport between him and the woman went—except for the fact he would have been sleeping with her well and truly by now and that hadn't happened with Tara. How on earth had the emotional stuff happened when they hadn't even slept together? Everything was upside down. Back to front. And confusing.

Maybe it was proximity. Of course it was incredibly hard not to get closer than normal when you were living in the same house and working in the same place and associating with the same people.

Um, except he had lived with other women and not got too emotionally involved. And he had the horrible suspicion he'd miss Tara if he created the distance he needed—either mentally or geographically.

That was the scariest thing of all. It hadn't happened before. He'd always felt the relationship was well and truly over by the time he began to see the signs of long-term planning on the side of his lady friend. Which was a good thing because that way he wasn't responsible for hurting anyone.

But this was different. The unease fluttered again as he turned off the shower tap. Silly thoughts of birthday cakes in the future still made him smile but that was not the sort of thing to do if he was deep in a relationship with his next woman.

Listen to himself. He doubted he'd ever been deep into a relationship ever—more floating along the surface with good sex, and with women who were still his friends.

But right at this moment he was abstinent and sinking. No utopia after what had been a truly delightful afternoon yesterday with loads of potential—until that bloody lyrebird had said she was his true love and he'd panicked. Well, at least he had seen the danger before they'd completely consummated their relationship.

He combed his hair with his fingers and opened the steamy bathroom door. Oops. He'd been in here a while. But at least he'd come to some conclusion. All he needed to do was pull away. Create some distance and see how it felt.

His stomach rumbled and he headed for the kitchen as he continued to mull over his dilemmas.

He just needed to let Tara know subtly that he wasn't a long-term prospect and then maybe they could just be friends. As in platonic. Hmm.

That brought up a whole new set of unpleasant dilemmas. If he and Tara were just friends that meant she could have other friends who were men. Maybe a lover. Someone else to take on her adventures. Someone else to do what he had knocked back. Strangely, not funny, idea at all.

He needed to think about that one.

'Hi, Simon.' He looked up from his preoccupation and saw a jeans-clad goddess.

'Hi, Tara.' He felt a smile spread across his face and then fall away as his previous conversations with himself came back.

'You okay?'

'Sure.' Hitched his smile back up. 'Of course. You?'

'Fine.' He could feel her concern. Saw her shrug.

'Okay. I'm going for a ride. To see one of my clients. Then maybe further afield. See you later.'

'Be safe.'

'High on my list. *Ciao.*'

He called after her, 'I didn't know you spoke Italian?'

'I don't.' She stopped. '*Ciao* and food items. Pizza, lasagne, *boccioni.*' She shrugged. 'The extent of my Italian. Anyway. See you.'

'Bye. When are you back?'

She stopped again and sighed. 'No idea.'

He opened his mouth to ask something else and closed it again. What was he doing? He lifted his hand to wave and turned away.

Geez. He was hopeless.

'Simon?' He spun back and she was there. Just behind him. And she was chewing on those gorgeous lips in a way that he wanted to touch her mouth with his fingers to stop her damaging anything.

'It's okay, Simon. I'm not expecting long term, you know. I'll be moving on soon.' She shook her head. 'Just wanted to let you know.'

'Me too,' he said helplessly.

And then she spun on her heel and walked away quickly. He was still staring after her when he heard the bike start and the roar as she rode away.

So why didn't he feel better? Basically she was saying they could have fun with no strings. Right up his alley. And he'd told her he felt the same. Liar.

When Tara drove into the driveway late in the afternoon of the next day Simon was sitting out at the manger, watching the animals.

She swung her helmet on her finger as she walked across the springy grass Louisa loved to water, and the smile he gave as she approached made the slight trepidation she'd started with worth the effort.

'Looking particularly fetching there, Miss Tara.'

He sounded relaxed. Thank goodness for that. Until

she'd given herself a stern talking to she'd been replaying the video of the dumb things she'd said in her head before she'd left. Dumb because she hadn't needed to put them out there, though he'd agreed—not dumb because she hadn't meant them, because she had. She sat down beside him on the bench and looked at the manger. 'Hi, Simon.'

'And what did you do today?'

She opened her eyes wide. 'I've had a very nice day, thank you. I visited my two postnatal mums, then rode all the way to the lighthouse. Watched the parachutists float from the sky. It was very beautiful.' Politely. 'What did you do?'

'I did a couple of hours for Dad in the general hospital while he took Mia to the airport to go visit a sick friend, and I had a decadent snooze this afternoon because I didn't sleep well last night.' He watched her face. 'I guess you're tired now?'

She looked at him over the top of sunglasses. 'No, Mr Old Man. I'm not tired. I am young and enthusiastic for adventure at all times.'

'Goody.' He grinned. 'And for the record that's the second time you've called me an old man.'

'Well, stop acting like one.'

He didn't offer any answers to that one. 'Trouble is I'm wide awake after my nap and could party all night. Got any ideas?'

She shrugged. 'What sort of things? Nature? Dining? Dancing? Astronomy?'

'Ah. Astronomy has potential.'

'For what?'

'Seeing stars.'

'I could help you with that right now.' She swung her helmet thoughtfully. He was teasing and it was fun. Until he said, 'I wondered if you were into violence.'

She thought about some of the people she knew and the way their demons seemed to lead them to violence. The fun went out of it and she stood up. They were from such different worlds. 'Nope. Much prefer to just walk away.'

She saw him reach out to stop her and then drop his hand and his mixed signals only confused her more.

Then he said, 'Sorry. I don't know what I said but I don't want to ruin the mood. So, before you go, what I've really been doing is sitting here waiting to ask you to dinner. Louisa and Maeve have gone to Dad's to stay overnight and mind the girls. I'd like to get dressed up and go on a date with you to the new restaurant down by the lake.'

She sat down again. 'Oh.' She looked at him. 'A date?'

'A fun date with a lady I like spending time with.'

She thought about that one. 'Fun', meaning 'not serious'. Wasn't that what she'd said she wanted, too? Hadn't they both agreed on that yesterday morning? 'Sure. I'd like that. What time?'

'When you're ready. I made a booking for six-thirty for seven.' She raised her brows at his presumption but he was ahead of her. 'It's not heavily booked and they don't mind if I cancel.'

She grinned at him. 'You really are a thoughtful man.'

'We old guys are like that.'

'I don't really think you're old.' She looked him over with mischief in her eyes. 'Far too sexy for an old guy.'

'Keep thinking that way. I thought we could have a drink before dinner at the bar, if you don't mind walking there.'

'Thank you. Sounds nice.' She glanced at her watch. 'I'd better have a shower and get changed, then.'

'No rush.'

'Sure. But I like to be on time. I was brought up that way.'

Simon watched her walk away, that sexy, determined little walk that had him squirming on his seat. And the crazy thing was she had no idea what she did to him. He wasn't much better at guessing why she affected him like she did but tonight he'd come to the conclusion he was going to try to figure it out by taking it to the next level. Regardless of the risk.

The new restaurant was built on a little knoll overlooking the lake. The grounds were surrounded by a vibrant green hedge with a latched gate. The entry had been landscaped into lots of little rock pools and greenery with a wide wooden boardwalk winding through to get to the restaurant door. There was even a little bridge they had to climb up and over and Tara couldn't keep the smile off her face. 'This is gorgeous. I can't believe it's here and I didn't know.'

'They've only just opened. Mia told me about it when I asked her where I should take you.'

She looked at him. Surprised. 'You told Mia we were going on a date?'

'That's what she said.'

Tara laughed. 'Your family is funny.' And gorgeous, but that was okay. She had settled a lot since her ride that afternoon. Decided that clarity came with enjoying the moment, not worrying about it. She was here with Simon now, and she was going to have a wonderful evening. 'I'm starving.'

'Excellent.'

They started with drinks at the bar, and behind the barman a huge window overlooked the water and showcased the sunset, and to the left a narrow curving terrace gave the diners a water view while they ate.

He watched Tara sigh with pleasure as she took a sip of her pina colada and gazed around. 'This place is amazing.'

You're amazing. He followed her gaze. Took in the colours on the lake. 'It is great.' He saw it through Tara's shining eyes and acknowledged that he hadn't let it soak in. He had been so busy with his thoughts and plans and second-guessing his own emotions he was missing the pleasure. Vowed to stop that right now. Vowed to enjoy the pleasure of company with the woman he wanted to be with—and be like Tara and enjoy things, without worrying about tomorrow. Imagine that!

It was easier than he expected when he tried it. Everything seemed suddenly brighter. Wow.

'How's your drink?'

She pretended to look at him suspiciously. 'Why? You want some?' So then he laughed. Because it was funny.

'No, I don't want some, Miss I'm-Not-Sharing. I have my own drink. Though mine doesn't look as flashy as yours, with its slice of pineapple and pretty pink umbrella.'

She grinned. 'Good. I've never had one before. And I like umbrellas.' She offered him her straw. 'But you can have a sip if you really want.'

I'll sip later, he thought, and suddenly the night was alive with promise and joy, and the conversation took off as he let go of worrying about the past and the future and just experienced Tara's company.

They flowed from the bar to their table, the most private one he could acquire, and the sun went down, as did the glorious seafood and the delightful sparkling wine in the bottle.

By the time he paid the bill they were both pleasantly mellow, and he had no hesitation in capturing her hand in his for the walk home around the lake.

The lake path from the restaurant to the hospital and Louisa's house was lit by yellow globes that matched the moon and it was almost as bright as day as they ambled along.

This time when there was a rustle in the bushes Tara just smiled at the noise and carried on walking.

He glanced back to where the undergrowth still crackled. 'So you're not afraid of snakes in the bushes now?'

'Nope.' She squeezed his hand. 'I'm going to believe it's a lyrebird who can sound like a motorbike. If he wants to, of course.'

'Of course.' And Simon realised he had become decidedly more trusting about other facets of lyrebird lore. He stopped and she stopped too. He pulled her by the hand until she faced him and lifted his fingers to her cheek. 'You look like a lake princess in the moonlight.'

She glanced up at the moon and the angles of her face shone like those of a perfectly carved silver goddess with the reflection of the moonlight shining Tara's truth at him.

She was frowning at him, trying to read him, and goodness knew what was flashing across his face as his mind raced, because she looked a little unsure. 'Thank you for the compliment. I like moonlit nights the best. Never been keen on the dark.'

He just wanted to hold her safe and never let her go. One day he would ask why she preferred to have a moonlit night than a dark one. Hopefully he would have the chance to ask.

He leant in and kissed her gently because if he did

it properly he wouldn't be able to stop and she didn't deserve that, but she lifted her hands up and held his head there.

Tara kissed him back with a warmth and generosity he remembered from the lookout and for a few minutes there he forgot his good intentions. Until they heard some people coming along the path and he put her away from him.

That's right. He had no intention of seducing Tara in a park. 'Let's go home now.'

There was something in the way he said 'home now' that sent a whisper of promise across Tara's skin. Home. Together. Now. That last kiss had been different, wonderful and absolutely intoxicating. Lucky Simon had heard the people coming because she'd been deaf to the world.

They were walking quite fast now. Seemed he'd decided caution was overrated and that was okay. Seriously okay because, no matter what, she wanted to sleep with this gorgeous, sexy, kind man at least once. She was not going to regret not spending time with Simon for the rest of her life. It might be her last chance.

Louisa and Maeve had gone to Mia's so they would be alone and that removed that last of her resistance, if she'd had any.

Simon held her hand tightly as they walked even more quickly along the lit path. She resisted the urge to run.

CHAPTER TWELVE

SIMON PUSHED OPEN the door and Tara reached up to turn on the lights but he stilled her hand.

'Can you see in the moonlight?'

Her hand fell away from the switch and instinctively they both slowed to draw out the moment. Tara's eyes adjusted and she could see easily as she stared into the strong features above her, cherished the fact that Simon found her very attractive, could almost feel herself unfurling in front of him. The silly, exciting, headlong rush to get here was completed and now it was time to savour their first moments.

Okay. Settle. Slow your breathing. Just soak it in.

He drew her to him, leaned in and brushed her mouth with his. Brushed again. Gently pulling on her lip with his teeth. A mingling of breath and promise and introduction to a Simon she didn't know. One she liked very much.

'You taste so beautiful.'

'Pina colada?'

'The taste of Tara. I like it.' He kissed her again.

'Mmm.' Closed her eyes at his reverence because it made her want to cry and he might think she did so for the wrong reasons. 'I like you tasting me.' Just a little bit gruffly.

He smiled, a brief flash of teeth in the moonlight, and then he was pulling her slowly down the hallway to his room. She wanted to lose herself like she had on the path, but she wanted to savour every moment, store up every stroke of his fingers as his hand trailed down her arm.

They passed her door. Good choice, she thought mistily. 'My room's a mess.'

'Mine's too tidy. I'm sure we'll find something in common.' He bent his body and slid one arm under her shoulder, the other behind her knee, and lifted her easily into his arms and against his chest. 'Something along the lines of I like to hold you in my arms and you like to be carried.'

'Not something I had previously been aware of.' She laid her head back and savoured it. 'It seems you're right.'

He squeezed her to him. Paused at his door. 'Will you spend the night with me, Tara?'

'That sounds very nice, Simon.'

He gave a small deep chuckle as he pushed open his door and closed it behind them. Then he stood her up in front of the bed and reached around behind her to ease the zipper down her back. A long leisurely unzipping that promised much.

He curved the fabric off her shoulders until it slithered into a heap at her feet, a rumpled puddle of material, then helped her step out. She looked back at this gorgeous man, burnished by the gentle light, and decided he looked like a magnificent knight as he stood in front of her. One who deserved something a little more romantic than her serviceable underwear but there wasn't much she could do about it except wish for a second she'd bought the lacy set she'd scorned last week.

Then Simon lifted her hands to his neck and traced them down his chest so that she too could undo fastenings, liking that she could follow his lead and lose the awkwardness of her lack of skill at this slow dance of undressing.

Surprisingly easily, she unfastened buttons until his shirt flapped open and she couldn't help an indulgent exploration of the ridges and hollows and bands of rippled muscles that she'd ached to stroke all evening— and while she was there she undid the silver buckle of his belt—such an unclick of commitment that made her smile a slow, wicked, womanly smile.

She felt his breath draw in as she slipped open the button of his trousers and carefully eased the teeth of his zip over the unmistakable bulge of his erection.

His fingers slid up her back and then around her neck and over her throat so she tilted her head, first a gentle brush of his lips over her throat and then a searing kiss that clouded her vision and had her matching the sudden flurry of movements they both made to remove the last of the clothing between them.

He lifted her again, placed her reverently like a prize across his bed and knelt down beside her, naked in the moonlight, a beautiful gilded warrior to claim his trophy.

The moonlight flooded across them, silvery streams of light with dark stripes where the branches from the tree outside blocked it, so when he lay down beside her the light rippled across his skin from silver to shadow and back to silver again.

She must have been in the stripes too, because he said softly, 'You still look like a mystical creature from the lake.'

'There's no mystery. Just me.'

He gathered her into his arms. Squeezed her to him. 'There's no "just" about you, Tara.'

And then he began to kiss her. Worship her. Inch by inch, kiss by kiss, stroke by stroke, accompanied by whispered murmurs of delight, discoveries that were marvelled over, and sudden indrawn breaths on Tara's side as she too discovered there was another world, a whispering, wonderful, wild world of worship at the hands of Simon Campbell.

As the sun peeped fingers of light towards the tangle of sheets on the bed Simon looked down at the woman he held in his arms. The warmth of sudden knowledge broke through to him like a beam from the dawn. Like

an epiphany. No warning. Just a moment in time between touching and looking—then he realised that, of
course, he loved her! Had done for days. Fool!

Tara was the one. It had been building since the lookout. And he'd denied it, the incredible dance of the lyrebird that had warned him about the truth.

Instead of panic, the relief was overwhelming because his body had been shouting in his ear for the last
torturous days and he'd been talking it down. Saying
they didn't know each other well enough, he couldn't
possibly, but that feeling of delight every time he'd seen
her should have warned him. Well, he knew her now,
in the biblical sense, and that was what it had taken for
him to know, without a doubt, that he'd fallen in love.

Simon tightened his hands around the waist he'd cradled through the night. The satin skin he'd held in his
arms and stroked with wondering hands. Kissed the tiny
intricate rose tattooed on her shoulder. He just knew
there would be a story about that.

Making love with Tara had been everything it had
never been with anyone else.

A revelation, a slow and gentle exploration that had
seen her unfurl like the tail of the lyrebird, he thought
whimsically, into a slow mesmerising dance of magnificent generosity that had enraptured them both. She
gave it all, held nothing back, and knowing her past only
made him more exultant about her generosity.

The trouble was, now he knew he loved her, what he

didn't know was if she loved him. All he could do was pray that Tara would see the same thing.

Prickly, determined, independent little Tara, and he discovered that when he loved, the feeling just grew, shifted, touched the whole world with its glow, irrevocably, from the depths of his soul, and there was no going back. So this was what his father had meant when he'd said it would happen one day and he'd recognise it.

He couldn't believe it. His sisters would be in whoops of laughter. His mother would be thrilled he was thinking of settling down.

Settling down?

That was why everything was so upside down and back to front. So unlike it usually was because he'd never fallen in love before. He was in love with Tara. No wonder he hadn't recognised it.

The last time Tara woke, because there had been several awakenings in more ways than one, Simon wasn't holding her and she felt the loss like a piece of herself was gone. And her heart began to pound. What would happen today?

Nothing or everything? Would he be kind but distant? Would he be loving and different towards her? She hugged herself and assured her newly awakened inner woman that everything would be fine, no matter what. But she didn't believe it.

Thankfully, before she could whip herself into too much of a state Simon poked his head around the door.

The smile on his face wasn't distant at all. Actually, his eyes said he wanted to jump in beside her and she was tempted to crook her finger at him. 'Your breakfast awaits you on the back veranda, my lady.'

She sat up. Realised she was naked. Clutched the sheet and blushed as Simon enjoyed the view with a decidedly proprietorial glint in his eye. 'Maeve and Louisa will be home soon, the girls leave for school in five minutes, and I thought you might like to get dressed before then.'

Absolutely. Crikey. 'Yes. Please.' She waved him away and he pulled his head back but not before he winked at her like a villain in a farce. Well, it didn't seem as though Simon regretted the night.

The tension slid from her shoulders and several unlimbered muscles twinged as she swung her feet out of the bed. Her cheeks heated as she caught a glance of a thoroughly sated woman in the mirror, and she tried one of Simon's winks on herself. She grinned. Felt silly.

But there was a curve to her lips she couldn't seem to move and she slid the same shirt around her shoulders that she'd removed from Simon last night, sniffed the collar, and recognised the faint cologne she would always associate with him, then gathered her own clothes with one hand and clutched the edges of the shirt together with the other hand as she let herself out of the room and into her own.

The fastest gathering on record of clothes for the

day and then she was safely behind the bathroom door before anyone else arrived home.

By the time she was out, dressed and confident, on the outside at least, Louisa and Maeve were home. Maeve was trying desperately to catch her eye but she refused to collide with the knowing looks that kept coming her way and Simon was whistling and avoiding his sister as well.

Diversion was needed. 'How are the girls?'

Louisa seemed oblivious to the undercurrents in the room. Thank goodness somebody was. 'As prettily mannered as you could wish for.' Louisa sighed blissfully. 'I do enjoy their company. And they're so excited about the carols tonight.'

'That's right. The carols by candlelight.' Tara was pretty excited about that too. She'd be with Simon. She wondered if he'd hold her hand in front of his family. The thought was nerve-racking and she stuffed it away to peek at later. 'What time does Mia get home?'

'Angus picks her up from the airport at lunchtime so she'll be back before they finish school.'

It was so weird having a normal conversation. Especially with Simon watching her. She could feel him. And then there were Maeve's eyes nearly bugging out of her head with curiosity. She tried to concentrate on Louisa. 'I've got two home visits this morning but can help any other time if you need me to do something.'

The older lady smiled serenely. 'Thanks, Tara. I'll let you know.'

Tara nodded and followed Simon out to the veranda, where he'd set a place and made her favourite herbal tea and raisin toast. He stood behind her chair and pushed it in when she sat down. Every time she glanced at him she could feel her cheeks heat. And her belly glow. Finally understanding the preoccupation a woman could have with sleeping with her man. Was Simon her man? He leaned across and kissed her and then he sat opposite and calmly sipped his tea.

Maeve arrived, hovered and Tara had a way to go before she reached that skill of composure Simon had. Sipped her tea, ate half a piece of toast and decided to bolt. She rose. 'I've got to go.'

The words sounded abrupt but Simon only smiled at her. Gave her a wink. Maeve looked thwarted and Tara decided exit had been an excellent idea as she walked hurriedly back into the house to get her gear, and knew the rest of the day would require some concentration if she wasn't going to end up staring into space every few minutes with a silly smile on her face.

Carols by candlelight began as the sun set. Angus and Simon had taken the trailer full of chairs and set them up to the left of the stage. It was a warm, sleeveless type of evening and the children were dressed in pretty red dresses and short-legged Santa helper suits, with Santa hats and flashing stars, and dozens of little battery-powered candles to wave in the darkening evening as families from all over the valley began to arrive.

Simon had been to the shops and Tara had never had so many Christmas-themed trinkets in her possession.

Her favourite was a long silver wand with a star on top that glowed silver in the darkening sky. Though the Christmas headband with reindeer made her laugh and the earrings shaped like Christmas trees that flashed on and off and matching bracelet were all very cool. When she'd demurred, Simon had laughed and said she could give them away if she had too much but he hadn't been able to resist buying them because every time he'd seen something new he'd thought she would like it.

Tara liked it. She'd never bought herself anything festive, had thought they were all for little children, but Simon said she looked like a Christmas angel so she hugged them to herself when what she wanted to do was hug Simon.

In the distance the lights from Louisa's house shone merrily and the carols began with a rousing rendition of 'Good King Wenceslas', and Tara turned with amazement as Simon began to sing in a deep, hilarious baritone that, despite his intention to make her smile, was incredibly rich and tuneful.

She had never thought she could ever be this happy, this excited, this included in a family night like tonight, and she shook her head at the gorgeous man beside her as he took her hand in his and hugged her to him.

She saw Louisa smile at them, and even Angus looked across at them warmly. Mia winked and Maeve grinned at her every time she saw them.

Tara was in love!

* * *

The day before Christmas Eve and Tara turned over in bed. Last night had been amazing. Simon had seemed so proud of her, so happy to show everyone that he cared, and just soaking up the night with Simon's arm around her had been one of the most magical evenings she'd ever had.

She was in love but instead of waking in the golden glow she should have, it was the terrified child from the orphanage who woke, and she felt like scooting down the hallway and crawling into Simon's bed for reassurance. She really, really hated that horrible feeling it was all too good to be true.

All those times as a kid when she'd thought maybe she could fall in love with a family, had waited for the call that only other children seemed to get—this was much worse, a thousand times worse.

What if something happened to this precious feeling between her and Simon?

To make it more terrifying, he was a part of the most amazing family of them all. A whole Christmas fairytale and Santa Claus stocking of loving people that she would give anything to be a part of. Could she possibly believe that good things like that could happen to her? She thought of the lyrebird and a little calmness came out of nowhere. Maybe she just needed to learn to believe it?

And then her phone rang, probably a mum with an unsettled baby, just as she was about to get out of bed and dress for work. It took her a moment to recognise the voice from her past. Mick.

That was when she knew it was the end.

She felt shock, and horror, and a queer almost relief from the impending doom she'd worried so much about. Karma-wise she'd probably talked herself into this bad luck. 'How did you find my number?'

'I didn't just find your number.' The smug tone sent icy shivers down her back. Not for herself. She wasn't afraid of Mick, or not much except when he was off his face on some substance, but she was afraid for Louisa getting a nasty shock when she opened the door. Or Maeve. For anyone else who got in his way. More afraid of the look of disgust when the people she cared about in Lyrebird Lake saw that she was the reason he was there.

Mick's gravelly voice recalled her to the present. 'I want my bike, Tara.'

The darned bike. 'The bike is mine. You owed me a lot more than it's worth.'

'It's mine. And I'm coming for it. And that's not all I'm coming for. You and me, Tara. Like old times.'

Like hell. He really was high. She glanced at the clock. 'Where are you?'

'Leaving Sydney soon.'

She didn't know what to do. What to think. Had to stall until she came up with a plan to keep Mick away from Lyrebird Lake and everyone in it until she could sort it.

She was crystal clear in her mind that she'd accepted

the bike wasn't worth it. Thankfully she had grown beyond defining herself because of a possession and was over her need to have a win over Mick for her self-esteem. If she wasn't so angry with him for risking her new-found friendships, let alone the precious jewel of her relationship with Simon, she'd feel sorry for Mick.

Even in her fog of anguish Tara could see he was missing out in life because of his bitterness about the past. But feeling sorry for Mick had led her into this mess of debt and negativity in the first place.

But she was slowly climbing out of that hole. Mentally she already had, and financially she was in the process, one small payment at a time.

And now, being with Simon had helped her find another stronger and prouder layer of herself. She was someone a wonderful man admired, and she could leave here a better person because of that.

The sigh that accompanied the thought seemed to tear itself loose from her soul. Because she would have to leave now that Mick had found her. Not with him, but after him, because he'd just keep coming back every time he wanted to extort something.

'You could pay me ten thousand dollars' worth of debts and it's all yours.'

Mick laughed and it wasn't a pleasant sound and Tara grimaced. He was high on something. 'You'll never get the money but I will get my bike. I know where you live. I'm coming to have Christmas with all your little families. I've seen the house where you live on Google Earth. Bet they don't know about me. But they will.'

'I'm negotiable on the bike, Mick. But there were never *old times* between you and me. Just a short time. I was your friend and you let me down. Nothing else is on the agenda.'

'What's up, Tara? You too good for your orphan buddies now?'

'The blood-sucking ones. Yes. I have a new life. One I've worked hard for. You're not a part of it.'

'That's what you think.'

'Forget it, Mick. I'll give you the bike, and you can get lost. But you can't have it now. I'm working this morning and don't finish until late this afternoon. I'll meet you tonight.'

Blow. That was family night at Mia and Angus's. 'About six.' The whole family was meeting for drinks to be there when the girls went to bed. Apparently they did it every year. She would just have to cry off and meet Mick somewhere out of sight while they all went on and had dinner.

Though how she'd smuggle the bike out of town would be tricky. That was the problem with Harleys. It wasn't like they didn't have a distinctive sound. Even lyrebirds noticed the noise. She'd say she had to go out for one of her women. Early labour. Simon would believe that. Except now she was lying to him. But she couldn't help that.

And then Mick upped the stakes. 'Nope. Think I'll

spend Christmas in Lyrebird Lake. Seems like as fine a place as any. With my good friend Tara.'

Tara felt a clutch of dread. What if she couldn't stop him? If it was too late? The cold wind of the real world was blowing through her life again. She could imagine the children frightened of Mick, Simon sticking up for her and Mick fighting him, Louisa terrified. Nightmare in Lyrebird Lake and she had to stop it all before any of it could happen.

She needed to stall him. Stop him the only way she could think of. 'If you come anywhere near my friends, my work or my home before I say so, I'll douse the bike in petrol and burn it.' Her voice lowered and she put every ounce of conviction she could muster into the threat. 'You know I will.'

A pause and then a bluster. 'You won't have the chance.'

'Try me.' There was a silence. 'Only on my terms and until then...leave me alone. Give me until tonight to figure something out. I'll meet you somewhere away from here and hand it over. Ring me around six some time but I don't want you in this town. Or I will destroy the bike.'

That morning at work Tara found it incredibly difficult to concentrate. She kept imagining Simon's face if he came face to face with wild-eyed Mick, who looked even worse than he was, except when he was high, and he really was a bad man. Why on earth anyone would tattoo their face was beyond Tara, though she didn't regret the tiny rose on her own shoulder, remembrance for the tragically short life of Mick's sister.

Maybe if she hadn't gone with Mick for that first tattoo he wouldn't have started painting his body but she would never know. The past was the past.

She just wished the past and the people from it would stay there! Especially now she'd glimpsed a future she'd foolishly thought she had a chance at.

The ward was quiet. They'd had a peaceful birth earlier in the day, one of Mia's mothers, and Tara spent the day sitting beside the new mum, gently praising her early breastfeeding skills. Everything was tidy and she was thinking she might even get off a little early when the phone rang to say her last due woman was coming in.

For the first time in her career she wished a baby would wait.

Of course, it didn't.

Tara didn't get home at three like she wanted, to give herself time to get organised. She arrived home at ten to six and Maeve and Louisa were busy in the kitchen, making finger food for tonight's family get-together at Mia's.

Simon had been out all day apparently, shopping, which was a good thing because every time someone spoke to her she jumped and he would notice more than anyone that she was preoccupied and nervous.

When she picked up her phone from her room she

grimaced at all the missed calls. When she tried to return the call on Mick's mobile, his phone was turned off
and she felt unease crawl up her neck. Missing his calls
wouldn't leave Mick in a good frame to negotiate with.

Frustration gnawed at her. She needed to get in contact before he took matters into his own hands.

What if he was already in town? What if he knocked
on the door and frightened Louisa? Or her greatest fear,
picked a quarrel with Simon?

Tara quickly typed in a message. Gave directions to
a place safely away from the town. Tried to imply he
couldn't come to the lake but without him knowing he
had her worried. This was her worst nightmare and she
threw on her jeans and grabbed her helmet.

Behind her eyes a dull throb of tiredness and strain
made her gulp the water beside her bed in the hope it
would help the headache, and she stared through the
curtains to the street as she drank.

Hell. Damn. Blast it. This was so unfair. She didn't
deserve this imploding of her dream town. She felt
like pulling her hair and stomping her feet. But that
had never been her way so she drew a deep breath and
straightened. It didn't matter about her. It was the people at the lake who mattered and she needed to stop
Mick from upsetting them. A sudden vision of Mick
and Simon fighting made nausea rise in her throat.

Just before she left, one last attempt as she paused in
the hallway, she finally managed to get through to Mick.

And as she'd dreaded, he'd borrowed a friend's car and trailer and had stopped for petrol only an hour away.

The dinner started at six-thirty and Tara estimated it would take her an hour to get to Mick, hand over the bike and get home.

Simon had gone to the next big town, shopping with his father, and still wasn't back so at least she could get away.

Tara repeated the directions to the local rubbish dump, on the inbound side of town, she could hand over the bike and walk the four miles home without anyone seeing her.

She had no idea what she'd say when everyone realised the bike was gone but that was the least of her worries. She'd just say she'd had to give it back.

CHAPTER THIRTEEN

SIMON HAD HAD a great day with his dad, had spent most of his time buying quirky gifts for Tara, and couldn't wait to hug her after a day with her filling his mind.

Then he saw Tara standing in the hallway talking on the phone. She hadn't seen him and he stood quietly and soaked in the vision. The light shone on her spiky silver hair, which exposed her gorgeous neck, and he wanted to trace that faint line behind her ear. Kiss that spot where her pulse beat gently against his mouth. He'd done a lot of that the other night. That hadn't been all he'd done and somehow they hadn't been able to recapture a moment when they could be together, alone, since then. He needed to do something about that.

She looked so good he wanted to drag her off to his room and have his wicked way with her right then and there but he guessed he'd have to wait until they could get away.

She'd finished the call so he moved towards her. 'Hi, Tara. Looking forward to tonight?' She jumped, and it wasn't a little one, it was a full-blown knee-jerk fright, and his own heart rate accelerated.

'Sorry.' He frowned, noticed the strain in her face he hadn't seen before, then remembered she'd been at work today. Not a good day? He knew how that felt.

He reached out and touched her shoulder with the idea of maybe sharing a little hug and she jumped again. Looked at him and then away and none of it was encouraging. What was going on? 'You okay?'

He tried to catch her eye but she turned her head. Now he was worried. Maybe she regretted the other night. He hoped not. He glanced at her jeans and boots. 'You going out on the bike?'

'Home visit. Early labour. Probably miss the dinner.'

Bummer. He'd been really looking forward to cuddling up to Tara while they all sat around and toasted the season. He guessed this had happened to all of his previous girlfriends and now the boot was on the other foot. 'Who is it? Want me to come? I could sit outside and reassure the man of the house.'

'You don't know her and, no, I don't want you to come.' A quick hunted glance and he was beginning to wonder if this was bigger than he thought.

Now what did he say? She looked like she was going to cry. 'You sure everything is okay?'

He watched her do that calming thing she did, a big breath, dropping the expression from her face, easing the tension from her shoulders. What had he done to make her that tense?

She shook her head. 'I'll see you later, Simon.'

And that was that. 'Okay.' Not a lot he could do about it except stalk her and that wasn't his style. 'I'll tell Mia you got called out.'

'Just leave it. I'll tell her.' She smiled but it wasn't one that made him feel good. 'Apologise for me. Maybe I'll get there before it all finishes, maybe not. Have a good night.'

'Sure.' He was anything but sure. Watched her go. But the feeling of unease glowed in his gut as he heard the sound of the bike start up. If he didn't know better he'd swear she'd looked panic-stricken for a minute there. Something was going on and he knew Tara well enough to suspect she was unhappy about where she was going. So why would that be? What could possibly make Tara unhappy about going to one of her women in labour? A poor domestic situation? Surely not. If that were the case she'd take someone else because that was the protocol. What if one of her women had a violent partner? Simon wished he'd asked a bit more. The unease grew in his gut and he decided to walk to Mia's and ask her if she knew anything.

Tara blinked back her tears. The wind on her face was achingly familiar and the throb of the engine hummed goodbye. Tara gained little enjoyment from her last ride but she was past lamenting over the loss.

She'd lied to Simon. To his face. But she couldn't see any other way of protecting those she'd come to love.

Yes, she loved Simon, she loved Louisa, she loved every darned person in Lyrebird Lake, it seemed, and all the sighs and shoulder drops in the world weren't going to lighten that load.

She'd let them down. And now she was going to sign away her only possession in the world to stop them finding out about her past, but she couldn't help feeling it wasn't going to stop disaster happening anyway.

She turned off the main road onto the quiet gravel road to the tip. It was good it was quiet because she really didn't want anyone from Lyrebird Lake wondering why she was driving this way at this time of the evening.

And maybe that was why she came round the corner just a little too fast. Hit a patch of gravel just a little bit deep.

And for the first time lost control of the big bike as the front wheel skidded in the gravel and went sideways. Tara fought to stay upright, fought the urge to hit the brake, skidded sideways up the road valiantly upright but at a dangerous angle. As the bike slowed she managed to stay upright and slowed more until she thought she'd manage to correct the angles in the end.

She concentrated, fiercely willing the front wheel to straighten as she pulled it around, but her luck ran out because she'd run out of straight road and didn't make the bend. She hit the grass and flew into the scrub until the bike caught on a strong branch and jerked to a stop, where it fell with lack of forward motion and went down, with Tara frantically shifting her bottom leg so she wouldn't be pinned underneath. Her ankle jerked and caught and she pulled frantically to get it clear and the pain shot up her leg as it twisted.

She could feel her heart racing in her ears. Tara pulled herself backwards on her bottom until she was clear of the bike as its massive weight sank slowly closer and closer to the ground, crushing the undergrowth with a sizzling crackle, until it was lying flat on its side. Tara's back came up against the trunk of a tree she was very glad to have missed. Her ankle throbbed but she wasn't trapped under the bike. Still some good to be found.

But she had no idea how she was going to lift the deadweight of the bike to get it off the ground.

After a minute of gathering her nerves, Tara crawled from her position against the tree and stood gingerly upright to brush herself off. She put a little weight on her ankle; it wobbled but stayed upright with a low-level throbbing. It could have been a lot worse.

At least she'd had jeans on. She'd refused to wear her leathers and walk home in them, but she hadn't escaped unscathed. As well as scratches on her arms as she and the bike had barrelled through the bushes, the areas where the stressed jeans had parted had let in tiny scratches and stings that would be annoying but not kill her. Her biggest dilemma was that she needed to get the bike upright and beat Mick to the rubbish dump before he decided she wasn't coming and head to Lyrebird Lake anyway.

She pulled her phone from her pocket and tried Mick's number but he wasn't answering. Peered at her watch but the screen was broken and she had to pick the plastic out to be able to read the numbers. It must have happened as she'd come through the bushes. She had ten minutes until she was supposed to be there.

She took a big, deep breath as she struggled to stand the bike while putting all of her weight on one leg. Ouch! No luck. Tara tried from the other side.

Pull! No luck, just a twinge of discomfort in her back from the effort and a fiercer ache from her ankle. She walked back again to the lifting side and tried jamming a stick as a lever to get it up. The stick broke.

No luck. She'd known it was going to be an unequal contest. It was all very well to sit astride a big bike. Even pulling it off its stand was fine when she was balanced evenly on her feet. But to lift a heavy motorcycle that was deadweight from lying on its side on the ground was just too much for her to achieve on her own. Even swearing was an effort after the last superhuman effort she'd made to no avail.

It was getting dark. She tried Mick again but he still wasn't answering his phone. The road was deserted, a fact she'd been happy about a few minutes ago and was not so thrilled about now.

It was past the agreed time and he hadn't rung her. Hopefully he had been held up somewhere too, or he'd decided he wouldn't answer the phone when she'd tried to ring him. It was the sort of pathetic thing he would do. There was nothing else she could do but ring for help—and the only person she could ring was Simon. Maybe they could get the bike upright before Mick came.

Simon had walked swiftly around to his father's house and cornered Mia in the kitchen to ask what she knew about Tara's due clients. Still concerned about the idea that one of Tara's birthing women might have a less than salubrious home life, he couldn't settle until he'd been reassured.

But Mia's comment that after her last birth Tara's only due woman was Maeve, had him thrust back into confusion.

So it couldn't be a premature labour because she'd be telling that woman to come for transfer. Which meant only one thing. She'd lied to him. To his face. And he couldn't think of one damn good reason why she'd had to do that.

And then his phone rang. 'Hello?'

'Simon?' It was her.

His hand tightened on the phone as he waved to Mia before he walked back towards the manse. 'Tara? Are you okay?'

Tara's 'Not really...' made his heart rate jump.

'What happened?'

'I came off my bike and I can't stand it up. I need help.'

'Where are you?' He looked up at Mia and pointed towards the manse. Mia nodded and waved him away.

There was a pause. 'I'm sorry about the dinner.'

He brushed that aside. 'Where are you?'

'On the old rubbish dump road.'

He hadn't thought there were any houses down that way. 'And you're all right? You're not hurt?'

'Pride's pretty banged up, my ankle is tender, but physically I'm scratched, that's all.'

He tried to hold them back but the words came out anyway. 'What are you doing out there?'

She sighed. 'It's a long story. I'll tell you when you get here. Turn onto the rubbish tip road and I'm about a kilometre in on the left just as you hit the low part of the road. Watch out for the loose gravel,' she added dryly.

'Twenty minutes!' And it had better be a good reason because he didn't like any of the ones he'd come up with.

CHAPTER FOURTEEN

'SIMON WILL BE here in time. He'll be here.' The words echoed eerily in the encroaching dusk and Tara huddled further into her thin top. It was summer, for pity's sake, and she hadn't had the forethought to bring warmer clothes, but down in the hollow the mist was cool. That's what happened when you forgot the way of the world.

She'd fallen into this trap s-o-o-o many times before you would think she'd have learnt her lesson. Why would Simon Campbell, darling of his two families and, in fact, all of Lyrebird Lake, forgive her for lying to him?

Especially when he didn't understand the reason.

Maybe the fault did lie a little with her. Come on, Tara, a lot with her. She didn't trust him enough to give him the tools to believe her. Hadn't let him into her dilemma because she'd been too afraid he'd turn away from her. So she'd lied instead.

Self-sabotage or what? If she was honest, somewhere in the back of her head the voices had been saying he would let her down. Maybe that was why she'd made this tryst so difficult.

Well, she was in trouble now. It was getting dark, miles from anywhere, and she didn't want to think about the possibility that she'd put her heart on the line again to be broken.

She lifted her chin. She wasn't some twelve-year-old orphan sent on her way. She was a grown woman. A grown professional woman and she would get over this just as soon as she figured a way to get back to civilisation, and she may as well start now because he wasn't going to come.

Then headlights crossed the tops of the trees and in the distance she heard an echo of a car roaring up the hill.

'Simon,' she whispered, and the words floated into the darkness. Now that he was coming, she dreaded seeing the disgust on his face. She'd let him down with her lies but she hadn't been able to think of anything else she could do to prevent her world crumbling. He'd probably think she was leaving with Mick. She may as well. There was nothing here for her now.

But it wasn't Simon. It was Mick. Towing a trailer behind a disreputable old sedan. Tara's heart sank and she considered throwing herself back into the bushes so he wouldn't see her, but it was too late.

He pulled up in a shower of gravel because he'd been driving far too fast as usual. She should have known it wasn't Simon with the car engine screaming up the hill in the dimness.

'Where's the bike?' The words flew out of his mouth

as fast as Mick got out of the car. He looked around suspiciously.

Tara sighed. She'd forgotten how childish he was. 'I lost it in the gravel so it's in the bush behind me.'

'Is it okay?'

'What about me?'

'Oh, yeah. You okay?' But his eyes were scanning the bush and he was on his way before she could answer.

'Fine,' she said to his back, and decided Mick was dumb enough and strong enough not to ask for help to extricate the bike.

She glanced up the road and wished like hell she'd never rung Simon. She considered phoning him back and saying, *Don't come. I'll be home soon.* Except that would involve more explanations and possibly more lies. She'd lied enough. All she could do was hope Mick would load the bike and go as soon as possible.

Mick did manage to get the bike on the trailer before Simon arrived but that was where Tara's luck ran out.

Simon turned off the main road and frowned at the deserted gravel road that stretched ahead in the dimness. He switched on his headlights and slowed right down. She'd said about a kilometre. Something was going on. And he was pretty sure he wasn't going to like it. But he was surprisingly unworried about that. Lots of people did things he didn't like and he got over it. Look at his parents lying to him. Look at Maeve. Though he hadn't got over Rayne's part in that. But this would be okay. Right.

Anyway, he loved Tara and the fact that she'd rung him for help was a big plus.

But he would be much happier when he found her and could see for himself she was unhurt.

And then he saw her. Standing in the gloom at the side of the road beside a dirty sedan and a trailer with her bike on the back. She must have found someone to help her get it home.

Well, that was one problem solved. She was standing, and apart from a limp when she came towards where he parked she looked okay. Thank goodness.

Then he saw the driver of the vehicle and his brows rose. Even in the poor light he could see the heavy tattoos and plaited beard. Noted Tara's guarded stance as he pulled up and climbed out of his vehicle. Thank goodness he'd hurried. The situation was not what he'd expected but as long as Tara was okay...

Mick waved him away. 'We don't need help, mate.'

Simon ignored him. 'You okay, Tara?' He crossed to her side, all the while noting the smudges of blood through the slits in her jeans, the abrasions on her arms and the extreme wariness on her face. He wanted to hug her but she was sending keep-off vibes like a missile launcher, telling him to stay away, and he frowned. 'How's the ankle?'

Mick lifted his head at that and took a step towards Simon. Towered over him. 'Who are you?'

Simon looked him up and down. Remained supremely unconcerned that he was outweighed. He'd faced down bigger men than this guy, and knew how not to antagonise. Usually. 'I'm a friend of Tara's. Who are you?'

'Mick. Me and Tara grew up together. We don't need your help.'

He smiled at Mick. 'Good to meet you, Mick. Then you'll understand if I ask Tara that.' He didn't wait for Mick's answer. 'Tara?'

'Ankle's fine. Sore but I can walk.' Tara was looking worried and he wished he could tell her how skilled he was at managing stroppy people. He was the one they called if a husband lost the plot in his concern for his wife. Though he wasn't feeling his usual detached self as he took in the full magnificence of this quite obnoxious guy, making ownership moves towards Tara.

'It's nice of you to take Tara's bike home for her.'

Mick laughed. 'Yeah. But it's my home. My bike. She gave it back.' He leered. 'I was thinking I might take Tara, too.'

Simon fought down his sudden out-of-character urge to knock the guy's teeth in and looked at Tara.

'And how does Tara feel about that?'

She glared at Mick. 'You've got the bike. Let's go, Simon.'

Simon did a double-take. 'You're giving him the bike?'

Tara straightened. To Simon she ground out, 'It's mine to give.' To Mick, 'I want you out of my life. Merry Christmas.'

Tara walked away from them both, climbed into Simon's car and slammed the door. She stared straight ahead, ignoring them, though her eyes were squinting sideways in the side mirror as she tried to catch a glimpse of what was happening. She'd had the desperate idea if she left they'd both look stupid if they started something, and she didn't think even Mick would drag her out of her chosen car with force. She was right.

Simon opened the car door just as Mick's car started up and drove ahead to find somewhere to turn around.

'What the hell was that all about?'

'Can we just turn the car around and get out of here first? Please!'

Simon reversed the car with very uncharacteristic roughness and speed, and they skidded away from the fateful corner in a shower of gravel, much like Mick's arrival. Tara sighed.

'Don't you sigh at me. What the hell were you thinking? You arranged that. Didn't you? To meet this man in a dark and deserted place, to hand over the bike. By yourself. After lying to me so I wouldn't demand to come with you.'

She looked at him. His face was set. His lips compressed. Those strong shoulders were rigid with disbelief. She'd done that to him. Hurt him. Made him uncharacteristically angry. Knocked herself off the pedestal she'd been trying to balance on. 'You're right. That just about covers it.'

'No, that doesn't just about cover it.' They turned off the road and onto the Lyrebird Lake road and Simon pulled over. Switched the engine off. They sat there for a few seconds and Tara gathered her thoughts. Behind them Mick's lights turned towards Sydney and disappeared. She guessed she did owe Simon an explanation but she wasn't happy with his high-handed tone or the fact that this had all backfired on her. She'd been trying to do the right thing but she'd had nowhere to go. She had lied to Simon.

So she gave it to him straight. No wrapping. It was all a mess now anyway. 'Mick wanted the bike back. He's not pleasant when he's in this mood. I didn't want him to upset anyone in Lyrebird Lake so I'd rather just give it to him.'

'So you arranged to meet him out here? On your own?'

She shrugged. 'I'm not afraid of Mick. He looks worse than he is but I didn't want him being horrible in front of Louisa.' She looked up at him. 'Or Maeve, or Mia.'

She sighed again. Almost defiantly. 'Or you.'

That just inflamed him more. 'And how were you going to get home after you handed this man your only possession?'

'Walk.'

'That's beautiful.' He grimaced in the darkness. 'Walk. On a dark road. What is it, four miles?' His hands tightened on the steering-wheel until his knuckles were white. Despite the quietness of his tone Tara could tell he was furious. 'You put yourself in danger. All the time.'

He shook his head. Flabbergasted as he ran over it in his mind. 'There's the motorbike I was getting used to, the controlled risk of skydiving. I get that, I really do. But then there's being wilfully, personally risky, meeting substance-affected men in deserted places at night. I can't believe you didn't ask me for help.'

'No. I didn't.'

He glared at her. 'Instead of telling me the truth, accepting my help and being safe?'

She shrugged. 'I'm used to looking after myself. I thought I would be safe.'

'See, now I have an issue with that.'

'I rang you in the end.'

'Far too little too late. Maybe we have rushed into this. Or maybe I have. This morning I would have sworn we had a future together but I'm not so sure now. If there's one thing I won't put up with it's being shut out and lied to, especially by someone I l—um...someone I care deeply for!'

Someone he cared deeply for. And she'd spoiled it all.

Tara risked a glance at him and he was staring straight ahead as if the road was going to open up and swallow them at any moment. She almost wished it would.

The silence was loaded with regret on both sides but neither of them seemed to be able to break it. It took for ever to get back to the empty manse.

Then they were home. Everyone else was at Mia's and as Simon helped her in she wondered if he'd go to the family dinner now. But he didn't say anything, just appeared with the cotton wool and disinfectant and bathed her cuts, despite the fact she wanted him to just leave her alone.

Ushered her to bed. But there was a huge distance between them of things that were said and unsaid as he closed her door and left her. On both sides.

CHAPTER FIFTEEN

TARA OPENED HER eyes at six o'clock on Christmas Eve morning and lay in her bed, staring at the ceiling full of ghosts from Christmas past, even though she didn't want to.

Long-gone children's faces, long-gone empty dormitories, less-than-wonderful foster-parent experiences. And all those Christmas Eves full of expectations. Well, she didn't have any of those today after last night.

She'd lost the one man who could have rounded out her world. She sat up and hugged her pillow to her chest.

Simon had been right. She should have faced the music earlier rather than later. Discussed her concerns rationally with the man who cared and had been nothing but supportive. She had a sudden memory of their morning with the breech birth. How safe she'd felt because Simon had been there. How supportive he'd been without being authoritative. How proud he'd been of her ability to understand what had needed to be done and doing it.

She'd thrown away her chance with Simon and

today was going to be a long, long day of tragedy of lost opportunities.

She should have trusted him to understand. She just didn't know how to trust people. Another hard, painful lesson learned. It was too late for her and Simon but she vowed she would try in the future.

But for now she needed to make sure she didn't spoil anyone else's day.

Apart from Simon hating her, today was going to be a good day. She would smile and play cheerful families one last time. She'd let go of the silly pipe dream of happily ever after with Simon that she should never have contemplated. He'd be gone soon and she'd see if she could settle back into the world of Lyrebird Lake. If she couldn't settle then what she'd learnt here would hold her in good stead for the future.

Starting from now, she needed to appreciate the fact that she could hear the cicadas in the tree outside her window. Savour the warmth that was already creeping into the morning. Sniff the air with the enticing fragrance of baking that had hung over the house like an aromatic fog for the last two days. Go outside onto the springy kikuyu grass and watch the nodding reindeer and manger animals gyrate as the sun rose.

Then she'd be ready for what today would bring and what it wouldn't bring.

The feeling of just-out-of-reach simple pleasures drew her out of bed. Today would have to look after itself and she would savour every moment because that was all she had control over.

There was a tinkle of music and she even managed a tiny, crooked smile into her pillow before she put it back on her bed. Louisa had the Christmas music on again. Maeve would be so glad tomorrow when it would be gone. Her eyes stung as she thought about losing Maeve as a friend and then pushed that thought too back into her mind.

She scooted down the hallway with her clothes under her arm. Ten minutes later she let herself out the front door into the misty morning light to start the day on her own. Build her walls of serenity so no one could see the lost little girl inside her.

Except that Simon was there on the seat in front of the manger. She almost turned around and ran back to her room—but instead she lifted her chin. Better to do this when no one else was there.

Simon felt some of his tension ease as Tara came across the grass. At least she was going to talk to him. 'Merry Christmas Eve, Tara.'

Her face said she didn't think so and his own interpretation said that was his fault. He'd done so many things wrong.

'Merry Christmas Eve, Simon.' She sat with a gap he could have driven a car through between them.

When he looked sideways at her a tiny silver tear

slid out of her eye and rolled down her cheek, and he thought his heart would break. 'Don't cry.'

She brushed it away. 'I'm not.' Sat up straighter and rubbed her face.

'Baby Jesus arrives at midnight tonight.'

She looked at him and frowned. And then he could see she imagined a tiny beautifully wrapped doll all tucked up in straw.

'That will be awesome.'

They sat there looking at the space for a physical sign of a new beginning and miraculously he saw the signs of her glimpsing that maybe there was still a chance of a new beginning between them too.

He shifted along the seat and closed the gap between them on the bench, and all the motorised animals nodded.

'You okay?' His hand came across and picked up her fingers. Squeezed them in his. For a few seconds she just let it lie there in his palm and he squeezed her fingers again gently until she returned the pressure.

'I guess you did come to save me.'

'I was later than I wanted to be. You need to learn to trust me.'

She looked down at their hands and then back at his face. 'You need to learn to trust me. I've looked after myself for a lot of years.'

He sighed. She was right. 'I thought I did but then things happened and I lost it again. I'm sorry.'

She smiled at that, a little mistily, and looked away.

He'd better be able to fix this because looking at her face and not kissing her was killing him. 'I'm sorry I was horrible to you last night.'

'You were horrible to me.'

Well, that didn't go as planned, he thought regretfully.

'But I can see why you were.' She straightened her shoulders. 'And I'm sorry I lied to you.'

She was so brave. His Tara. 'You did lie to me. But I can see why you did.'

She nodded in the morning light. 'I didn't want you to meet Mick.'

He smiled ruefully at that. 'I didn't really want to meet Mick either. But I do want you to lose the ridiculous idea that any obnoxious person who comes looking for you is going to affect the way we feel about the Tara we know and care about. You have the whole of Lyrebird Lake behind you. Mick needs to see that. You need to see that.'

He looked at her under her brows. 'And he's not getting your bike.'

'I don't care about the bike.'

'I do. It's yours. I've given his number plate to the police and told them if he gives it back we won't press charges. They checked and it's your name on the paperwork.'

He saw her look of cautious hope but she said again, 'I don't care about the bike. What if he comes back? He can be very aggressive.'

He shook his head. Not the answer. 'Giving him the bike won't stop that. If he comes back we make him welcome. There must have been a reason he was your friend.

'But Mick's really not the bad man here. I am. Can you forgive me? For being angry?' He shook his head. 'I'm having a hard time forgiving myself. I never lose it.'

'You lost it.' She was teasing him now. Typical. 'Pretty controlled kind of guy, eh?' And he deserved it.

'I thrive on it. Usually. Like to have my world lined up and the bases covered.' He glanced at her. It was always good to look at Tara. 'Do you know why I lost it?'

She nodded. 'You were worried about me?'

'That too. But mainly because I've just discovered if I lose you I lose everything.'

He could see she didn't know how to answer that. All he could hope for was that when she did figure it out he'd like the answer.

Finally she did. 'I didn't want you to meet Mick in case I lost you.'

Now, that was good to hear. She did care and she squeezed his hand and turned towards him. A fresh, beautiful, Christmas Eve morning face with far less shadows than it had had a few minutes ago. 'Thank you for understanding, Simon. It's just that he can be very intimidating.'

'So can you.'

She shook her head. 'You're not intimidated by me.'

He had to laugh at that. He who had a burning question he couldn't ask.

'Tara.'

'Yes, Simon?'

'Do you love me?'

She looked away. Then back at him and her face seemed to glow. Even he could see that. His heart leapt. 'I might.'

She was so brave. Braver than him. Thank the stars for that. Time for him to be brave. 'Will you kiss me?' He puckered his lips. She looked at him like he was mad.

'No.'

'Please.'

She leaned over and did a reasonable job considering they were out in the street.

Fearless woman. Yep, there was love in that. He could feel his heart lift and swell and he just wanted to crush her to him. Finally he said it. 'Tara. I absolutely, one hundred percent, irrevocably love you.'

She blinked and chewed those gorgeous lips, and slowly an incredulous and painfully disbelieving smile grew on her beautiful mouth.

He didn't stop while he was ahead. 'And I want to marry you. As quickly as I can because you've spent too much of your life alone and, despite all my dozens of relatives, I've been alone too.'

She nodded. Quite vigorously. Apparently dumbstruck but he could work with that.

'But I need to marry you mostly because I love you, you crazy, adventurous woman.'

She swallowed and it must have helped because finally she said the words he wanted to hear.

'And I love you too, you too-sane, too-careful, too-bossy and will-learn-to-be-adventurous, man.'

She leaned over and kissed him again but this time he took over. Kissed her so thoroughly they forgot where they were until Maeve called from the veranda, 'Hey, you two. Come inside and do that.'

They broke apart and Simon was glad it was still too early for the neighbours to be around.

Tara grinned as Maeve turned and went back into the house. Asked thoughtfully, 'Just how many relatives have you got?'

'We have two sets. Which, now that I come to think of it, is perfectly designed for us.'

She wasn't really taking this in. She was gazing more at the love that was dusting her as it radiated from Simon. The way he looked at her, held her hand as if it was the most precious hand in the world. Hers?

She let the words resonate. 'Perfectly designed? How so?'

His eyes met hers with an exuberance she couldn't help smiling at. 'We have our Lyrebird Lake family, your new mama, Mia...' he grinned at that '...and Angus as dad. He's a very cool dad to come on late in life, let me reassure you there.'

Tara knew that but she loved the way Simon was

painting the picture. His pleasure at this the most precious gift he could share with her, his family, and her heart felt like it was opening like a flower starved of sunlight. One petal at a time.

'You'll have a new grandmother in Louisa, who will be over the moon. And will sew beautiful blankets for our children.' This was said smugly.

Louisa would be her grandmother. A huge lump rose into her throat with that incredible thought.

But Simon had only started as he kept adding depth to the picture. 'And two new little sisters in Layla and Amber, who I hope you will consider as bridesmaids. They look very pretty all dressed up. And Maeve will want to be maid of honour.'

She hadn't even thought about a wedding but suddenly she realised she would have one of those too. And sisters-in-law of her own.

So much to take in, to get used to, to be nervous about even.

But while the joy of a family would be hers, it was nothing compared to the thought of waking up beside Simon in the morning, every morning, and going to bed at night together for the rest of their lives. Spending their lives together. Everything was a wonderful, amazing Christmas tree of bonuses on top of everything. And Simon was her shining, love-filled star.

But he hadn't finished. 'And for your other family, we'll met the sisters and then we'll fly to America. See my dad and mum—it might take a while, but you'll grow to love her. Totally different from Mia, and she has fabulous taste because she thinks the sun shines out of me.'

He looked quite satisfied at that and she laughed. 'Imagine that. I think you're going to be quite a needy husband.'

His eyes darkened. 'I love the thought of being your husband. And I am needy. I need you because I've finally found what's been missing in my life. You're my heart, my love, my future. I look at you and feel the smile shine inside me like Louisa's blue star.'

'I'm your blue star.' He could see she liked that. Good.

'Shining at me as you save me. I love you, Tara.'

Tara could feel tears prickle and swallowed them back. The thought floated across her mind that Simon wouldn't mind her tears, she didn't have to hold back anything, or hide anything, or wait for anything. Simon knew all about her, warts and all, the only person who really did, and he was here and still loved her, and maybe everything that had gone before had been preparing her for this moment.

'I know you said you didn't expect evermore. But I wish you would. Stay with me for ever.'

Yes, please. 'And beyond.' They, she and Simon, were the future. She could see it and it was magic.

'And we are having a wedding cake with candles.'

She blinked and looked back at him. 'What? You can't have candles on a wedding cake.'

He lifted his chin and she recognised the tiny streak of stubbornness that stopped him from being perfect. Thank goodness he wasn't perfect. 'It's our cake. We can have what we want. And on our anniversary every year we'll have a cake with candles, and including your birthday, when you will definitely have candles, in twenty years' time you'll have blown out the same number of candles as everyone else in your life.'

'You're crazy.'

'About you.'

'And I am crazy about you, Simon Campbell.'

'Mrs Campbell.'

'Not yet.'

And suddenly he was serious. Intent. 'I love you, Tara. I'm not blind. I know we'll have our disagreements but I love the woman inside you. The survivor. The nurturer who has never had a chance to share that gift of nurturing. Share it with me, with the children I can't wait to have with you. We're going to have so much fun with our children.'

He was serious again. 'I can't wait to buy the toys you never had.' She could feel her frown but he'd known it was coming. 'Before you fire up, it's not pity, it's love. I can't wait to play the games you never played—with you, when we play with our children. And I know I'm going to love you more every single day. In fact, even thinking about this is driving me crazy. This has to happen as quickly as I can arrange it.'

She laughed. 'We have to finish Christmas first.'

'Yes, we'll have Christmas, our first Christmas together. And Maeve will have her baby. But inside, when all the revelry is around us, I'll know that you are my future. And ahead is a whole life of joy and adventure with you.'

He took her hand and drew her to her feet. 'Thank you, Tara.' He stroked her face and his eyes were solemn as he stared down into her face. 'My Christmas is here because you have given me your love and that is the greatest gift I could ever wish for.'

* * * * *

MIDWIFE'S
MISTLETOE BABY

BY
FIONA McARTHUR

Dear Reader

Welcome to Rayne and Maeve in Lyrebird Lake at Christmas time.

Wow. I hope you have fun with this. I was grinning all the way through. Rayne and Maeve wrote their story and I was just trying to keep up with them—two people with *sooo* much sexual chemistry between them, and both of them such determined people in their own right, with really tough dilemmas.

Most of my heroes and heroines are pretty private, and they prefer it if I leave the bedroom door firmly closed—but, while still avoiding anatomical explanations, Rayne and Maeve are so aware of the physical in each other they just can't keep their hands off and sometimes forget to shut the door. But it's still sweet.

So it's not surprising that after an explosive first night, right at the beginning, Maeve falls pregnant. As Rayne says, 'If there was one night when, no matter how many precautions were used, a determined sperm would get through *that* was the night.'

Fast forward nine months and Rayne returns, unaware that Maeve is about to have his baby—and as a guy emotionally scarred by his childhood and with no male role model he can't see how he can become the kind of father Maeve's baby deserves.

Maeve has to come to terms with the fact that Rayne walked away, didn't answer her letters, and let her down in her pregnancy. But he's here now—exactly what she so desperately wanted for Christmas—and after the first day with him back she believes in him...believes that Rayne has the potential to share the love he's never had a chance to share. She just has to help him to see it, and hopefully he'll become a believer before she has this baby. Thankfully she's in Lyrebird Lake, and with all the people she needs around her this is the place to do it.

I'd really love to hear what you think of Rayne and Maeve's journey.

Warmest wishes

Fi

PS I really loved Simon giving Tara, from the previous book, Russian dolls for Christmas!

Dedication

Dedicated to my darling husband, Ian.
Because I love you
xx Fiona

Praise for
Fiona McArthur:

'CHRISTMAS WITH HER EX is everything a good
medical romance should be, and it tells a story which
resonates with everything Christmas stands for.'
—*HarlequinJunkie*

'McArthur does full justice to an intensely emotional
scene of the delivery of a stillborn baby—
one that marks a turning point in both the characters'
outlooks. The entire story is liberally spiced with
drama, heartfelt emotion and just a touch of humour.'
—*RT Book Reviews* on
SURVIVAL GUIDE TO DATING YOUR BOSS

'MIDWIFE IN A MILLION by Fiona McArthur
will leave readers full of exhilaration.
Ms McArthur has created characters
that any reader could fall in love with.'
—*CataRomance*

PROLOGUE

March

RAYNE WALTERS BREATHED a sigh of relief as he passed through immigration and then customs at Sydney airport, deftly texted—I'm through—and walked swiftly towards the exit. Simon would be quick to pick him up. Very efficient was Simon.

He'd had that feeling of disaster closing in since the hiccough at LA when he'd thought he'd left it too late. But the customs officers had just hesitated and then frowned at him and waved him through.

He needed to get to Simon, the one person he wanted to know the truth, before it all exploded in his face. Hopefully not until he made it back to the States. Though they were the same age, and the same height, Simon was like a brother and mentor when he'd needed to make life choices for good rather than fast decisions.

But this choice was already made. He just wanted it not to come as a shock to the one other person whose good opinion mattered. He wasn't looking forward to

Simon's reaction, and there would be anger, but the steps were already in motion.

A silver car swung towards him. There he was. He lifted his hand and he could see Simon's smile as he pulled over.

'Good to see you, mate.'

'You too.' They'd never been demonstrative, Rayne had found it too hard——but their friendship in Simon's formative years had been such a light in his grey days, and a few hilarious hell-bent nights, so that just seeing Simon made him feel better.

They pulled out into the traffic and his friend spoke without looking at him. 'So what's so urgent you need to fly halfway around the world you couldn't tell me on the phone? I can't believe you're going back tomorrow morning.'

Rayne glanced at the heavy traffic and decided this mightn't be a good time to distract Simon with his own impending disaster. Or was that just an excuse to put off the moment? 'Can we wait till we get to your place?'

He watched Simon frown and then nod. 'Sure. Though Maeve's there. She's just had a break-up so I hope a sister in my house won't cramp your style.'

Maeve. Little Maeve, Geez. It was good to think of someone other than himself for a minute. She'd been hot as a teenager and he could imagine she'd be drop-dead gorgeous by now. All of Simon's sisters were but he'd always had a soft spot for Maeve, the youngest. He'd bet, didn't know why, that Maeve had a big front of confidence when, in fact, he'd suspected she was a lot softer than the rest of the strong females in the house.

Though there'd been a few tricky moments when she'd made sure he knew she fancied him—not politic when you were years older than her. He'd got pretty good at not leaving Simon's side while Maeve had been around. 'I haven't seen Maeve for maybe ten years. She was probably about fifteen and a self-assured little miss then.'

'Most of the time she is. Still a marshmallow underneath, though. But she makes me laugh.'

She'd made Rayne laugh too, but he'd never mentioned his avoidance techniques to Simon. He doubted Simon would have laughed at that. Rayne knew Simon thrived on protecting his sisters. It had never been said but the *Keep away from my sisters* sign was clearly planted between them. And Rayne respected that.

'How are your parents?' It was always odd, asking, because he'd only had his mum, and Simon had two sets of parents. Simon's father, who Rayne had known as a kid, had turned out to be Simon's stepdad and he remembered very well how bitter Simon had been about all the lies. Bitter enough to change his last name.

But Simon's mum had chosen to go with someone she'd thought could give her accidental child the life she wanted him to have, and had been very happy with Simon's wealthy stepdad. Simon's birth father hadn't known of his son's existence until Simon had accidentally found out and gone looking for him.

No such fairy-tale for himself. 'Your father is dead and not worth crying over,' was all his mother had ever said.

'You know Dad and Mum moved to Boston?' Simon's voice broke into his thoughts. 'Dad's bypass went well and Mum's keeping us posted.'

'Good stuff.' Rayne glanced at his friend and enjoyed the smile that lit Simon's face. Funnily, he'd never been jealous of Simon's solid family background. Just glad that he could count this man as his friend and know he wouldn't be judged. Except maybe in the next half-hour when he broke the news.

Simon went on. 'And Angus and the Lyrebird Lake contingent are great. I saw them all at Christmas.' More smiles. He was glad it had all worked out for Simon.

Then the question Rayne didn't want. 'And your mum? She been better since you moved her out to live with you?' Another glance his way and he felt his face freeze as Simon looked at him.

'Fine.' If he started there then the whole thing would come out in the car and he just needed a few more minutes of soaking up the good vibes.

Instead, they talked about work.

About Simon's antenatal breech clinic he was running at Sydney Central. He'd uncovered a passion for helping women avoid unnecessary Caesareans for breech babies when possible and was becoming one of the leaders in re-establishing the practice of experienced care for normal breech births.

'So how's your job going?' Simon looked across. 'Still the dream job, making fistloads of money doing what you love?'

'Santa Monica's great. The house is finished and looking great.' Funny how unimportant that was in the big picture. 'My boss wants me to think about becoming one of the directors on the board.' That wouldn't happen now. He shook that thought off for later.

'The operating rooms there are state-of-the-art and we're developing a new procedure for cleft pallet repair that's healing twice as fast.'

'You still doing the community work on Friday down at South Central?'

'Yep. The kids are great, and we're slipping in one case a week as a teaching case into the OR in Santa Monica.' He didn't even want to think about letting the kids down there but he did have a very promising registrar he was hoping he could talk to, and who could possibly take over, before it all went down.

They turned off the airport link road and in less than five minutes were driving into Simon's garage. Simon lived across the road from the huge expanse of Botany Bay Rayne had just flown in over. He felt his gut kick with impending doom. Another huge jet flew overhead as the automatic garage door descended and that wasn't all that was about to go down.

He'd be on one of those jets heading back to America tomorrow morning. Nearly thirty hours' flying for one conversation. But, then, he'd have plenty of time to sit around when he got back.

Simon ushered him into the house and through into the den as he called out to his sister. 'We're back.'

Her voice floated down the stairs. 'Getting dressed.' Traces of the voice he remembered with a definite womanly depth to it and the melody of it made him smile.

'Drink?' Simon pointed to the tray with whisky glass and decanter and Rayne nodded. He'd had two on the plane. Mostly he'd avoided alcohol since med school but he felt the need for a shot to stiffen his spine for the conversation ahead.

'Thanks.' He crossed the room and poured a finger depth. Waved the bottle in Simon's direction. 'You?'

'Nope. I'm not technically on call but my next breech mum is due any day now. I'll have the soda water to keep you company.' Rayne poured him a glass of the sparkling water from the bar fridge.

They sat down. Rayne lifted his glass. 'Good seeing you.' And it was all about to change.

'You too. Now, what's this about?'

Rayne opened his mouth just as Simon's mobile phone vibrated with an incoming call. Damn. Instead, he took a big swallow of his drink.

Simon frowned at him. Looked at the caller, shrugged his inability to ignore it, and stood up to take the call.

Rayne knew if it hadn't been important he wouldn't have answered. Stared down into the dregs of the amber fluid in his glass. Things happened. Shame it had to happen now. That was his life.

'Sorry, Rayne. I have to go. That's my patient with the breech baby. I said I'd be there. Back as soon as I can.' He glanced at the glass. 'Go easy. I'll still be your mate, no matter what it is.'

Rayne put the glass down. 'Good luck.' With that! He had no doubt about Simon's professional skill. But he doubted he'd be happy with his friend when he knew.

Rayne watched Simon walk from the room and he was still staring pensively at the door two minutes later when the woman of his dreams sashayed in and the world changed for ever.

One moment. That was all it took. Nothing could have warned him what was about to happen or have prevented him, after one shell-shocked moment, standing up. Not all the disasters in the universe mattered as he walked towards the vision little Maeve had become.

A siren. Calling him without the need for actual words. Her hair loose, thick black waves dancing on her shoulders, and she wore some floating, shimmering, soft shift of apricot that allowed a tantalising glimpse of amazing porcelain cleavage—and no bra, he was pretty sure. A flash of delicious thigh, and then covered again in deceptive modesty. He could feel his heart pound in his throat. Tried to bring it all back to normality but he couldn't. Poleaxed by not-so-little Maeve.

Maeve paused before entering the room. Drew a breath. She'd spent the day getting ready for this moment. Hair. Nails. Last-minute beauty appointments that had filled the day nicely. When Simon had told her yesterday that Rayne was coming she'd felt her spirits lift miraculously. Gone was the lethargy of self-recriminations from the last month. She really needed to get over that ridiculous inferiority complex she couldn't seem to shake as the youngest of four high achieving girls.

Here was one man who had never disappointed her. Even though she'd been embarrassingly eager to pester him as a gawky teenager, he'd always made her feel like a princess, and she wanted to look her best. Feel good about herself. Get on with her life after the last fiasco and drop all those stupid regrets that were doing her head in.

She hoped he hadn't changed. She'd hero-worshiped the guy since the day he'd picked up the lunch box she'd dropped the first time she'd seen him. Her parents' reservations about Rayne's background and bad-boy status had only made him more irresistible. At fifteen, twenty had been way out of her reach in age.

Well, things should be different this time and she was going to make sure they were at least on an even footing!

Maybe that's where the trill of excitement was coming from and she could feel the smile on her face from anticipation as she stepped into view.

That was the last sane thought. A glance across a room, a searing moment of connection that had her pinned in the doorway so that she stopped and leant against the architrave, suddenly in need of support—a premonition that maybe she'd be biting off more than she could chew even flirting with Rayne. This black-shirted, open-collared hunk was no pretty boy she could order around. And yet it was still Rayne.

He rose and stepped towards her, a head taller than her, shoulders like a front-row forward, and those eyes. Black pools of definite appreciation as he crossed the room in that distinctive prowl of a walk he'd always had until he stood beside her.

A long slow smile. 'Are you here to ruin my life even more?'

God. That voice. Her skin prickled. Could feel her eyebrows lift. Taking in the glory of him. 'Maybe. Maybe I'm the kind of ruin you've been searching for?'

Goodness knew where those words had come from but they slid from her mouth the way her lunch box had dropped from her fingers around ten years ago. The guy was jaw-droppingly gorgeous. And sexy as all get-out!

'My, my. Look at little Maeve.'

And look at big Rayne. Her girl parts quivered.

'Wow!' His voice was low, amused and definitely admiring—and who didn't like someone admiring?—and the pleasure in the word tickled her skin like he'd brushed her all over. Felt impending kismet again. Felt his eyes glide, not missing a thing.

She looked up. Mesmerised. Skidded away from the eyes—too amazing, instead appreciated the black-as-night hair, that strong nose and determined jaw, and those shoulders that blocked her vision of the world. A shiver ran through her. She was like a lamb beckoning to the wolf.

Another long slow smile that could have melted her bra straps if she'd had one on, then he grew sexy-serious. 'Haven't you grown into a beautiful woman? I think we should meet all over again.' A tilt of those sculpted lips and he held out his hand. 'I'm Rayne. And you are?'

Moistened her lips. 'Maeve.' Pretended her throat wasn't as dry as a desert. Held out her own hand and he took her fingers and kissed above her knuckles smoothly so that she sucked her breath in.

Then he allowed her hand to fall. 'Maeve.' The way he said it raised the hair on her arms again. Like ballet dancers *en pointe*. 'Did you know your name means *she who intoxicates*? I read that somewhere, but not until this moment did I believe it.'

She should have laughed and told him he was corny but she was still shaking like a starstruck mute. Finally she retaliated. 'Rain. As in wet?'

He laughed. 'Rayne as in R.A.Y.N.E. My mother hated me.'

'How is your mother?'

His eyes flickered. 'Fine.' Then he seemed to shake off whatever had distracted him and his smile was slow and lethal. 'Would you like to have a drink with me?'

And of course she said, 'Yes!'

She watched him cross the room to Simon's bar and that made her think, only for a millisecond, about her brother. 'Where's Simon?' Thank goodness her brother hadn't seen that explosion of instant lust between them

or he'd be playing bomb demolition expert as soon as
he cottoned on.

'His breech lady has gone into labour and he's meeting her at the hospital.'

Maeve ticked that obstacle out of the way. A good
hour at least but most probably four. She was still languid with residual oxytocin from the Rayne storm as
she sank onto the lounge. Then realised she probably
should have sat in Simon's favourite chair, opposite,
because if Rayne sat next to her here she doubted she'd
be able to keep her hands off him.

He sat down next to her and the force field between
them glowed like the lights on the runway across the
bay. He handed her a quarter-glass of whisky and
toasted her with his own. Their fingers touched and
sizzled and their eyes clashed as they sipped.

'Curiouser and curiouser,' he drawled, and smiled
full into her face.

OMG. She licked her lips again and he leaned and
took her glass from her hand again and put it down
on the coffee table. 'You really shouldn't do that.'
Then lifted his finger and gently brushed her bottom lip with aching slowness as he murmured, 'I've
been remiss.'

He was coming closer. 'In what way?' *Who owned
that breathy whisper?*

'I didn't kiss my old friend hello.' And his face filled
her vision and she didn't make any protest before his
lips touched, returned and then scorched hers.

In those first few seconds of connection she could feel a leashed desperation about him that she didn't understand, because they had plenty of time, an hour at least, but then all thoughts fled as sensation swamped her.

Rayne's mouth was like no other mouth she'd ever known. Hadn't even dreamt about. Like velvet steel, smoothly tempered with a suede finish, and the crescendo was deceptively gradual as it steered them both in a sensual duel of lips and tongue and inhalation of whisky breath into a world that beckoned like a light at the end of the tunnel. She hadn't even known there was a tunnel!

Everything she'd imagined could be out there beckoned and promised so much more. She wanted more, desperately needed more, and lifted her hands to clasp the back of his head, revel in his thick wavy hair sliding through her fingers as she pulled him even closer.

His hands slid down her ribs, across her belly and up under and then circling her breasts through the thin fabric of her silk overshirt. His fingers tightened in deliciously powerful appreciation then he pulled away reluctantly.

'Silk? I'd hate to spoil this so I'd better stop.'

'I'll buy another one,' she murmured against his lips.

Rayne forced his hands to draw back. It was supposed to be a hello kiss. Holy hell, what was he doing? He'd barely spoken to the woman in ten years and his next stop was definitely lower down. They'd be naked on the floor before he realised it if he didn't watch out. 'Maybe we should draw a breath?'

She sat back with a little moue of disappointment, followed by one of those delicious tip-of-the-tongue lip-checks that drove him wild. He was very tempted to throw caution to the winds, and her to the floor, and have his wicked way with the siren. Then he saw Simon's glass of sparkling water sitting forlornly on the table and remembered his unspoken promise. Forced himself to sit back. He'd be better having a cold glass of water himself.

'I'm starving!' He wasn't, but appealing to a woman's need to feed a man was always a good ploy to slow the world down.

She shrugged and he wanted to laugh out loud. Still a princess. Gloriously a princess. 'Kitchen's through there.' A languid hand in vague direction. 'I'm not much of a cook but you could make yourself something.'

Observed her eyes skid away from his. Decided she was lying. 'Don't you know the way to a man's heart is through his stomach?'

'And the way to a woman's heart is more of that hello kissing.' She sighed and stood up. 'But come on, I'll feed you. And then I'm going to kiss you again before my brother comes home. You'll owe me.'

He did laugh at that. 'I'll pay what I have to pay.' And he thought, I am not sleeping with this woman but thank God I brought condoms.

* * *

Maeve had lied about not being able to cook. She'd done French, Italian and Spanish culinary courses, could make anything out of nothing, and Simon's fridge was definitely not made up of nothing. 'Spanish omelette, French salad and garlic pizza bread?'

'Hold the garlic pizza bread.'

She grinned at him, starting to come down from the deluge of sensations that had saturated her brain. She'd planned on being admired, building her self-esteem with a safe yet sexy target, not ending up in bed with the guy. 'Good choice.' Heard the words and decided they applied to herself as well. It would be a good choice not to end up in bed either.

Then set about achieving a beautifully presented light meal perfect for a world traveller just off a plane.

'Oh, my.' He glanced down at his plate in awe. 'She cooks well.'

'Only when I feel like it.' And spun away, but he caught her wrist. Lifted it to his mouth and kissed the delicate inside skin once, twice, three times, and Maeve thought she was going to swoon. She tugged her hand free because she needed to think and she hadn't stopped *feeling* since she'd seen this man. She mimicked him. 'He kisses well.'

He winked at her. 'Only when he feels like it.'

She leaned into him. 'We'll work on that. Eat your dinner like a good boy.' *While I get some distance, fan*

*my face and figure out why I'm acting like he's my
chance at salvation. Or is that damnation?*

Five minutes later Rayne sat back from his empty plate.
He had been hungry. Or the food was too good to possibly leave. 'Thank you.'

He needed a strategy of space between him and this
woman. What the heck was going on to cause this onslaught of attraction between them? His own dire circumstances? The thought that she might be the last
beautiful thing he would see or touch for a long time?

And her? Well, she was vulnerable. Simon had suggested that. But vulnerable wasn't the word he would
have used. Stunning, intoxicating, black-widow dangerous?

He stood up and put his plate in the sink. Rinsed it,
like he always did because he'd been responsible for
any cleaning he'd wanted done for a long time, and in-
ternally he smiled because she didn't say, *Leave that,
I'll do it*, like most women would have. She leant on
the doorframe and watched him do it.

'Simon said you've just finished a relationship?'
Seemed like his subconscious wanted to get to the bottom of it because his conscious mind hadn't been going
to ask that question.

'Hmm. It didn't end well, and I've been a dishrag
poor Simon had to put up with for the last month. You've
no idea the lift I got when Simon said you were coming.'

No subterfuge there. He had the feeling she didn't

know the meaning of the word. 'Thank you. But you know I'm here only for one night. I fly back tomorrow.'

She turned her head to look at him. 'Do you have to?'

That was ironic. 'No choice.' Literally. 'And I won't be back for a long time.' A very long time maybe.

She nodded. 'Then we'd best make the most of tonight.'

He choked back a laugh. 'What on earth can you mean?'

'Catch up on what we've both been doing, of course. Before Simon monopolises you.' She was saying one thing but her body was saying something else as she sashayed into the lounge again, and he may as well have had a leash around his neck because he followed her with indecent haste and growing fatalism.

'Simon will be back soon.' A brief attempt to return to reality but she was standing in the centre of the room looking suddenly unsure, and that brief fragility pierced him like no other reaction could have. Before he knew it he had his arms around her, cradling her against his chest, soothing the black hair away from her face. Silk skin, glorious cheekbones, a determined little chin. And she felt so damn perfect in his arms as she snuggled into him.

'Take me to bed, Rayne. Make me feel like a woman again.'

'That would be too easy.' He kissed her forehead. 'I don't think that's a good idea, sweetheart.'

'I'm a big girl, Rayne. Covered for contraception. Unattached and in sound mind. Do I have to beg?'

He looked at her, squeezed her to him. Thought about the near future and how he would never get this chance again because things would never be the same. He would never be the same. Searched her face for any change of mind. No. Bloody hell. She didn't have to beg.

So he picked her up in his arms, and she lifted her hands to clasp him around his neck, and he kissed her gorgeous mouth and they lost a few more minutes in a hazy dream of connection. Finally he got the words out. 'So which bedroom is yours?'

She laughed. 'Up two flights of stairs. Want me to walk?'

'Much as I have enjoyed watching you walk, I'd prefer to carry you.'

And with impressive ease he did. Maeve rested her head back on that solid shoulder and gazed up at the chiselled features and strong nose. And those sinful lips. OMG, did she know what she was doing? Well, there was no way she wanted this to stop. This chemistry had been building since that first searing glance that had jerked and stunned them both like two people on the same elastic. She tightened her hands around his neck.

He felt so powerful—not pretty and perfect like Sean had been—but she didn't want to think about Sean. About the pale comparison of a man she'd wasted her heart on when she should have always known Rayne would stand head and shoulders above any other man.

Speaking of shoulders, he used one to push open the door she indicated, knocked it shut with his foot, and strode across the room to the big double bed she thought he would toss her onto, but he smiled, glanced around the room and lowered her gently until her feet were on the floor.

His breathing hadn't changed and he looked as if he could have done it all again without working a sweat.

Ooh la la. 'I'm impressed.'

He raised his brows quizzically and freed the French drapes until they floated down to cover the double window in a flounced bat of their lacy eyelids and the room dimmed to a rosy glow from the streetlights outside. Slid his wallet out of his pocket and put it on the windowsill after retrieving a small foil packet.

Then he pulled her towards him and spun her until her spine was against the wall and her breasts were pressed into his hardness. Shook his head and smiled full into her eyes. Felt her knees knock as he said, 'You are the sexiest woman I have ever seen.'

She thought, *And you are the sexiest man*, as she lifted her lips to his, and thank goodness he didn't wait to be asked twice. Like falling into a swirling maelstrom of luscious sensation, Maeve felt reality disappear like a leaf sucked into a drainpipe then she heard him say something. Realised he'd created physical distance between them. Her mind struggled to process sound to speech.

'Miss Maeve, are you sure you want to proceed?'

It was a jolting and slightly disappointing thing to say

in the bubble of sensuality he'd created and she looked up at him. Surprised a look of anguish she hadn't expected. 'Are you trying to spoil this for a particular reason?'

A distance she didn't like flashed in his eyes. 'Maybe.'

She pulled his head forward with her hands in his hair. 'Well, don't!'

Rayne shrugged, smiled that lethal smile of his, and instead he lifted her silk shift over her head in a slow sexy exposure, leaving the covering camisole and the dark shadow of her breasts plainly visible through it.

He trailed the backs of his fingers up the sides of her chest and she shivered, wanted him to rip it off so she could feel his hands on her skin. And he knew it.

This time the backs of his fingers trailed down and caught the hem of the camisole, catching the final layer, leaving her top half naked to the air on her sensitised skin.

She heard him suck in his breath, heard it catch in his throat as he glimpsed her body for the first time— and the tiny peach G-string that was all that was left.

Her turn. He had way too many clothes on and she needed to look and feel his skin with a sudden hunger she had no control over.

She reached up and danced her fingers swiftly down the fastening of his black shirt, as if unbuttoning for the Olympics way ahead of any other competitor, because she'd never felt such urgency to slip her hands inside a man's shirt. Never wanted to connect as badly as now with the taut skin-covered muscle and bone of a man. The man.

This was Rayne. The Rayne. And he felt as fabulous as she'd known he would and the faster she did this the faster he would kiss her again. Her fingers seemed to glow wherever she touched and she loved the heat between them like a shivering woman loved a fire.

While her fingers were gliding with relish he'd unzipped and was kicking away his trousers. They stood there, glued together, two layers of mist-like fabric between their groins, two flimsy, ineffectual barriers that only inflamed them more, and his mouth recommenced its onslaught and she was lost.

Until he shifted. Moved that wicked mouth and tongue lower, a salutation of her chin, her neck, her collarbone, a slow, languorous, teasing circle around her breast and exquisite tantalising pleasure she'd never imagined engulfed her as he took the rosy peak and flicked it with delicate precision.

She gasped.

His hands encircled her ribs, the strong thumbs pushing her breasts into perky attention for his favours. Peaks of sensitive supplication and he took advantage until she was writhing, aching for him, helpless against the wall at her back, unable to be silent.

She. Could. Not. Get. Enough.

Rayne lifted his head, heard the moan of a woman enthralled, saw the wildness in her eyes, felt his own need soar to meet hers, dropped his hands to the lace around her hips and slid those wicked panties slowly down her legs, savoured the silk of her skin, the tautness of her thighs under his fingers, and then the scrap of material fell in a ridiculously tiny heap at her feet. There was something so incredibly sinful about that fluttering puddle of fabric, and he'd bet he'd think about it later, many times, as he reached for the condom and dropped his own briefs swiftly.

Then his hands slid back to her buttocks. Those round globes of perfection that fitted his hands perfectly. Felt the weight of her, lifted, supported her body in his hands, and the power of that feeling expanded with the strain in his arms and exultantly, slowly, her back slid up the wall and she rose to meet him.

Rayne slowly and relentlessly pinned her with his body and she wrapped her legs around him the way he had known, instinctively, she would, and it felt as incredible as he'd also known it could be, except it was more. So much more. And they began to dance the ancient dance of well-matched mates.

The rising sun striped the curtains with a golden beam of new light and Maeve awoke in love. Some time in the night it had come to her and it was as indestructible as a glittering diamond in her chest. How had that happened?

Obviously she'd always loved him.

And it was nothing like the feelings she'd had for

other men. This was one hundred per cent 'you light my fire, I know you would cherish me if you loved me back, I want to have babies with you' love. So it looked like she'd have to pack her bags and follow the man to the States.

At least her mother lived there.

But Rayne was gone from their tumbled bed and someone was talking loudly downstairs.

Maeve sat up amidst the pillows he'd packed around her, realised she was naked and slightly stiff, began to smile and then realised the loud voice downstairs was Simon's.

A minute later she'd thrown a robe over her nakedness and hurried into Simon's study, where two burly federal policemen had Rayne in... handcuffs?

The breath jammed in her throat and she leant against the doorframe that had supported her last night. Needed it even more now.

Simon was saying, 'What the hell? Rayne? This has to be a mistake.'

'No mistake. Just didn't get time to explain.' Rayne glanced across as Maeve entered and shut his eyes for a moment as if seeing her just made everything worse. Not how she wanted to be remembered by him.

Then his thick lashes lifted as he stared. 'Bye, Maeve,' looked right through her and then away.

Simon glanced between the two, dawning suspicion followed swiftly by disbelief and then anger. 'So you knew they'd come and you...' He couldn't finish the sentence. Sent Maeve an, 'I'll talk to you later' look, but the federal policemen were already nudging Rayne towards the door.

Simon was still in the clothes he'd left in last night so he hadn't been home long. Rayne was fully dressed, again in sexy black, and shaved, had his small cabin bag, so it looked like he'd been downstairs, waiting. She would never know if it was for Simon or the police.

She wondered whether the police hadn't come he would have woken her to say goodbye. The obvious negative left her feeling incredibly cold in the belly after the conflagration they'd shared last night and her epiphany this morning.

He'd said he was going and wouldn't be back for a while but she'd never imagined this scenario.

Then he really was gone and Simon was shaking his head.

CHAPTER ONE

Nine months later.
Looking for Maeve.

RAYNE'S MOTHER DIED of a heroin overdose on the fifteenth of December. He was released from prison the day after, when the posted envelope of papers arrived at the Santa Monica police station, and he put his head in his hands at his inability to save her. The authorities hadn't been apologetic—he should have proclaimed his innocence, but he'd just refused to speak.

Her last written words to him…

My Rayne
*   I love you. You are my shining star. I would never have survived in prison but it seems I can't survive on the outside either with you in there. I'm so sorry it took me so long to fix it.*

With the other letter and proof of her guilt she'd kept, the charges on Rayne were dropped and he buried her a week later in Santa Monica. It had been the only place she'd known some happiness, and it was fine to leave her there in peace.

He had detoured to see his old boss, who had been devastated by the charges against him, explained briefly that he'd known she wouldn't survive in jail, and the man promised to start proceedings for the restoration of his licence to practise. Undo what damage he could, and as he'd been able to keep most of the sensation out of the papers, that was no mean offer.

Then Rayne gave all his mother's clothes and belongings to the Goodwill Society and ordered her the biggest monumental angel he could for the top of her grave. It would have made her smile.

Then he put the house up for sale and bought a ticket for Australia and Maeve. The woman he couldn't forget after just one night. Not because he was looking for happily ever after but because he owed it to her and Simon to explain. And if he was going to start a new life he had to know what was left of his old one. If anything.

All he knew was the man he was now was no fit partner for Maeve and he had no doubt Simon would say the same.

On arrival it had taken him two days of dogged investigation before he'd traced Maeve to Lyrebird Lake and he would have thought of it earlier if he'd allowed himself to think of Simon first.

Simon's birth father lived there and Simon often

spent Christmas with them—he should have remembered that. With Maeve's mother in the US it made sense she was with her brother.

Who knew if she'd say yes to seeing him after the way he'd left, if either of them would? He guessed he couldn't blame them when they didn't know the facts, but he had to know they were both all right. Maybe he should have opened the letters Maeve had sent and not refused the phone calls Simon had tried, but staying isolated from others and keeping the outside world out of his head had been the only way he'd got through it.

Looked down at the wad of letters in his hand and decided against opening the letters now in case she refused to see him in writing.

Two hundred miles away from Lyrebird Lake, and driving just over the legal speed limit, Rayne pressed a little harder on the accelerator pedal. The black Chev, a souped-up version of his first car from years ago, throttled back with a throaty grumble.

He didn't even know if Maeve had a partner, had maybe even married, but he had to find out. She would refuse to see him. It was ridiculous to be propelled on with great urgency when it had been so long, but he was. He should wait until after the holiday season but he couldn't.

The picture in his head of her leaning against the doorframe as he'd been led away had tortured him since that night. The fact that he'd finally discovered the woman he needed to make him whole had been there all the time in his past, and he'd let her down in the most cowardly way by not telling her what would happen.

He couldn't forgive himself so how did he think that Maeve and her brother would forgive him? All he just knew was he had to find her and explain. Try to explain.

So clearly he remembered her vulnerability before he'd carried her up those stairs. Blindingly he saw her need to see herself the way he saw her. Perhaps it was too late.

If she had moved on, then he would have to go, but he needed her to know the fault was all his before they said a final goodbye. It wasn't too late to at least tell her she couldn't have been more perfect on that night all those months ago.

A police highway patrol car passed in the opposite direction. The officer glanced across at him and Rayne slowed. Stupid. To arrive minutes later after nine months wouldn't make the difference but if he was pulled over for speeding then the whole catastrophe could start again. International drivers licence. Passports. He didn't want the hassle.

It was lucky the salesman had filled the fuel tank last night because he'd only just realised it was early Christmas morning. Every fuel stop was shut. He had no food or drinks except the water he'd brought with him. Big deal except he was gatecrashing Simon's family at a time visitors didn't usually drop in. Hopefully the rest of the family weren't assembled when he arrived.

It wasn't the first time he'd done this. He remembered Simon taking him home to his other parents' one year while they'd been in high school. Rayne's mother had ended up in rehab over the holiday break, it had always been the hardest time of the year for her to stay straight, and his friend, Simon, had come to check on him.

He'd been sixteen and sitting quietly watching television when Simon had knocked at the door, scolded him for not letting him know, and dragged him reluctantly back to his house for the best Christmas he'd ever had.

Simon's parents had ensured he'd had a small Christmas sack at the end of his bed on Christmas morning and Maeve had made him a card and given him a Cellophane bag of coconut ice she'd made for everyone that year. He'd loved the confectionary ever since.

Well, here he was again, gatecrashing. Unwanted.

It was anything but funny. The truly ridiculous part was that in his head he'd had an unwilling relationship with Maeve for the last nine months. She'd made an irreversible imprint on him in those hours he'd held her in his arms. Blown him away, and he was still in pieces from it. He'd kept telling himself they'd only connected in his last desperate attempt to hold onto someone good before the bad came but he had no doubt she would always hold a sacred piece of his heart.

In prison he'd separated his old life out of his head. Had kept it from being contaminated by his present. Refused any visitors and stored the mail. But when his defences had been down, when he'd drifted off to sleep, Maeve had slid in beside him, been with him in the morning when he'd woken up, and at night when he'd dreamt. He'd had no control over that.

But he'd changed. Hardened. Couldn't help being affected by the experience, and she didn't need a man like he'd become—so he doubted he'd stay. Just explain and then head back to Sydney to sort out his life. Start fresh when he could find some momentum for beginning. Wasn't even sure he would return to paediatrics. Felt the need for something physical. Something to use up the coil of explosive energy he'd been accumulating over the last nine months.

So maybe he'd go somewhere in between for a while where he could just soak up nature and the great outdoors now that he had the freedom to enjoy it.

Funny how things were never as important until you couldn't have them. He'd lusted after a timeless rainforest, or a deserted mountain stream, or a lighthouse with endless ocean to soothe his soul.

Or Maeve, a voice whispered. No.

CHAPTER TWO

Maeve

MAEVE PATTED HER round and rolling belly to soothe the child within. Christmas in Lyrebird Lake. She should have been ecstatic and excited about the imminent birth of her baby.

Ecstatic about the fact that only yesterday Simon had declared his love to Tara and was engaged to a woman she couldn't wait to call her sister. She put her fingers over the small muscle at the corner of her eye, which was twitching. But instead she was a mess.

Her only brother, or half-brother, she supposed she should acknowledge that, seeing she was living in Lyrebird Lake where his birth father lived, was engaged to be married. That was very exciting news.

And it wasn't like Simon's family hadn't made her welcome. But it wasn't normal to land on people who didn't know you for one of the biggest moments of your life even if Simon had always raved about Lyrebird Lake.

The place was worth raving about. She'd never been so instantly received for who she was, even in her own family, she thought with a tinge of uneasy disloyalty, but that explained why Simon had always been the least judgemental of all her siblings.

Until she'd slept with Rayne, that was.

Simon's other family didn't know the meaning of the word judgmental. Certainly less than her mother, but that was the way mum was, and she accepted that.

And she and Simon had re-established some of their previous closeness, mostly thanks to Tara.

The fabulous Tara. Her new friend and personal midwife was a doll and she couldn't imagine anyone she would rather have in the family.

She, Maeve, was an absolute bitch to be depressed by the news but it was so hard to see them so happy when she was so miserable.

She gave herself a little mental shake. Stop it.

Glanced out the window to the manger on the lawn. It was Christmas morning, and after nearly four weeks of settling in there was no place more welcoming or peaceful to have her baby.

So what was wrong with her?

It was all very well being a midwife, knowing what was coming, but she had this mental vision of her hand being held and it wasn't going to be Simon's. Have her brother, in the room while she laboured? Not happening, even if he was an obstetrician.

No. It would be Tara's hand that steadied her, which

was good but not what she'd secretly and hopelessly dreamt of.

That scene she'd replayed over in her head a thousand times, him crossing the floor to her after that first glance, and later the feel of his arms around her as he'd carried her so easily up the stairs, the absolutely incredible dominance yet tenderness of his lovemaking. Gooseflesh shimmered on her arms.

She shook her head. The birth would be fine. It was okay.

She tried to shake the thought of needing Rayne to get through labour from her mind but it clung like a burr and refused to budge as if caught in the whorls of her cerebral convolutions.

Which was ridiculous because the fact was Rayne didn't want her.

He'd refused to answer her letters or take the call the one time she'd tried to call the prison, had had to go through the horror of finding out his prison number, been transferred to another section, the interminable wait and then the coldness of his refusal to speak to her.

Obviously he didn't want her!

Simon had told her he'd found out he would be in prison for at least two years, maybe even five, and that the charges had been drug related. She, for one, still didn't believe it.

But she hated the fact Rayne didn't want to see her.

Her belly tightened mildly in sympathy, like it had been tightening for the last couple of weeks every now and then, and she patted the taut, round bulge. *It's okay, baby. Mummy will be sensible. She'll get over your father one day.* But that wasn't going to happen if she stayed here mooning.

Maeve sat up and eased her legs out of the bed until her feet were on the floor. Grunted quietly with the effort and then smiled ruefully at herself for the noisy exertion of late pregnancy.

She needed to go for a walk. Free her mind outside the room. Stay fit for the most strenuous exertion of her life.

It was time to greet Christmas morning with a smile and a gentle, ambling welcome in the morning air before the Queensland heat glued her to the cool chair under the tree in the back yard. The tables were ready to be set for breakfast and later lunch with Simon's family and she would put on a smiling face.

She wondered if Tara was up yet. Her friend had come in late last night with Simon, she'd heard them laughing quietly and the thought made her smile. Two gorgeous people in love. The smile slipped from her face and she dressed as fast as she could in her unbalanced awkwardness and for once didn't worry about make-up.

Self-pity was weak and she needed to get over herself. She was the lucky one, having a baby when lots of women ached for the chance, and she couldn't wait.

It wasn't as if she didn't have a family who loved her, even if her mum was in the States.

But she had dear Louisa, Simon's tiny but sprightly grandmother, spoiling them all with her old-fashioned country hospitality and simple joy in kinfolk. She, Maeve, was twenty-five and needed to grow up and enjoy simple pleasures like Louisa did.

Once outside, she set off towards the town and the air was still refreshingly cool. Normally she would have walked around the lake but it was Sunday, and Simon liked the Sunday papers. Did they print newspapers on Christmas Day? Would the shop even be open? She hadn't thought of that before she'd left but if it didn't then that was okay.

It was easier not to think in the fresh air and distractions of walking with a watermelon-sized belly out front cleared the self-absorbtion.

Maeve saw the black, low-to-the-ground, old-fashioned utility as it turned into the main street and smiled. A hot rod like you saw at car shows with wide silver wheels and those long red bench seats in the front designed for drive-in movies. It growled down the road like something out of *Happy Days*, she thought to herself. The square lines and rumbling motor made it stand out from the more family-orientated vehicles she usually saw. Something about it piqued her curiosity.

She stared at the profile of the man driving and then her whole world tilted. Shock had her clutching her throat with her fingers and then their eyes met. Her heart suddenly thumped like the engine of the black beast and the utility swerved to the edge of the road and

pulled up. The engine stopped and so did her breath—
then her chest bumped and she swayed with the shock.

It was Maeve! The connection was instantaneous. Like
the first time. But she was different. He blinked. Pregnant! Very pregnant!

Rayne was out of the car and beside her in seconds,
saw the colour drain from her face, saw her eyes roll
back. He reached her just as she began to crumple.
Thank God. She slumped into his arms and he caught
her urgently and lifted her back against his chest, felt
and smelt the pure sweetness of her hair against his
face as he turned, noticed the extra weight of her belly
with a grimace as he struggled with the door catch
without dropping her. Finally he eased her backwards
onto the passenger seat and laid her head gently back
along the seat.

He stared at the porcelain beauty of the woman he'd
dreamed about throughout that long horrible time of
incarceration.

Maeve.

Pregnant by someone else. The hollow bitterness of
envy. The swell of fierce emotion and the wish it had
been him. He patted her hands, patted her cheek, and
slowly she stirred.

Unable to help the impossible dream, he began to
count dates in his head. He frowned. Pushed away a
sudden, piercing joy, worked out the dates again. But
they'd both used contraception. It couldn't be…

She groaned. Stirred more vigorously. Her glorious long eyelashes fluttered and she opened her eyes. They widened with recognition.

Then she gagged and he reached in and lifted her shoulders so she was sitting on the seat and could gag out the door. She didn't look at him again. Just sat with her shoulders bowed and her head in her hands.

He reached past her to the glove box and removed a small packet of tissues. Nudged her fingers and put them into her hand. She took them, but even after she'd finished wiping her mouth she still didn't look at him and he glanced around the street to see if anyone had noticed. Thank God for quiet Sunday mornings. Quiet Christmas morning, actually.

Well, that was unexpected. Something going right!

Seeing Maeve outside and alone. So unplanned. Looking down at her, he couldn't believe she was here in front of him. His eyes were drawn to the fragile V of the nape of her neck, the black hair falling forward away from the smoothness of her ivory skin, and he re-alised his heart was thumping like a piston in his chest. Like he'd run a marathon. Like he'd seen a vision of the future that was so bright he was blinded. Fool.

It felt like a dream. A stupid, infantile, Christmas fantasy… In reality, though, the woman of his dreams had, in fact, fainted and then thrown up at the very sight of him! He needed to get a grip.

CHAPTER THREE

After faint...

'WHERE DID YOU come from?' Maeve opened her eyes.
Barely raised her voice because her throat was closed
with sudden tears. She kept her head down. Couldn't
believe she'd fainted and thrown up as a first impression. Well, he shouldn't have appeared out of nowhere.

'America. Earlier this week. You're pregnant!'

Der. 'Does Simon know?'

'That you're pregnant?'

She sighed. Her head felt it was going to explode.
Not so much with the headache that shimmered behind
her eyes but with the thoughts that were ricocheting
around like marbles in her head. Just what she needed.
A smart-alec answer when she had a million questions.

Awkwardly she sat straighter and shifted her bottom on the seat in an attempt to stand. Frustratingly
she couldn't get enough purchase until he put his hand
down and took hers.

She looked at his brown, manly fingers so much

larger than the thin white ones they enclosed. Rayne was here. She could feel the warmth from his skin on hers. Really here.

He squeezed her fingers and then pulled steadily so she floated from the car like a feather from a bottle. She'd forgotten how strong he was. How easily he could move her body around. 'I assume you caught me when everything went black?'

'Thank goodness.' She looked up at the shudder in his voice. 'Imagine if I hadn't.'

She instantly dropped her other hand to her stomach and the baby moved as if to reassure her. Her shoulders drooped again with relief.

'You're pregnant,' he said again.

Now she looked at him. Saw the rampant confusion in a face she'd never seen confusion in before. 'I told you that. In the letters.'

His face shuttered. A long pause. 'I didn't open your letters.'

Maeve was dumbstruck, temporarily unable to speak. He hadn't opened her letters? The hours she'd spent composing and crunching and rewriting and weeping over them before she'd posted them. Wow!

That explained the lack of reply, she thought with a spurt of temper, but it also created huge questions as to just how important she'd been to him. Obviously not very. Not even being locked away in prison had been enough to tempt him to open her letters. She felt the nausea rise again.

He'd refused to talk to Simon too and she knew her brother had been hurt about that. He had hoped for some reassurance from Rayne that somewhere there was an explanation.

The guy was lower than she thought. She needed to protect Simon from being upset a day after his happiest day. That was a real worry. Or a diversion for her mind.

She tried to compose herself, get her thoughts together...

'I don't think you should see Simon until I can warn him you're back.'

Rayne straightened. Lifted his chin. 'I'm not going to hide.'

'It's not about you.' She could feel the unfairness expand in her. This was not how she dreamed their first meeting would be. Why couldn't he have warned her he was coming? Given her a chance to have her defences sorted? Dressed nicely? Put her make-up on, for goodness' sake? She'd just walked out of the house in her expander jeans and a swing top. And trainers. She groaned.

'Are you okay?'

She looked up. Saw the broad shoulders, bulging muscles in his arms, that chest she'd dreamt of for three quarters of a year. He was here and she wanted to be scooped up and cradled against that chest but he wasn't saying the right things. 'You can't see Simon yet. He's just got engaged. He's happy. I won't let you do that. You've upset him enough.'

He'd upset her too, though upset was an understatement. Hurt badly. Devastated. But then you reappeared at the right moment, a tiny voice whispered. The exact right moment. Just in time.

She saw a flicker of pain cross his face and she closed her eyes. What was she doing? Why was she being like this? Was she trying to drive him away?

She needed to think. It overwhelmed her that Rayne was here. As if she'd conjured up him by her need this morning and now she didn't know what she should think. And he hadn't known she was pregnant!

Rayne was having all sorts of problems keeping his thoughts straight. He could see she was at a loss too. 'Maeve!'

'What?'

He needed to know. Couldn't believe it but didn't want to believe it was someone else. 'Are you pregnant with my baby?'

She hunched her shoulders as if to keep him out. 'It's my baby. You didn't want to know about it.'

He pulled her in close to him and put both arms around her. Lifted her chin to look at him. 'For God's sake, woman.' Resisted the urge to shake her. 'Are you pregnant with my baby?'

'Yes. Now let go of me, Rayne.' His loosened his fingers. Felt her pull away coolly. Create distance between them like a crack from a beautiful glacier breaking away from its mountain, and his heart, a heart that had been a solid rock inside him, cracked too.

Maeve turned her back on him and climbed awkwardly into his car. The realisation that she couldn't protect Simon from this shock forever hit her.

'Come on. Let's get it over with. You need to see Simon and then we need to talk.'

Simon came out of the house when the car pulled up and a petite blonde woman followed him. Rayne remembered now that Maeve had said Simon was engaged. This would be some first introduction.

Rayne climbed out and walked around to open the passenger door; he glanced at his old friend, who looked less than pleased, and then back at the woman's hand he wanted to hold more than anything else in the world.

For an icy moment there he thought she wasn't going to allow him that privilege—right when he needed her most—but then she uncurled her closed fist and allowed her fingers to slide in beside his. By the time Simon had arrived she was standing beside him. Solidarity he hadn't expected.

'They let you out?' There was no Christmas spirit in that statement, Rayne thought sardonically to himself, though couldn't say he could blame him, considering Maeve's condition.

He stared into Simon's face. Felt the coolness between them like an open wound. 'I wanted to explain.' He shrugged. 'It just didn't happen.'

'Instead, you slept with my sister.'

'There's that.' To hell with this.

He just wanted it over. Tell Simon the truth. Let Maeve know at least the father of her baby wasn't a criminal. At the very least. Then get the hell away from here because these people didn't deserve him to infect their live with the disaster that seemed to follow him around.

'When my mother died there wasn't a reason for me to be in there any more. She told them the truth before she overdosed and they dropped the charges.'

Maeve's breath drew in beside him. 'Your mother died?' Felt her hand, a precious hand he'd forgotten he still held, tighten in his. She squeezed his fingers and he looked down at her. Saw the genuine sympathy and felt more upset than he had for the last horrific year. How could she be so quick to feel sorry for him when he'd ruined her life with his own selfishness? That thought hurt even more.

'You took the rap for your mother!' Simon's curt statement wasn't a question. 'Of course you did.' He slapped himself on the forehead. Repeated, 'Of course you did.'

He didn't want to talk about his mother. Didn't want sympathy. He spoke to Simon. 'I understand you not wanting me here.'

He forced himself to let go of Maeve's hand. 'Take Maeve inside. She fainted earlier, though she didn't fall.' He heard Simon's swift intake of breath and saw the blonde woman, from hanging back, shift into gear to swift concern.

He felt Maeve's glance. Her hand brushed the woman's gesture away. 'No. We need to talk.'

'I'll come back later when you've had a chance to rest. I'll find somewhere to stay for tonight.'

And give myself a chance to think, at least, he thought. He reached into his wallet and pulled out a piece of paper on which he'd written his number. 'This is my mobile number. Phone me when you've rested.' And then he spun on his heel and walked away from the lot of them, wishing he had warned them he was coming, though he wasn't sure it would have gone over any better if he had.

Well, they knew the truth now. He'd done what he'd come to do. Learnt something he'd never envisaged and was still grappling with that momentous news. He allowed himself one long sweeping glance over the woman he had dreamed about every night, soaking in the splendour that was Maeve. Her breasts full and ripe for his child, her belly swollen and taut, and her face pale with the distress he'd caused her.

Maeve allowed Tara to steer her back inside, up the hallway to her bedroom, because suddenly she felt as weak as a kitten. Simon was still standing on the street, watching the black utility disappear down the road with a frown on his face, but she'd worry about Simon later.

An almost silent whistle from Tara beside her drew

her attention as she sat down on her bed. 'So that's Rayne. Not quite what I imagined. A tad larger than life.' Tara squeezed her arm in sympathy. 'You look pale from shock.'

Maeve grimaced in agreement. Glanced at Tara, calm and methodical as usual as she helped her take off her shoes. 'It was a shock. And highly embarrassing. Not only did I faint but then proceeded to throw up in front of him.'

She felt the assessing glance Tara cast over her. 'For a very pregnant lady you've had a busy morning and it hasn't really started yet.'

It was barely seven o'clock. 'Lucky I got up early. It was supposed to be a gentle Christmas morning walk for Simon's newspaper.'

'The shop won't be open. But your Rayne is a Christmas present with a difference.' Tara laughed. 'What was it you said when you described him to me? A head taller and shoulders like a front-row forward and those dark eyes. No wonder you fell for him, boots and all.'

A fallen woman. And still in love with him, boots and all. 'Is it mad that even after ten minutes with him after all this time, I wanted to go with him? That I feel like we've been together for so much more than one night? That I can even feel that when he's just been away? When even I know that's too simplistic and whitewashed.'

She saw Tara look towards the bedside table, cross to her glass of water and bring it back for her. 'Even from where I was standing, I could feel the energy between you two. I wouldn't be surprised if Simon felt it too.'

'Thanks for that, at least.' She took a sip of water and it did make her feel a little clearer. 'Problem is, I was okay to sleep with but not okay to tell that he was going to prison.'

'Well.' Tara looked thoughtful. 'It seems he has got an explanation if he took the blame for his mother. And things are different now. He can't just walk away and think you'll be better off without him without even discussing it.'

She touched Maeve's shoulder in sympathy. 'And you have been carrying his child. So I guess at least a part of him has been with you since then.' Tara gave her a quick hug. 'He looks tough and self-sufficient but doesn't look a bad man.'

She knew he wasn't. From the bottom of her heart. 'He's not. I believe he's a good man.' She stroked her belly gently. 'I have to believe that if he's going to be part of our lives. And until this…' she patted her belly again '…Simon wouldn't hear a wrong word said about him.' She glanced at Tara and smiled to lighten the dramatic morning. 'And we both know Simon has good taste.'

Tara blushed but brushed that aside. 'Did he say he wants to be a part of your lives?'

In what brief window of opportunity? 'We didn't get that far. What with me fainting like a goose at the sight of him.' Maeve shook her head. Thought about it. 'He said he hadn't opened my mail. That he didn't know I was pregnant.' She thought some more. 'But he didn't look horrified when I told him.'

'Helpful. Though why he wouldn't open your mail has me puzzled.'

Me, too. 'I'll be asking that when he comes back. And it's Christmas morning.' She suddenly thought of the impact of her commotion on everyone else's day. That's what Lyrebird Lake did to you. Made you begin to think more of other people. 'I hope it doesn't spoil your first Christmas with Simon. I feel like I'm gatecrashing your engagement celebrations with my dramas.'

'Nothing can spoil that.' A lovely smile from Tara. 'I'm just glad we're here for you. No better time for family. And Simon will be fine.'

Tara had said family. The idea shone like a star in a dark night sky. It was a good time for family. Tara had probably meant Simon's family but Maeve was thinking of her own. Rayne and her and their baby as a family.

To Maeve it had felt like she'd been marking time for Rayne to arrive and now he was here he was her family. As long as he could handle that idea. Well, he'd just have to get used to it.

She heard Simon's footsteps approaching and as he paused at her bedroom door Maeve felt his assessing glance.

She looked at him. 'Rayne went to gaol for his mother! That's what he'd come to tell you that night.'

Simon nodded. 'So it seems. Fool. He didn't get around to it and if he had I would have tried to talk him out of it. I'm not surprised he didn't rush into an explanation. He knew I would have told him that taking the blame for his mother wouldn't help her at all.'

What kind of man made that sort of sacrifice without flinching? Actually, her man. 'He went to prison for her. Lost his job and his reputation.' And me, she thought, but didn't say it. Well, he hadn't lost her yet.

Simon rubbed the back of his head. 'That news just makes me more angry with him. But I'll get over it.' He rubbed again. 'Obviously I'm still battling with the idea I didn't suspect Rayne would do that. Now it's glaringly obvious. So I let him down too.'

He put his finger up and pointed at her. 'Maybe you should do what he suggested. Lie down. You're as pale as a ghost and the family won't be here for another two hours for breakfast.'

Maybe she would. Because she had plans for tonight. 'I want Rayne to spend Christmas with us.'

Simon didn't look as surprised as she'd thought he would. He glanced at Tara and Maeve caught the almost imperceptible nod between them. 'Thought you might—just don't rush into anything,' was all he said.

Rayne threw his duffle bag on the floor of the sparse hotel room and himself onto the single bed on his back. He'd had to knock on the residence door to ask if they were opening today. The guy had said not officially and let him in. Given him a room and said he'd fix him up tomorrow.

Rayne pulled the packet of letters from his pocket and eased open the first one. Started to read about Maeve's pregnancy. After ten minutes, and an aching, burning feeling in his gut, he loosened his belt and lay down on the bed. His mind expanded with images, good and bad, of his time with Maeve and what she'd gone through because he hadn't been there for her. He couldn't stomach it. He searched for something else to think about until he got over the pain.

He reached his hands arms up behind his head and sighed. One thing about prison, you lost your finicky ways about where you could sleep.

It was a typical country pub. With typical country hospitality, seeing he could be sleeping on a park bench if they hadn't let him in.

Squeaky cast-iron bedframe with yellowed porcelain decoration in the middle, thin, lumpy mattress, used-to-be white sheets and a wrinkled bedspread. A hook for clothes and a bathroom down the hall to share, except that no one else was such a loser they were in there for Christmas.

He wouldn't be here long. Wasn't sure he should be in Lyrebird Lake at all. But thank God he'd come.

Maeve was having his baby. Maeve, who was anything but 'little Princess Maeve'. How the hell had that happened when they'd been so careful?

Funnily, he didn't even consider it could be anyone

else's because the dates matched and after what they had shared—Lord, what they had shared in one incredible night—if a persistent sperm was going to get through any night that would be the one. He half laughed out loud—a strangled, confused noise—thankful that nobody else would hear or care about it.

A ridiculous mix of horror that a child had been dumped with him for a parent, regret at how distressed Simon must have been at his supposed friend's perfidy, ghastly regret that Maeve had had to face Simon without him and spend a pregnancy without his support.

But on top, like a life-raft shining light in the dark ocean, was an insidious, floating joy that glorious Maeve had kept his child and he was going to be a father. And she'd held his hand in front of Simon.

Though the next steps held a whole bag of dilemmas. What was he going to do about it? What could he do about it? Of course he would support them, money wasn't a problem. Hell, he'd buy her a house and put it in her name, or the baby's name, whatever she wanted. But what else?

Suddenly his whole world had changed, from that of a lost soul who hadn't been able to help his own mother—the one person he'd tried so hard to save—to a social pariah without any commitments and little motivation to slip back into his previous life, and now to a man with the greatest responsibility of all. Protecting another woman, keeping in mind he hadn't been able to save the last one, and this time his child as well, was something which scared him to the core.

Of course, that was if they could possibly work something out, and if she'd let him, but at least she wanted to talk. He wasn't so sure Simon wanted to and he really couldn't blame him.

It was a lot to take in. And a lot to lose when you thought you'd already lost it all.

Maeve saw Rayne arrive because she was standing at the window of her bedroom, waiting. It was nine-thirty and everyone had arrived for breakfast and the huge pile of family presents were to be opened after that.

She shook her head as the black car stopped, so antique it was trendy again, big and bulky and mean looking, very *James Dean, I'm a bad boy*, Rayne really needed to get over that image. Especially now he was going to be a father. She smiled ironically through the window. Though if Rayne had a son her child would probably love that car as he grew up.

She turned away from the window and glanced at the mirror across the room. So it seemed after only one sight of Rayne she was thinking of her child growing up with him.

She saw her reflection wincing back at her. The worried frown on her brow. Saw the shine reflected on her face and she crossed the room to re-powder her nose.

Was she doing the right thing, going with her feelings? she thought as she dabbed. Should she believe so gullibly that there might be a future with Rayne? Take it slowly, her brother had said. Maybe Simon was right.

She reapplied her lip gloss. At least she'd been the first point of call as soon as he was free, and that had been before he'd known she was having his baby.

Or was she having herself on. Maybe it was Simon, his best friend from his childhood, not her he'd really come to see. He had travelled across the world last time for a conversation with Simon that hadn't happened. This morning he'd just seen her on the side of the road first.

When it all boiled down to it. how much did Rayne know about her or could care after just one night? One long night when they hadn't done much talking at all.

Nope. She wasn't a stand-out-in-the-crowd success story.

With a mother who expected perfection and three older, very confident sisters, she'd always wanted to shine in the crowd. Had hidden her shyness under a polished and bolshie exterior that had said, *Look at me*, had forced herself to be outgoing. Maybe that was why her relationships with men had seemed to end up in disaster.

Once they'd got to know her and realised she wasn't who they'd thought she was.

That was her problem. Being the youngest of five very successful siblings, she'd always seen herself falling a little short. But finally, when she'd settled on midwifery, incredibly she'd loved it. But her job had gone

down the tube with this baby for a while yet—so she'd
blown that too.

The hardest thing about Rayne walking away without
a backward glance had been those voices in her head
saying it had been easy for him to do that. Too easy.

She turned away from the mirror with a sigh. And
then there was Rayne's consummate ease in keeping
the whole impending disaster of his court appearance
and sentencing from her.

But what if she had the chance to show him the real
woman underneath? Maybe he'd show her the real man?
Maybe it could work because there was no doubting
physical chemistry was there in spades between them.
Or had been before she'd turned into a balloon. They'd
just have to see if that was enough to build on with
their child.

She slid her hand gently over the mound of her stomach and held the weight briefly in her palm.

*You are the most important person, baby, but maybe
your daddy just needs to have someone with faith in
him to be the perfect father. And I do have that faith
and he'll have to prove otherwise before we are going
to be walked away from again.*

CHAPTER FOUR

Christmas Day

RAYNE PULLED UP outside the place Maeve had called the manse. The phone call had come sooner than he'd expected. Apparently he was down for family breakfast *and* lunch. He wasn't sure if could mentally do that but he'd see how it turned out.

As he gently closed the door of the car he glanced at motorised nodding animals in the Christmas manger on the lawn and shook his head. There was a little straw-filled crib with a tiny swaddled baby in it, and for a minute he thought it was a real baby; rubbed his eyes and, of course, it was a doll. He was seeing babies everywhere. Not surprising really.

But there were definite adoring looks and nods from the mechanical Mary and Joseph, and the three wise men and those crazy manger animals nodded along.

He could imagine during the weeks leading up to Christmas it wouldn't be unusual for children to drop by on the way home from school to check out the display.

He'd sort of noticed the display but not really when he'd been here earlier. He stopped for a moment and took in the full glory of the scene. Geez. Now, that was schmaltz with a capital S.

It was so over the top, with the solar mini-train circling the yard carrying fake presents, the fairy-lights all over the house and around the manger, and the giant blue star on the main building roof, totally the opposite of Maeve and Simon's mother's idea of colour-coordinated, understated elegance. Or his own poor mother's belief it was all a waste of time.

Imagine a family who was willing to put that much effort into decorations that only hung around for a month and then had to be packed away again. He couldn't help but speculate how much they'd be willing to put into things that were really important.

It was so hard to imagine that sort of close-knit caring. The kind he'd seen between Maeve and Simon's family every time he'd visited their house.

He'd always told Simon he was lucky, having two families and six sisters, and Simon had said he could share them as long as he didn't chat them up.

Well, that one had been blown out of the water with Maeve, he thought with a grimace, though he and Maeve hadn't done much chatting.

He sighed. Pulled back his shoulders and lifted his chin. Started to walk again. Not something to be proud of. Well, that's what he was here for. To make right what he could. Maeve had said they needed to talk but he wasn't so sure Simon was going to come to the party.

The front screen door opened and Simon met him as he came up the steps. And held out his hand. There was a definite welcome there he hadn't expected. Holy hell. Rayne's throat burned and he swallowed.

Simon shrugged and smiled. 'Can't say I've been happy but it is good to see you.' Then he stepped in and hugged him.

Rayne's choked throat felt like someone had shoved a carpenter's wood rasp down his neck, not that he'd ever cried, even when he'd buried his mother, so it was an unfamiliar and uncomfortable feeling, but he hadn't expected this. He gripped Simon's hand so hard his friend winced and he loosened his fingers. Dropped the handshake.

'Um. Thanks. That was unexpected.'

'I've had time to cool down. And I'm sorry about your mother.' A hard stare. 'You taking the blame for her is something we'll talk about another time.'

His throat still felt tight. He so hadn't expected this. 'Maeve is incredible.'

Simon snorted. 'Or incredibly stupid. We'll see which one.' He shrugged, definitely warmer than earlier that morning, and gestured to the door. 'Now come in. It's Christmas and you're about to meet the rest of the family. By the way, my dad knows all about you.' Simon raised his brows.

Raised his own back. 'Nice.' Not. Rayne glanced

over his shoulder at the road but there was only his car on the street. He'd hoped as there were no other cars he could come and go before the family arrived.

Simon must have seen his look because he said, 'Everyone walks most places around here. They're all out the back.'

They walked through the house down a central hallway, past some mistletoe he needed to avoid unless Maeve was there, with at least three rooms each side, and into a large kitchen, heavily decorated for Christmas, complete with multi-coloured gifts under the tree. At the kitchen bench a tiny, round, older lady with a Santa hat on her white hair was carving ham slices onto a plate. The young blonde woman he'd seen earlier that morning was piling fried eggs onto another carving plate.

'This is Rayne, Louisa. My grandmother, Rayne.'

The older lady looked up and glowed at Simon and then with twinkling eyes skimmed Rayne from head to toe with apparent delight. 'Maeve's mystery man. You are very welcome, my dear. And just in time for breakfast. Merry Christmas.'

Just in time for breakfast? His stomach rumbled. He hadn't even thought about food. She was a jolly little thing and jolliness had been hard to come by lately. He couldn't help a small smile. 'Merry Christmas to you.'

Simon's voice warmed even more. 'And this divine being is my fiancée, Tara. Tara's a midwife at the birth centre and has been looking after Maeve's pregnancy since she arrived. If you're good, we might even invite you to our wedding.'

'Hello, Rayne. Welcome. Merry Christmas.' And Tara, a much younger small blonde woman with wise eyes, smiled a smile that said, *I know how hard it is for you at this moment.* And, incredibly, he actually believed her. Now, that was strange.

Tara handed him the heaped plate. 'Take this out with you when you go, could you, please, and try to find a spot on the table for it.'

He took the plate and she gestured Simon to a basket of rolls, which he obligingly picked up right after he'd kissed her swiftly on her mouth. She laughed and shooed him off and Rayne looked away. He couldn't ever imagine being so easy with Maeve.

There was a brief lull in the conversation when they opened the screen door out into the back yard, but Rayne had spotted Maeve and the voices were fading anyway as his eyes drank in the sight of her.

Damn, she looked amazing in a red summer dress, like a ripe plum, the material ballooned over her magnificent belly and shimmered when she shifted. A green Christmas scarf draped her gorgeous shoulders. She looked like his fantasy Mrs Santa Claus and he had to hold himself back as Simon introduced him to his other family.

A tall, powerfully built man crossed to them. He put his hand out to Rayne and he took it. Shook firmly and stepped back. Yep. That had to be Simon's natural father. Same mouth and nose. A chip off the old block, and he reminded him of an army major he'd know once. 'Pleased to meet you, sir.'

'Angus, not sir. And I understand you're a paediatrician?'

'Not for nearly a year.'

'Maybe we'll get a chance to talk about that while you're here. You could think of having a breather here while you settle back into some kind of routine.'

Not likely. He already wanted to run. 'Perhaps.'

A vivacious redhead swooped in and gave him a hug. He tried awkwardly to return it but he'd never been a hugger. Her head only came up to his chin. 'Merry Christmas, Rayne. I'm Simon's stepmother, Mia.'

She stepped back and waved to two young miniatures of herself at the table. 'And our daughters Amber and Layla. So there will be nine of us for breakfast.'

It felt like a lot more but, really, the only person he wanted to talk to there was Maeve, who was watching him with an enigmatic expression, and it looked like they'd have to eat before he'd get any chance of that.

Tara and Louisa brought the last two plates and they all began to sit at the long table under the tree, but as he crossed to Maeve she moved towards the table as if she felt more confident there. With definite intent he held her chair and then settled himself beside her.

He glanced around and hoped nobody could see he really didn't want to be here, then he pulled himself up. It was Christmas.

One of the little girls said grace, and he acknowledged the nice touch, especially as he would have
been stumped if someone had asked him, and the table
groaned with food. He hadn't seen this much food since
that Christmas at Simon's all those years ago.

When grace was over he turned to Maeve. She was
why he was here. Funny how Simon had slipped back
into second place, though it was good to see him too.
His only friend in the world, and he'd thought he'd lost
him.

But Maeve. She looked even better up close. Much
more colour in her cheeks than earlier. He lowered his
voice because he imagined she wouldn't want to draw
attention to the fact she'd fainted that morning. 'Are
you okay?'

A brief glimpse of her confusion as she looked at
him. 'I'm fine.'

'Fine as in Freaked Out, Insecure, Neurotic and Emotional?' He tried a poor attempt at a joke.

A longer look. 'They been showing you movies in
there?'

He felt his face freeze. His body go cold with the
memories. 'No.'

Then he saw the distress that filled her eyes and her
hand came across and touched his. Stayed for a second, warmed him like an injection of heat up his arm,
and then shifted back to her lap. 'I'm sorry. It was a
stupid joke.'

'Ditto. From another movie.' He forced a smile. 'It's fine.'

Her face softened. 'You sure? You know what "fine" means?'

He so didn't want to play, even though he'd started it. 'How long do we have to stay? I need to talk to you.'

She glanced around to make sure nobody had heard. It wasn't a problem because everyone was talking and laughing full steam ahead and the little girls were bouncing in their seats. Maeve's eyes softened when she looked at them. 'Until after the presents, and then I don't have to be back here until this afternoon.'

'So you'll come with me for a couple of hours. Talk in private? Sort what we can?'

He felt her assessing look. 'We can do that. Not sure how much we can sort in a couple of hours. As long as you get me back here before Christmas lunch at three o'clock. I promised to make the brandy sauce.' She glanced under her brows at him. 'I can cook when I feel like it, you know.'

'Oh. I know.'

It was all still there. Maeve could feel the vibration of chemistry between them. Just an inch or two between her skin touching his skin and even then his heat was radiating into her shoulder in waves without the contact. And all this at the Christmas breakfast table in front of Simon's family.

How could this man make her so aware of every part

of her body, and why him? He curled her toes, made her nipples peak, her belly twist and jump, and that was without the baby doing its own gyrations in there. It was darned awkward and the only consolation was he didn't look any more comfortable than she was.

But this was way more important than incredible sex. This was about the future, and even she had to admit she hadn't given the future a thought last time they'd been together. He'd been pretty adamant there hadn't been a future if she remembered rightly, though she had expected a little more pillow talk the next day rather than him being marched away by federal police.

She caught Tara's concerned eyes on her and shrugged. She'd be okay. Early days yet. But to think that this morning she'd been crying into her pillow, wanting him to be here for the birth, and here he was within an inch of her. It was a lot to take in. And she couldn't help the tiny beam of light that suggested she'd been given a blessing to be thankful for.

Someone asked her to pass a plate of tomatoes. There was a lot of eating going on all around them and she and Rayne hadn't started yet. Maybe they'd better.

Rayne must have thought the same because he passed her the ham and she took a small piece, glanced at his plate, and saw at least he was preparing to be fed. Then he passed her the eggs and she took one of those as well. Though she didn't feel like putting anything into her mouth. Her belly was squirming too much.

People were putting their knives and forks together

and sitting back. Leaning forward again and pouring coffee and juice. Maeve reached over and brought the rolls over in front of her, gave one to Rayne and one to herself without thinking and then realised she was acting like an old housewife looking after her husband.

He lifted his brows and smiled sardonically at her and she shrugged. 'Enjoy.' Reminded herself that she'd been a confident woman the last time he'd seen her and she needed to keep that persona even more now she was fighting for her baby's future. But what if she wasn't enough? What if he still left after their talk today? Surely he wouldn't leave this afternoon after just getting here.

'How long can you stay around here?'

He paused with his fork halfway to his mouth. Good timing at least. 'When is the baby due?'

'Tomorrow.'

His face paled and she thought, *Tell me about it, buster, I'm the one who has to do it.* 'But I expect I'll go overdue. Does it matter what date?'

He shook his head, clearly rattled by the impending birth. Put his fork down. Couldn't he see her belly looked like it was about to explode?

Then he said quietly, aware that a few ears were straining their way, 'I have no commitments, if that's what you mean.'

She sniffed at that. 'You do now.'

He glanced around the table. Saw Simon and his

father watching them. 'I'll be here for as long as you want me to be here. It's the least I can do.'

If only he hadn't added that last sentence. The relief she'd felt hearing him say he'd stay as long as she needed him was lost with the tone of sacrifice. Before she could comment, and it would have been unwise whatever she'd been going to say, at the very least, he touched her hand.

'Sorry. That came out wrong. It's just that I'm still getting used to you expecting a baby. And this table is killing me.'

Just then Mia stood up. 'The girls want to know how long before everyone is finished.'

Maeve pushed her plate away thankfully. 'I'm done.'

Rayne stood up. 'Let me help clear.' And he began very efficiently scraping and collecting plates, and she remembered him rinsing his plate at Simon's house.

At least he was house-trained, she thought with an internal smile as she began to gather up side plates, probably a lot more than she was. It was a warming thought that maybe there was stuff that they could do for each other, maybe there were things they could share between them that they'd find out and enjoy as well.

Within a very short time the dishwasher was loaded, the leftovers were stowed in the fridge and the kitchen clean. The big sunroom area of the back room at the end of the kitchen had been cleared when the kitchen table had gone outside and the Christmas tree was surrounded by lots of presents, as well as chairs and cushions so everyone had a niche to perch to watch the fun.

Simon had Tara on his lap, Mia and Angus were sitting with Louisa on the lounge they'd pulled in, and the girls were hopping and crawling around the tree as they shared out the presents one at a time.

Everyone sat except Rayne. He leant against the wall to the left of Maeve so he could watch her face, and he knew she wished he'd take the chair Simon had offered and sit down next to her. But he didn't. He didn't deserve to be a part of the circle. Felt more of an outsider than he ever had, despite the efforts of others. It was his fault he felt like that and he knew it. Just couldn't do anything about it.

He watched Simon take a present from the eldest child and hand it solemnly to Tara. When she opened it he saw her eyes flash to Simon's, saw the tremulous smile and the stroke of her finger down the painted face of the Russian doll. Those dolls that had other dolls inside. This looked like a very expensive version of those.

Cute. But a strange present to give. Though he had no idea about giving presents himself. He frowned, realising he should have thought about that on the way here. He didn't have any to give.

Tara didn't seem to know about the tinier dolls inside and Simon laughed and showed her how they came apart and another pretty painted doll was removed from the centre. And another and another. Until there was a dozen little painted dolls in a line along the arm of the chair. Simon's little sisters had eyes wide with wonder and he suspected there was a little moisture in Tara's eyes, and even Maeve's. He was missing something here.

Maeve shifted her body so she was closer to him and gestured for him to lean down.

'Tara's parents died when she was six. So she was in an orphanage until she grew up. Since then she's never owned a doll.'

Damn! No wonder she understood a little of his awkwardness on arrival. He wasn't the only one who'd had it hard. He'd always been grateful his mum had stayed straight long enough to keep him out of care. Even though he'd been the one doing the caring at home. At least it had been his home and he had had a mother.

The present-giving moved on and Maeve was given a little hand-made wheatpack, a drink bottle with a straw, and a pair of warm socks as comfort aids for labour, and they all laughed.

He watched Maeve smile and thank Tara, but the little twitch in her eyelid made him wonder just how calm the woman having his baby really was about the approaching birth.

His own uneasiness grew with the thought. It wasn't like neither of them didn't know a lot about birth. He'd been at many, but mostly he had been the paediatrician there for Caesarean babies or other newborns at risk.

And Maeve had done her midwifery so she was well versed in what would happen. But it was a bit different when it was this close to home. There were those other times when the unexpected happened.

He really needed to talk to her about that. He glanced at the clock. Fifteen minutes since last time he'd looked at it. Not too bad. And then it was over. The paper was collected, hugs were exchanged and everyone sat back. Louisa asked about fresh coffee or tea and Maeve shifted to the edge of her chair. He put out his hand and helped her up.

Her hand felt good in his. He tightened his grip.

'We're going for a drive.' She said it to the room in general and there was a little pause in the conversation. Then she looked at Louisa and smiled. 'I'll be back by two-thirty to make that brandy sauce.'

Simon groaned. 'Make sure you are. That sauce is to die for.' Everyone laughed again and Rayne wondered, with dry amusement, if he really was the only one who got the warning directed their way.

Louisa said, 'Hold on for a minute.'

And Maeve shrugged and said, 'I'll just go to the loo before we go.' He thought they'd never get away.

Then Louisa was back with a small basket. Quickest pack he'd ever seen. 'Just a Thermos of tea and a cold drink. Some Christmas cake and rum balls in case you get hungry.'

He looked at her. 'I'm pretty sure nobody could be hungry leaving this house.' Looked at her plump cheeks, pink from exertion. Her kind eyes crinkled with the pleasure of giving her food. 'Thank you.' He lowered his voice so that nobody else heard. 'I was going to take Maeve to the seats by the boatshed. This is perfect.'

She held up a finger. 'One more thing, then.' And within seconds was back with a small brown paper bag. 'Bread scraps for the ducks.'

He shook his head. He had never ever met anyone like her. 'You are my new favourite person.'

Then Maeve came back and he tucked the paper bag into his pocket so he could take her hand and carried the basket in the other.

CHAPTER FIVE

The lake

DRIVING AWAY FROM the house, he felt like a load fell from his shoulders. He never had done other people's family events well and the feeling of being an outcast had grown exponentially when he'd had to add the words 'ex-inmate' to his CV.

He realised Maeve was quiet too, not something he remembered about her, and he looked away from the road to see her face. Beautiful. She was watching him. He looked back at the road. Better not run over any kids on Christmas morning, riding their new bikes.

'So where are we going?'

'I saw a boathouse down on the lake. Thought we'd just sit on one of the park benches beside the water.' He looked at her again. 'That okay?' He could smell the scent of her hair from where he was sitting. He remembered that citrus smell from nine months ago.

'Sure.' She shrugged and glanced at the seat between them. 'What's in the basket?'

He had to smile at that. Smile at the memory of Louisa's need to give. 'Emergency food supplies Simon's grandmother worried we might need.'

Maeve peered under the lid and groaned. 'She put in rum balls. I love rum balls. And I can't have them.'

He frowned. She could have what she liked. He'd give her the world if he had the right. 'Why can't you have rum balls?'

She sighed with exasperation. 'Because I'm pregnant and foetuses don't drink alcohol.'

He looked at her face and for the first time in a long time he felt like laughing. But he wasn't sure he'd be game to.

Instead, he said, trying to keep his mouth serious, 'I hope our baby appreciates the sacrifices its mother has been through.'

Tartly. 'I hope its father does.'

That was a kick to the gut. He did. Very much. He turned into the parking area of the boatshed and parked. Turned off the engine. Turned to face her.

'Yes. I do. And I am sorry I haven't been here for you.'

She sighed. 'I'm sorry you didn't know. That I couldn't share the pregnancy with you.'

He thought of his state of mind in that prison if he'd known Maeve was pregnant and he couldn't get to her. God, no. 'I'm not.' He saw her flinch.

'Surely you don't mean that now. That's horrible.' She opened the car door and he could feel her agitation.

Regretted immensely he'd hurt her, but couldn't regret the words. Saw her struggle to get out of the low car with her centre of balance all haywire from the awkwardness of the belly poking out front.

Suddenly realised it sounded harsh from her perspective. He didn't know how to explain about the absolute hell of being locked up. About the prospect of staying locked up for years. About his guilt that his mother had died to get him out and he'd actually been glad. He still couldn't think about the load of guilt that carried. He opened his own door and walked swiftly round to help her out.

Finally Rayne said very quietly, 'I would have gone mad if I'd known you were pregnant and I couldn't get to you. There was a chance I wasn't coming out for years and years.'

She stopped struggling to get herself from the car. Wiped the tears on her cheek. Looked up at him. 'Oh. Is that why you didn't read the letters?'

'I lost access to everything, Maeve. I was a faceless perpetrator surrounded by men who hated the world. I'd never hated the world before but I hated it in there. The only way I could stay sane in that toxic environment was to seal myself off from it. Create a wall and not let anything in. The last thing I needed was sunshine that I couldn't touch and that's what your letters were to me. That way led to madness and I had to stay strong behind my wall.'

'I shouldn't have sent them, then?'

It certainly hadn't been her fault for sending them. She was an angel—especially now he'd read them. 'You couldn't have known. But they were something I looked forward to. I was going to open them when I got out. As soon as I got out. But then I got scared you would tell me not to come and I needed to see you and Simon one more time to explain. So I decided to open them after I saw you.' He rubbed the back of his neck. 'I'm so sorry I caused you pain.'

Maeve looked up at Rayne and saw what she'd seen nine months ago. Big shoulders under a black shirt, black hair cut shorter to the strong bones of his head, dark, dark eyes, even more difficult to read, but maybe they were only easy to read on the way to the bedroom. And that wicked mouth, lips that could work magic or drop words that made her go cold.

This was going to be tougher than she'd expected it to be. Something Tara had said to her a couple of days ago filtered back into her memory. Something about her knowing men who had been to prison and were harder, more distanced from others when they got out.

The problem was Rayne had already been distanced from people before he'd been wrongly convicted.

But when he'd said he was glad he hadn't opened her letters, and she'd responded emotionally with the hurt of it, she'd been thinking about herself. Not about why he would say something hurtful like that. Not about what he'd been through. She promised herself she would try to help heal the scars that experience had left him with—not make the whole transition more difficult.

Guess she'd have to learn to filter her reactions through his eyes. And that wasn't going to be easy because she liked looking at things her way.

But it should be easier with him here, not harder. The thought made her feel cross. 'For goodness' sake, help me out of this damn car.' Not what she'd intended to say but now she thought about it she'd be a whole lot more comfortable with him not standing over her.

The dirty rat laughed.

But at least he put his hand out and again she sailed upwards with ridiculous ease until she was standing beside him.

'You really are a princess, you know that?'

She glared at him as she adjusted her dress and straightened her shoulders. Re-establishing her personal space. 'You have a problem with that?'

He looked at her, and if she wasn't mistaken there could even be a little softening in that hard expression. 'Nope. I love it.'

Warmth expanded inside her. There was hope for the man yet.

Rayne shut the door behind her and picked up the basket. Tucked her hand under his other arm, and she liked that closeness as they sauntered across to the lakeside seats.

Like nothing was wrong. She let it go. She'd always been a 'temper fast and then forget it' person so that was lucky because she had the feeling they had a bit of getting used to each other to come.

Further down the shore, a young boy and his dad were launching an obviously new sailing boat into the lake and a small dog was barking at the ducks heading their way away from those other noisy intruders.

'I love ducks,' Maeve said. 'Always have. I used to have a baby one, it grew up to be an amazing pet. Used to waddle up and meet me when I came home from school.'

'What did you call it?'

She could feel a blush on her cheeks. He was going to laugh. Maybe she could make up a different name. A cool one.

He bumped her shoulder gently with his as if he'd read her mind. 'I want the real name.'

She glared at him. 'I was going to give you the real one.'

'Sure you were.'

Quietly. 'Cinderella.'

Yep, he laughed. But it was a good sound. And so did she. Especially for Christmas morning, from a man only a few weeks out of prison who'd recently lost his mother and found out he was going to be a father. Going to be a father very soon. It felt good she'd made him laugh.

'Imagine,' he said. Then he turned and studied her face. His eyes were unreadable but his voice was sombre. 'Thank you for even thinking of giving me a chance.' And when she saw the sincerity, and just a touch of trepidation, now she felt like crying.

Wasn't sure she should tell him about this morning—what if she scared him?—but couldn't resist the chance. 'You know, I woke up today and all I wanted for Christmas was to be able to talk to you.'

His eyes widened in shock. And something else— she wasn't sure but it could have been fear. Yep, she'd scared him. Fool.

She felt her anger rise. Anger because it shouldn't be this hard to connect with a guy she'd been powerless to resist and it wasn't like he'd been doing something he hadn't agreed to either that night they'd created this baby together. So there was a force greater than them that she believed in but she wasn't so sure it worked if only one of them was a convert. 'It's not that hard to understand. I'm having a baby and there is supposed to be two of us. And if you don't hate me, think about it.'

She turned away from him. Didn't want to see anything negative at this moment. She watched the little boy jumping up and down as his little sailing boat picked up the breeze and sailed out towards the middle of the lake.

Nope. She needed to say it all. Get it out there because if it wasn't going to happen she needed to know now. She turned back to him. 'So what I'm saying is thank you for coming, even though you didn't know I was pregnant, thank you for driving all this way on Christmas to see us.'

'That's nothing.'

'I haven't finished.'

He held up his hands. 'Go on, then.'

'If you want to do the right thing, do something for me.' She took a big breath. 'I'm asking you to stay. At least until after the birth. Be with me during the birth, because if you're there I will be able to look forward to this occasion as I should be—not dreading the emptiness and fear of being alone.'

Rayne got that. He also got how freaking brave this woman was. To lay herself out there to be knocked back—not that he would, but, sheesh, how much guts had it taken for her to actually put that request into words? He felt the rock in his heart that had cracked that morning shift and crack a little more.

Heck. 'Of course I'll stay. Just ask for anything.' Well, not anything. He didn't think he was the type of guy to move in with, play happy families with, but he could certainly see himself being a little involved with the baby. He was good with babies. Good with children. For the first time in a long time he remembered he had an amazing job helping children and their parents and maybe it was a job he should go back to some time.

But he had no experience about making a family. No idea how to be a father. No idea what a father even did, except for those he'd seen at work. Simon's father had just seemed to be 'there'. He didn't know how to do 'being there'.

He glanced around the peaceful scene. Another little

family were riding shiny pushbikes along the path. They all wore matching red helmets. The dad was riding at the back and he guessed he was making sure everyone was okay. That seemed reasonable. Maybe he could do that. The birds were chirping and hopping in the branches above his head like the thoughts in his brain.

This place had an amazing vibe to it. Or it could be the collective consciousness of celebrating Christmas with family and friends creating the goodwill. But he'd never felt anything like it. He looked at Maeve. Or seen anyone like her.

She was staring over the water into the distance but there was tension in her shoulders. Rigidity in her neck. And he'd put that there. He'd need to be a lot better at looking after her if he was going to be her support person in one of the most defining moments of her life. Of both their lives.

He stepped up behind her and pulled her back to lean into his body. Lifted his hands to her shoulders and dug gently into the firm muscles, kneaded with slowly increasing depth until she moaned and pushed her bottom back into him until her whole weight was sagged against him.

She moaned again and he could feel the stir of his body as it came awake. Down, boy. Not now. Definitely not now. He could barely get his head around any of this, let alone lose the lot in a fog of Maeve sex.

'That feels *so-o-o* good,' she said.

He just knew her eyes were closed. He smiled. 'I'd

need to get lots of practice to build up my stamina for the event.'

'Mmm-hmm,' she agreed sleepily.

He shifted his fingers so that they were circling the hard little knot in her neck and she drooped even more.

'You might need to sit down.' He could hear the smile in his voice. Drew her to the bench they were standing beside and steered her into a sitting position. Went back around the bench so he was standing behind her—which helped the libido problem as he wasn't touching her whole body now.

He began again. Slow circular rotations of his fingers, kneading and swirling and soothing the rigidity away, for her, anyway. His body was as stiff as a pole.

He'd never had this desire to comfort and heal a woman before. Plenty of times he'd wanted to carry one to bed with him, but this? This was different. His hand stilled.

'Don't stop.'

He stepped back. Created distance from something he knew he wasn't ready for. Might never be ready for. 'I remembered the bread.' Pulled the brown paper bag from his pocket and gave it to her. A heaven-sent distraction to stop her interrogation into why he'd stepped back.

'For the ducks,' he said.

'Oh.' He heard the disappointment fade from her voice. Watched her straighten her shoulders with new enthusiasm. She was like a child. And he envied her so much. He couldn't remember when he'd felt like a child.

Then she was into planning mode again. 'You'll have to stay at the manse so I can find you when I need you.'

Just like that. Room, please. 'I can't just gatecrash Simon's grandmother's house.'

She threw a knobby crust of bread at a duck, which wrestled with it in a splash of lake water. 'Sure you can. Locum doctors and agency midwives come all the time when one of the hospital staff goes away. That's where they stay. The manse has lots of rooms and Louisa loves looking after people.'

Unfortunately too easy. He'd said he'd be there for the birth. He said he'd be her support person. He'd said he'd do anything and the second thing she asked for he was thinking, No!

H pushed back the panic. It would be better than the hotel. And not as bad as just moving into a house with Maeve and having her there twenty-four seven as his responsibility not to let anything happen to her.

Now, that was a frightening thought.

He wasn't on a good statistical run with saving people, which would be why he was an orphan now, and he went cold. Couldn't imagine surviving if anything happened to Maeve on his watch.

He did not want to do this. 'Sure. If Simon's grandmother says it's fine.' He thought about his friend. 'If Simon doesn't think I'm pushing my way into his family.'

'Simon spends every available minute with Tara.

Which reminds me. Tara is my midwife. I might ask
her to run through some stuff with us for working together in labour. She's done a course and it works beautifully for couples.'

His neck tightened and he resisted the impulse to
rub it. Hard. Or turn and run away. Couple? Now they
were a couple? She must have sensed his withdrawal
because she made a little sound of distress and he threw
her a glance. Saw a pink flood of colour rise from her
cleavage. Was distracted for a moment at the truly glorious sight that was Meave's cleavage, and then looked
up at her face.

She mumbled, 'I meant a couple as in you are my
support person in labour.'

Hell. He nodded, dropped his hands back onto her
shoulders. Tried not to glance over the top of her so
he could see down her dress. He was an emotionally
stunted disgrace, and he had no idea what Maeve saw
in him or why she would want to continue seeing him.
He needed to be thankful she was willing to include
him at all.

But he couldn't come up with any words to fix it.
He watched her throw some more bread scraps to a flo-
tilla of black ducks that had made an armada towards
Maeve. They were floating back and forth, their little
propeller legs going nineteen to the dozen under the
water. A bit like he was feeling, with all these currents
pulling him every which way.

Across the lake the Christmas sailboat was almost

at the other side. He could see the father and the little boat boy walking around the path to meet it. That father knew what to do. He wasn't stressing to the max about letting his kid down. What training did he have? Maybe, if bad things didn't happen, if he didn't stuff up, if Maeve didn't realise she deserved way better than him, he'd do that one day with his own son.

Or kick a ball. Ride bikes with him and buy him a little red helmet.

Or maybe Maeve's baby would be a little miniature Maeve. That was really scary. Imagine having to keep her safe? The air around him seemed to have less oxygen that it had before, leaving him with a breathless feeling.

'Want to see what's in the basket?' Maeve was pulling it onto the seat beside her. 'We'd better eat something out of it before we go back.'

She handed him the rum balls. 'Eat these so I don't.' Began to put mugs and spoons out.

He took them. Battened down the surge of responsibility that was crowding in on him as Maeve began to make a little picnic. Like any other family at the side of the lake. He didn't know where the conversation should go or what he was supposed to do. She handed him a cup of tea and he almost dropped it.

He felt her eyes on him. 'Relax, Rayne.' Her voice was soft, understanding, and he wasn't sure he deserved that understanding but he did allow his shoulders to drop a little. 'It's all been a shock for you. Let's get through the next week and worry about long term later. I'm just glad you're here and that you've said you'll stay for the labour.'

She was right. He felt the stress leach away like the tea seemed to have soaked into the brown dirt. He sat down beside her.

She handed him the bag of crumbs. 'Bread-throwing is therapeutic.'

Like a child. 'You are therapeutic.' But he took the bag. Before he could throw more crumbs, a tiny, yapping black-curled poodle came bounding up to them, the red bow around his neck waving in the slight breeze. He raced at the ducks and stopped at the edge of the water, and the black ducks took off in a noisy burst of complaint because they'd just found another benefactor in Rayne and now they had to leave.

A little girl's tremulous cry called the dog from further down the street and the black dog turned, cocked an ear, and then bounded off towards his mistress.

'So much for duck therapy.'

'Poor Rayne. Come, snuggle up to me and I'll make you feel better.'

He smiled and was about to say something when they heard the quack of another duck from the bushes beside them. He frowned and they both looked.

'Is it a nest?'

'Could be tangled in something.' He was about to stand up and check the bush when the sound came again and the branches rustled with movement. He stilled in case he frightened whatever was caught in there and they watched the bushes part until a little brown bird appeared, not a duck at all, a slim bird with a long drooping tail that shook itself free of the undergrowth.

'Ohh...' Maeve whispered on a long sigh of delight. 'It's not a duck making that noise—it's a lyrebird.'

Rayne watched in amazement. 'A lyrebird mimic? As in Lyrebird Lake? I guess that figures.' But there was something so amazing about the pure fearlessness of a wild creature glaring at them as it moved a step closer and cocked his head to stare their way.

Then the little bird, no larger than a thin hen, straightened, spread his fan-shaped tail in a shimmer of movement and proceeded to dance at the edge of the lake for Maeve and Rayne.

A gift for Christmas.

Backward and forward, shimmering his harp-shaped tail as it swayed above his feathered head, and Rayne had never seen anything like it in his life as he clutched Maeve's hand in his and felt the tight knot in his chest mysteriously loosen the longer it went on. He glanced at Maeve and saw silver tears glistening.

He hugged her closer, drank in the magic without questioning why they were being gifted with it. All too soon it was over and the tail was lowered. One more stern look from the bird and he stepped nonchalantly back into the bush and with a crackle of foliage he disappeared.

They didn't speak for a moment as the moment sank into both of them.

'Wow,' whispered Maeve.

'Wow is right,' Rayne said, as he turned and wiped away the silver droplets from Maeve's face. Leant over and kissed her damp cheek. 'I feel like we've just been blessed.'

'Me, too.' And they sat there in silence for a few minutes longer, in an aura of peace between them that had been missing before, and slowly the real ducks came floating back.

CHAPTER SIX

Back at the manse

WHEN THEY GOT back Maeve disappeared into the kitchen
to make her brandy sauce. Most of the family were out
in the back yard—apparently the Christmas lunch table
was set out there again—and the little girls were en-
grossed in their new possessions.

Simon waylaid Rayne and steered him back out the
door away from the family. 'So what have you two
decided?'

Rayne wasn't sure he'd decided anything. Maeve had
done all the planning and now it was up to him to keep
his end of the bargain. 'Maeve wants me to stay for the
birth. I've said I will.' Simon looked mildly pleased.
'It's the least I can do.' There was that statement that
had upset Maeve and it didn't do anything positive to
Simon's frame of mind either if the frown across his
friend's brow was an indication. He had no idea why it
kept popping out.

'Is it that hard to commit to that? You slept with her.' His friend was shaking his head.

He held up his hand. 'Simon, I'm sorry. The last time I saw you it was an awful night. My world was about to implode. I didn't intend to end up in bed with Maeve.' He paused. Looked back in his mind and shook his head. 'But you should have seen her. She was like some peach vision and she poleaxed me.'

Simon glanced sardonically at him. 'And she dragged you off to bed?'

'Nope.' He had to smile at that memory. 'I carried her.' And she'd loved it.

Simon raised his brows. 'Up two flights of stairs?' Then he put his hand up. 'Forget I asked that. Tara says the sparks from you two light up the room. I get that. I get being irresistibly drawn to someone. And I get that you don't do commitment.'

Simon laughed dryly. 'But I thought I didn't do commitment until my Tara came along.'

Rayne looked at his friend's face. Had never seen it so joyous. As if Simon had finally found his feet and the whole world. Rayne couldn't imagine that. 'I meant to say congratulations. Tara seems a wonderful woman.'

Simon's smile grew. 'She is. And she so tough and...' He stopped, shook his head ruefully. 'Nice diversion. But this is about you.' Simon searched his face and he flinched a little under the scrutiny. 'Are you in for the long haul?'

Freaking long haul. Geez. He didn't know if he would last a week. 'I'm in for the labour. I'm in for what I can do to help Maeve for the birth. But as soon as I cause problems in her life I'm out of here.'

'And if you don't cause problems in her life?' The inference was he had already let her down, and he guessed he had.

'I didn't know she was pregnant.' Thank God.

Simon shrugged. 'Tara said you didn't open the mail. And I know you wouldn't answer my calls. Why?'

It was his turn to shrug but his bitterness swelled despite his effort to control it. 'I didn't want to bring her into that place. Either of you. I had to keep the good things pure. And when I got out, I didn't want to read that she might refuse to see me. So I came here first.'

'Have you read the letters now?'

'Yes.' Could feel the long stare from Simon. Those letters just reiterated how much he was capable of stuffing up other people's lives.

Simon sighed long and heavily. 'I love you, man. I'm even getting used to the idea that you will be in Maeve's life now. In all our lives. But don't stuff this up.'

So he'd read his mind? Rayne almost laughed, even though it was far from funny. 'That's the friend I remember.'

'Yeah. Merry Christmas.' Simon punched his shoulder. 'Let's go ask Louisa if you can stay. She'll be over the moon. She likes you.'

'I get the feeling your grandmother likes everyone.'
Simon laughed. 'Pretty much.'

Maeve had already asked Louisa.

'Of course he can stay,' Louisa enthused. 'So he'll
be with you when you have the baby.' She sighed happily. 'Things have a way of working out.'

Maeve grimaced on the inside. *Things weren't 'working out' yet.*

There were a lot of things she and Rayne had to sort
yet, not the least his attitude of *It's the least I can do.
Grrr.* But, she reminded herself, this morning she'd
been on her own. And he was here!

The magnitude of that overwhelmed her for a moment and she paused in the rhythmic stirring of thickening liquid in the bowl and just soaked that in. Rayne
was here. And he was staying. At least until after the
birth, and that was all she could ask for. Yet! She wondered if they would actually get much alone time.

Wondered if he was up for that. Wished she was
skinny and gorgeous and could drag him off to bed. Or
be carried there by her gorgeous sex object 'partner',
round belly and all.

Partner. She'd always been uncomfortable with that
sterile word. Not that Rayne was obviously sterile. And
he wasn't her boyfriend. He certainly wasn't her lover.

'You want me to do that?' Louisa's worried voice.
Maeve jumped and stirred again in the nick of time before she made lumps in the sauce.

'Wool-gathering.' Louisa's favourite saying and she'd picked it up. It described her state of mind perfectly. Little floating fibres of thought creating a mess of tangles in her brain. Mushing together to make a ball of confused emotions and wishes and fears and silly impossible dreams. Like the flotsam of leftover wool collected from the bushes where the sheep had walked past.

Well, Rayne was nobody's sheep. He'd never been a part of the flock, had never followed the rules of society except when he'd taken his incredibly intelligent brain to med school at Simon's insistence.

Men's voices drifted their way.

And here they came. Simon and Rayne. Two men she loved. The thought froze the smile on her face. She really loved Rayne. Did she? Fancied him, oh, yeah. The guy could light her fire from fifty paces away. But love?

Maybe brotherly love. She looked at her brother, smiling at something Louisa had said. Nope. She didn't feel the way she felt about Simon. And there was another bonus. She could stop fighting with Simon now that Rayne was back. Fait accompli.

Her mind eased back into the previous thought. The scary one. That she did really love Rayne. There was no 'might' about it. She really was in no better spot than she had been this morning because though Rayne was physically here she wasn't stupid enough to think he was in love with her. And he could leave and have any woman he wanted any time he wanted.

The sauce was ready and she poured it into the jug.

The beauty of this recipe, the reason she was the only one who made it in her family, was the secret ingredient that stopped the film forming on the top. So it didn't grow a skin.

That was a joke. She needed the opposite. She needed to grow ten skins so she could quietly peel away a new layer of herself to show Rayne so that she didn't dump it all on him at once. Because she knew it would require patience if she wanted to help him see he had a chance of a future he'd never dreamed about.

That he could be the kind of man any child would be proud to call his or her father. The kind of man any woman wanted to share her full life with—not just the bedroom.

What was with these pregnancy hormones? She needed to stop thinking about the bedroom. She ran her finger down the spoon handle on the way to the sink. Coated her finger in the rich golden sauce. Lifted it to her lips and closed her eyes. Mmm…

Rayne tried not to stare at Maeve as she parted her lips to admit a custard-covered fingertip. Watched her savour the thick swirl. Shut her eyes. Sigh blissfully as she put the spoon in the sink. Geez. Give a guy a break. If the day hadn't been enough without the almost overwhelming urge to pick her up from amidst all these people and ravish a heavily pregnant woman.

Louisa was talking to him. 'Sorry.' He blinked and turned to the little woman and he had the idea she wasn't blind to what had distracted him if the twinkle in her eyes was anything to go by.

'I said if you would like to follow me I'll show you your room. It's small but I think you'll like the position. And all the rooms open out onto a veranda and have their own chair and table setting outside the door.' She bustled out of the kitchen and he followed.

'That's the bathroom. It's shared with Maeve and Simon and Tara.'

He nodded and paid a bit more attention to the fact that this old country manse had to be at least a hundred years old. The ceilings were a good twelve feet high and the wood-panelled walls looked solid and well built.

Louisa gestured to a door. 'Maeve said she didn't mind there was a connecting door between the two. Do you?' She twinkled up at him.

'Um. No. That will be fine.'

'I thought it might be. Especially as she's getting near to her time and if she wanted to she could leave the door open between you.'

It was a good idea. That look of nervous anticipation he'd seen in Maeve's eyes this morning, he didn't like to call it fear, did need addressing. And it wasn't like he hadn't seen her without clothes. He brought his mind sternly back to the present.

If he could help by being close then that would give him purpose as he tried to come to grips with becoming an unexpected part of a large, noisy, hugging family— all that contact took a bit of getting used to.

He still couldn't believe they weren't all wishing him back to prison away from Maeve. But he knew for a fact Maeve was glad to see him. Maybe too glad, considering the prize she'd won.

Louisa opened the door next to Maeve's and, sure enough, it was a small room, but it did have a double bed against the wall and a chest of drawers. All he needed. 'Thanks, Louisa. It's great. Can I fix you up for it?'

'Lordy, no. I don't need money. I'm well looked after. But you may end up working every now and then for Angus at the hospital if he gets stuck. Everyone helps everyone in Lyrebird Lake.'

Well, not where he'd come from. He felt like he'd fallen into some religious sect and they were going to ask for his soul soon, except he knew that Simon was regular. And Maeve. And this sweet, generous older lady was obviously sincere. So it looked like he had a casual job as well as a place to lay his head. Though he couldn't see him being needed much at the hospital. 'Maybe I can help around the house. Or the garden? I wouldn't say no to be able to burn off some energy.'

She looked at him, a good once-over that had him wishing he'd tucked his shirt in and shaved, but she nodded. 'I have a pile of wood I need chopped before winter. The axe is in the wee shed under the tank stand. It's a bit early in the year but whenever you feel the need you just go right ahead and chop.'

He grinned. Couldn't help himself. Of all the things he'd thought might happen as he'd driven through the night to get here, getting a job as a woodcutter hadn't figured in the speculations.

He followed her out. 'Have I got time to nip back to the pub and let them know I won't be staying?'

'Have you left anything there?'

'No.' You didn't leave things in pub accommodation. Or maybe you did in Lyrebird Lake. Who knew?

'Well, that's fine. Denny Webb will be over visiting his wife at the hospital. Angus will pass the message on to the ward sister.'

Louisa waved to his car out in the street. 'You could bring your things in and then wash in the bathroom if you want.' She had noticed the bristles. 'And we'll see you back in a few minutes because it's nearly time for Christmas lunch.'

Obediently Rayne walked out to his car and brought in his overnight bag. The rest of his stuff—one small suitcase—was under the tarpaulin in the back of the truck. Not that he had much. He'd pretty well given everything else away. Had never been one for possessions. Wasn't quite sure what had influenced him to buy the old Chev. He'd passed it in a car yard on his way in from the airport and it had reminded him of his mother in happier times.

After his sleep in the motel for eight hours he'd walked back to the car yard an hour before closing time. Had told the guy if he could arrange a full mechanical check by a third party, transfers and insurance and tank of petrol in the time they had left, he'd pay the full price.

By the time he'd had a feed and returned, his car was waiting for him. So he did have one possession.

And an exit strategy. Both good things.

Walking back through the kitchen and outside, it seemed that Christmas lunch would be even noisier than breakfast.

Simon offered him a beer before they all sat down and, to hell with it, he took the glass and it was icy cold, and even though they were in the shade from the trees, it was pretty warm outside.

It was Christmas in Queensland and the beer tasted like Australia. Strong and dry and producing a sigh of momentary content. He noted some corny Christmas music on the CD player and Maeve was holding one hand over her left ear, pleading for it to stop. Tara was laughing and Louisa looked offended.

He leaned towards her. 'So you don't like carols?'

'Not twenty-four seven for the last month,' she whispered. 'Save me.'

He laughed. And gave her a quick squeeze as she went past with another jug of sauce to put on the end of the table. She glanced back and she looked at him like he'd given her a present. *Be careful there,* he thought to himself. Expectations and what he could actually deliver could differ.

Angus came up and stood beside him. Raised his glass. 'Lemonade. I'm on call.' He grimaced. 'But cheers. I hear you're staying.'

'Cheers.' He lifted his beer. 'Staying until after the baby at least.'

'Good.'

That was unexpected approval. 'Thank you.'

'It's for Maeve. And Simon. But I'm guessing it's not all easy on your side either. Not easy to get used to all this when you didn't expect it.'

Rayne glanced around. 'It's taking some.'

Angus nodded. 'Just chill. This place is good at helping the chill factor. Maeve has a lot of support so you won't be doing it on your own. And Tara is a good midwife.'

Change of subject. Great. 'Which reminds me. Congratulations on your new daughter-in-law-to-be. I haven't seen Simon look this happy, ever.'

Angus nodded. Glanced at his son, who had Tara's hand clasped firmly in his. Tara was laughing up at him. 'Best Christmas present I could wish for.' Then he glanced at his own wife and daughters. 'Finding the right woman is hard but incredibly worth it.'

'Okay, everyone,' the woman he was regarding said. 'Sit.' He inclined his head at her, gave Rayne a faint smile, and moved away to hold Louisa's chair, and then his wife's. He sat at the head of the table and Louisa sat on his left, with Mia on his right.

Simon sat at the other end with Tara next to him and Maeve on the other side. Rayne was in the middle opposite the two little girls, who were giggling at something Simon had said.

After this morning, he wasn't surprised when the elder of the two girls said grace, and for a fleeting moment he wondered with an inner smile whether, if he had a daughter, he would ever hear her piping little voice bless this table at Christmas. His throat thickened and he drew a quiet breath, and in a reflex he couldn't control he blocked it all out. Blocked out the tinny Christmas music, the laughing people, the beautiful woman expecting his baby beside him.

Maeve felt the distance grow between her and Rayne and wanted to cry. There had been moments there when he'd seemed to be settling into the day better than she'd expected. Especially when she'd noted his obvious rapport with Louisa, but, then, who didn't feel that? Louisa was a saint. Even when she'd first arrived and been at her most prickly and morose, Louisa's gentle, good-natured kindness had won her round before she'd known it.

She'd seen him talking to Angus. Well, since she'd arrived she'd decided Angus was a man's man, so that wasn't surprising. Rayne hadn't really spoken to the girls or Mia since they'd been introduced, but in fairness he hadn't had much chance. She couldn't help hoping he would exhibit some signs he was good with children. The guy was a paediatrician, for goodness' sake. And soon to be a father.

Tara leaned across the table and distracted her by offering the end of a Christmas cracker to pull. 'I'm not sure how many of these I'm supposed to pull,' she said in a quiet aside. 'I just did it with Simon and of course he won. And with Amber and she won. But I want a hat.'

Maeve smiled. 'You can pull any bon-bon offered. It's the bon-bon owner's choice who they want to pull them with. So take any you can.' Maeve had pulled a lot of bonbons in her time. The two young women had tested their strength against each other, and Tara had been a little more competitive than Maeve had expected, and that made her smile.

Maeve pulled harder and the bon-bon banged and split in half. Tara got the bigger half and the hat and prize. This time Tara crowed as she won. Simon clapped. He didn't miss much where Tara was concerned, Maeve thought with a pang. She glanced at Rayne. He was watching but his face was impassive and she got the feeling he wasn't really there.

Not so flattering when she was sitting beside him. 'Would you like to pull a bonbon with me?' Darn, did she have to sound so needy?

He blinked. 'Sorry?'

'A Christmas cracker.' She waved the one that was on her plate. 'See who wins.'

'Oh. Right. Sure.'

Such enthusiasm, she thought, and realised she was becoming a crotchety old woman by waiting for Rayne to behave like her fantasies.

'It's okay. Don't worry. I'll pull it with Tara. She loves them.' She meant it. No problem. Then he surprised her.

'Oi. I love them, too.'

That was the last thing Maeve had expected him to say. 'You love bon-bons?'

'Yeah. Why not?' His eyes crinkled and she sighed with relief that he was back with her. 'Not like I had that many family lunches over the years. That Christmas at your place was the first. You made me coconut ice.'

He remembered. The thought expanded in ridiculous warmth. 'I made everyone coconut ice at Christmas. For years. But it's very cool that you remembered.'

He held his hand out for the end of her Christmas cracker and she waved it around at him. 'I want to win.'

They pulled it and Rayne won. 'Oops,' he said. 'Try mine.' They realigned themselves to pull again and she could tell he tried hard to let her win but the cracker broke the larger end on his side. He got the prizes. Life sucked when you couldn't even win in a cracker-pull.

'Can I give it to you?'

'Not the same.' Shook her head. Pretended to be miffed.

He raised his brows. 'But I can't wear two hats.'

Then she said, 'Men just don't understand women.'

Rayne looked at the woman beside him, 'I'm hearing you.' He held out the folded hat. She took it reluctantly, opened it out and put it on. He'd given her the red one to match her dress and she looked amazing in a stupid little paper hat. How did she do that? He felt like an idiot in his.

He decided to eat. It seemed they were last to reach for the food again but, then, they'd made inroads into the basket Louisa had sent with them to the lake. He was starting to feel sleepy and he wasn't sure if it was the fact he'd driven all night, though he'd slept most of yesterday after the flight. Or maybe Louisa's rum balls were catching up with him. He stifled a yawn.

'I'm a bitch.'

The piece of roast turkey that was on the way to his mouth halted in mid-air. 'Sorry?'

'You're tired. I'd forgotten you haven't slept.'

He had to smile at her mood swings. The idea that life would not be boring around Maeve returned with full force.

They ate companionably for a while, he answered a question from Louisa on how the drive had been and gradually relaxed a little more with the company. 'I'll snooze later. Isn't that what everyone does after Christmas lunch? Wash up and then lie around groaning and doze off until teatime?'

'You're eating off a paper plate. The washing up's been done.' She smiled at him and his belly kicked because he was damned if there wasn't a hint of promise in that smile. More than a hint.

She bent her head and spoke softly into his ear. 'Not everyone sleeps.'

Geez. He wasn't making love with Maeve when Simon's room was two doors down. Imagine if she went into labour and everybody knew he'd been the one responsible for the induction. His neck felt hot and he couldn't look at anyone at the table.

'Rayne?' She laid her hand on his leg and it was all he could do not to flinch. Since when had he ever been at this much of a loss? The problem was his libido was jumping up and down like a charged icon on a computer.

She yawned ostentatiously and stood up. 'Happy Christmas, everyone. I think I'll go put my feet up.'

'Bye, Maeve.' From Simon and the girls.

'Don't go into labour, Maeve. I'm too full,' Tara said.

She turned back to Rayne. 'You coming? I think we need to talk some more.'

His ears felt hot. He needed to get himself back on an even footing here. It seemed she'd turned into a militant dominatrix and while the idea of submitting to sex wasn't too abhorrent, it didn't fit with the very late pregnancy visual effect. And he wasn't enamoured by the smothered smiles of his lunch companions.

'Sure. I'll just help Louisa clear the table first.'

She narrowed her eyes at him. 'Fine.'

Hell. She'd said, '*Fine.*' Which meant she was emotional and he might just have heard a tiny wobble in the word, which meant maybe he should go and comfort her.

Louisa shooed him away. 'You cleared at breakfast. Off you go and help that girl put her feet up.'

He caught Simon's perplexed glance at his grandmother and then at him. They both shrugged. How did you help someone put their feet up? Either way, he'd had his marching orders from two women. Maybe he should get his own place or they'd have him emasculated before New Year.

He stood up. Gave Simon a mocking smile and walked after Maeve.

CHAPTER SEVEN

Resting after lunch

MAEVE HAD GOT as far as slipping her shoes off, she'd been stupid, telling him to follow her, and she'd better learn from her mistakes pretty damn quick if she didn't want to drive him away.

She stewed on that thought for a minute until she heard Rayne's quiet footsteps coming down the hall and she didn't know whether to sit on the bed, stand at the window, looking decorative, or just freeze where she was looking at the closed door like a rabbit in headlights.

Time took care of that because Rayne knocked, paused and then opened the door and put his head around. She didn't get time to do anything except feel her heart thumping like a bass drum.

It was the Rayne from nine months ago. Black brows slightly raised, eyes dark and dangerous, a tiny amused tilt to those wicked lips. 'Louisa said you needed a hand to get your feet up?'

She licked dry lips. 'You can come in.' But when he did push open the door and shut it again the room shrank to the size of a shoebox and they were two very close-together shoes. 'Um. I am a bit tired.'

He glanced at the queen-sized bed then back at her. Looked her over thoroughly. 'Want a hand getting your dress off?'

'Thanks.' She turned her back and once he'd worked out there was no zip and she only wanted him to help her lift it over her head, the task was accomplished in no time.

No real seduction in that swift removal. She tried not to sigh. While he was draping the dress carefully over the chair she was thinking as she sat on the bed, *Thank goodness I changed my stretchy granny undies for the cute lace pair.*

He seemed to be staring at her chest. 'Nice cleavage.' Well, at least he appreciated something.

He was so big and broad standing over her and she patted the quilt she was sitting on. She wished he'd take off *his* shirt. 'Are you staying?'

'Staying? As in coming to bed with you?'

'You did say everyone lies down after Christmas lunch?'

He sat on the bed beside her. Then he turned his head and looked her full in the face. 'I'm not going to have sex with you but I'm happy to lie beside you while you rest.'

She pulled a face at him. Her own desire to snuggle

up to him was withering like a dehydrating leaf. 'I wouldn't want to force you to do anything you didn't want to.'

He grinned at her but there was a definite flare in his dark eyes that left her in no doubt she was wrong. A flare that made all the saggy disappointment feelings sit up and take notice again. 'It's not that I don't want to get closer.' He was telling the truth and at least that made her feel a little bit better. 'But I think we need to talk a whole lot more before we fall into...' he hesitated, didn't even offer a word for what they were both thinking about '...first.'

Talk? When she was sitting here in her lacy bra and panties—admittedly with a huge shiny belly out in front—behind a closed door with all those pregnancy hormones saying ooh-ah. 'Talk?' She fought back another sigh. 'That sounds more like a girl thing than a guy thing.'

He shrugged, stood up again and then leaned down, slipped an arm behind her knees and the other under her shoulders and placed her in the middle of the bed. Oh, my, she loved the way he did that.

Then he bent, unlaced his shoes and removed them, loosened his belt and then sat back down on the bed in his jeans. Reached for the folded light sheet at the bottom of the bed she'd been resting under in the afternoons, swung his legs up and draped the sheet over both of them.

Then he slipped his arm around her shoulders so her head was resting on his chest and settled back.

She was still smarting from the 'not having sex with you' comment. 'Is this the pillow talk I missed out on last time?'

He didn't seem perturbed. 'You do have a nasty little bite when you don't get your own way, don't you?'

She hunched her shoulders. 'It comes with not knowing where I stand.'

'Well,' he said slowly, 'I see that. But I can't tell you what I don't know. And if you want me to make something up then you're resting your head on the wrong chest.'

It was not what she wanted to hear and yet it was. And this particular chest felt so good to lean on. She relaxed and snuggled in a little closer. 'So you're saying you won't lie to me.'

The sound of his heart beating in a slow, steady rhythm reverberated under her ear. God, she'd missed this. 'I won't lie to you.'

She lifted her other hand slowly and ran her fingertip down the strong bulge of his bicep. An unfairly sexy bicep. Her girl parts squirmed in remembered ecstasy. Conversation. Remember conversation. 'Not lying to me is a good start.'

'You're supposed to say you won't lie to me either.' She could tell he was dead serious. Fair enough.

She wriggled awkwardly, trying to shift her weight

until she'd managed to roll and could see his whole face. Said just as seriously, 'I will not lie to you.'

She couldn't read the expression in his eyes but his mouth was firm. 'So if you want me to go, you tell me. Not telling me is a lie too.'

She frowned at him. 'I'm not sure I want to hear about it if you want to go.' Then she sighed and lay back down again. 'But I guess that's fair.'

He was shaking his head. 'You don't understand and you need to get where I'm coming from. I may not be good at this whole father thing, Maeve. I'll try but I don't have a lot of family experience, and no paternal role model, to draw on.' She could hear the slight thread of panic in his voice. Had to remind herself that a few hours ago this guy had had no idea he would be having a child some time in the next few days.

She thought about his 'no family experience' statement. Well, she guessed he'd never had a father to learn from or even subconsciously copy. Maybe he was finding that pretty daunting. 'Did you know your father at all?'

'Nope. I asked. All my mother said was he was dead and didn't offer any clues. Not even his name. And my mum wasn't into men staying over so no "special" uncles. If she spent the night with a man, she usually stayed out.'

Maeve thought about that. 'So when you were young you stayed home alone? At night?'

Maeve squeezed his arm in sympathy and Rayne

could feel himself begin to freeze her out. Had to force himself to let her offer comfort because if he was going to try to make this work he had to at least attempt to learn to do these things too. Apparently it was what families did and he needed to at least give it a shot.

He dispelled the myth that he had been alone. 'We lived in a dingy block of flats. You were never alone. You could always hear people in the other units.'

She nodded against him. 'So you never got scared on your own at night?'

He nearly said no. But he'd said he wouldn't lie. 'When I was younger I got scared. Especially if someone was shouting or I could hear someone yelling on the footpath. The worst was if a woman screamed down on the street. I always worried it was my mum and I wasn't doing anything to help her.'

He'd never told anyone that. Didn't know why he'd told Maeve. He moved on and hoped she would forget he'd said it. 'Guess I'd make sure my kid was never left alone until they wanted to be left.'

She squeezed him again. 'Perhaps your mum thought the people she was with were more disturbing than the idea of you being alone.'

His mum had actually said something like that. He hadn't believed her. Had there been a grain of truth in it after all? And Maeve had picked up on it all these years later. 'You don't judge her, do you? My mother?'

Maeve shrugged on his chest. 'Who am I to judge? I know nothing about her. I just know I've always admired you and she must have had a part in that. She was your mother.'

That heavy carpenter's rasp was back down his throat. Sawing up and down and ripping the skin off his tonsils. Or at least that's what it felt like as his throat closed. He searched for some moisture in his mouth. 'Even when I said I'd been in prison because of her, you were sad for me that she was dead.'

He'd been thinking about that a lot. Couldn't get his head around the fact that Maeve saw the part of him he hadn't shown to many people. Except Simon. But he doubted her brother would have discussed it with his little sister.

She snuggled harder and his arm protested and began to cramp. He told it to shut up.

Then she said, 'Even though you didn't meet your father, I think you'll be a good dad. And you certainly tried to look after your mum from a very young age. You're probably better father material than many men who had dads.'

He grimaced at the fact that maybe he had become a little parental with his mum, but that didn't change the fact he hadn't been able to save her.

Maeve was like a dog with a bone. 'You'll be fine. You're a paediatrician so at least you're good with kids.' She settled back. The law according to Maeve.

'At least I'm that,' he said dryly. 'I'm good with sick kids.' And especially the ones who were left alone and needed company.

She went on, 'I was too young to understand about how you grew up. You always looked tough and capable when I saw you.'

Rayne listened to her voice, the husky tigress lilt tamed a little now, and thought about what she'd said. So he'd appeared tough and capable. He guessed he had been. By the time she'd been in her early teens he'd almost grown out of his, and his mum had begun to need a bit more care taken of her. A couple of dangerous overdoses. A problem with her supplier that had left her badly bruised. The way she'd forgotten to eat. She'd had two close shaves with the law and had told him if she ever got convicted she would die if she went to prison.

The last years had been a downward spiral and he'd tried most things to halt it. The number of rehab centres, fresh towns, health kicks they'd tried. Things would go well for a few months and he'd get tied up at work. Miss a couple of days dropping in then she'd start to use again.

The best she'd been had been in Santa Monica. She'd looked young for the first time in years. Had got a job as a doctor's receptionist at one of the clinics he worked from in the poorer area, a place where kids who needed care they normally couldn't afford could access a range of different doctors. And she'd been good at it.

She had connected well with the people who didn't need anyone to look down on them. He'd valued the once a week he'd donated his time there, away from the upmarket private hospital he'd worked in the rest of the time. And he'd cheered to see her making a life for herself. Fool.

Until the day she'd worked and gone home early. It had been his day as well and he'd finished late. Locked up. The investigation had been well in progress by the time he'd found out all the drugs had been stolen. Had known immediately who it had been. He hadn't been able to track her down anywhere until finally she'd rung him. Pleading. Promising she would never, ever, touch anything ever again, if he would say it was him. That this was her chance to go clean for life.

He'd hoped maybe it was true and that she would stop using. Then had begun to realise the fingers had been pointing to him anyway. So he'd made a conscious decision to try a last attempt at saving her.

He'd tried ringing Simon so he wouldn't find out from someone else that he would probably be going to prison. Hadn't been able to give the explanation on the phone and had had that ridiculous idea to fly out, explain and then fly back in twenty-four hours. He'd thought he should have just about that much time before it all came crashing down. Before the police came for him!

'Hey,' Maeve whispered, but she wasn't talking to him. The belly beside him rolled and shifted and his eyes fixed on the movement, mesmerised. He glanced quickly at Maeve, who was watching him with a gentle smile on her face, lifted his hand and put his palm on the satin skin. And the creature below poked him with something bony.

Geez. He looked back at Maeve.

'Cool, isn't it?' she said softly. And put her hand over his. And he realised with a big shift of emotion that the three of them were together for the first time. 'He likes you.'

His eyes jerked to her face. 'It's a he?'

She laughed. 'I really don't know. Just find myself calling him he. Maybe because you weren't here.' He winced at that.

'Might be a girl.' She shrugged. 'I really don't care which.'

'I hope she looks like you.'

She looked at him as if she were peering over a pair of glasses at him. 'Why on earth would you want your son to look like me?'

'Okay. A boy could be like me but it would be very sweet to have a little girl who looks like you.' Then he spoilt it all by unexpectedly yawning.

She laughed. 'You need a nap more than I do. Why don't you take your jeans off? We can talk more later. Then you can roll over and I'll cuddle you.'

'Bossy little thing.' But suddenly he felt morbidly tired and he did what he was told, not least because his arm had gone totally to sleep now and his jeans were digging into him.

When he climbed back onto the bed and rolled to face the door, she snuggled up to him as close as her big tummy would allow. It actually felt amazing when his child wriggled against him. Geez.

Maeve listened to Rayne's breathing change and she lay there, staring at his dark T-shirt plastered against his strong shoulders as he went to sleep.

She tried to imagine Rayne as a little boy, from a time when his first memories had begun to stick. Dark, silky hair, strong little legs and arms, big, dark eyes wondering when Mummy would be home.

It hurt her heart. She wanted to hug that little boy and tell him she'd never leave him scared again. How old had he been when his mother had begun to leave him? She had a vague recollection of hearing Simon say to her parents that Rayne's mum hadn't started using drugs until after something bad had happened when Rayne had gone to school.

She wondered what had happened to Rayne's poor mum. Something that bad? It couldn't have been easy, bringing up a child alone with very little money.

Her childhood had been so blessed. Always her hero brother Simon and three older sisters to look after her, as well as both well-adjusted parents, although her mum was pretty definite on social niceties.

Her dad was a fair bit older than her mum, but he'd always been quietly there, and her mother had come from a wealthy family and always been a determined woman. She'd been spoilt by her dad, but had sometimes felt as if she wasn't quite enough of a star for her mother. Hence the try-hard attitude she really needed to lose.

She would be thankful for all her blessings of family and now having this gorgeous, damaged man appear just when she needed him. He hadn't run. He'd promised to stay at least until after the birth. Had tried to fit into a strange family's Christmas Day, which must be pretty damn hard when he was still reeling from being in prison and adjusting to society again, and he'd just found out he'd fathered a child.

She stared again at the powerful neck and short hair in front of her eyes and the way the thick strands clung to his skull like heavy silk. Resisted the urge to move her hand from around his chest to touch it as she didn't want to wake him, but her fingers curled.

She could imagine her baby having hair just that colour, though, of course, hers was black like her dad's as well, so the kid didn't have much choice. But she would think of it as his father's hair. Would he have Rayne's eyes and mouth too?

Imagine.

A long slow pulling sensation surged in her belly from under her breasts down to her pubic bone, growing tighter and then after a while easing off. Just one.

Braxton-Hicks. Practice contractions. Not painful. Just weird, as if the baby was stretching out straight. But she knew it wasn't. Soon they would come more frequently. Maybe for a couple of hours at a time and then stop. For a few days probably. She'd told other women this so many times, but it was strange when it was yourself you were reassuring.

This time she'd welcomed it without the accompanying flare of nervousness she'd been fighting for weeks. Giving birth was a job that needed to be done and now that Rayne was here the time was right. Whatever happened, whatever her birth journey was meant to be, Rayne would be there to share it all. The best Christmas present of all.

Rayne woke an hour later, straight from dreaming about Maeve. Like he'd woken nearly every day for the last nine months. Except this time he really had her in his arms, his hands really were cupping her glorious breasts, her taut backside really was snuggled into his erection, which was growing exponentially with confirmation of the contact.

They must have rolled in their sleep.

She murmured drowsily, not yet awake, and languidly backed into him a little more. Unconsciously, his hands slid over her belly, pulling her closer.

The little person inside that belly nudged him and he recoiled in startled appreciation of where his actions were leading. 'Sorry,' he murmured, and slid his hands down to the sides of Maeve's abdomen, but Maeve was having none of it. Took his hands and placed them back on her breasts. Wriggled into him.

'Have mercy, Maeve,' he whispered in her ear, but he couldn't help the smile that grew on his face. She wriggled against him again and he groaned. Slid his rear end across the bed to make room for her to shift and turned her to face him. 'You are a menace.'

'And you feel so good against me,' she whispered back drowsily. Then tilted her face for a kiss, and there was no way he could resist those lips, that mouth, or keep it to one kiss. And the gentle salute turned into a banquet of sliding salutations and memories that resurfaced from all those months ago. How they matched each other for movements, timing, a connection between them that had him pulling her closer, but the big belly in the middle made everything awkward, yet erotic, and he must be the most debauched man on earth to want to make love to this woman who was so close to giving birth.

As if she'd read his mind, she said, 'If we don't make love now, you'll have to wait for ages.'

He really hadn't thought of that. 'Maybe we should wait.' But he seriously didn't want to. And she obviously didn't. Nine months of fantasy and the woman of his dreams was demanding he make love to her.

No-brainer really.

In the Maeve fog that was clouding his mind he wasn't really sure what he'd been thinking to knock her back before.

Still in the fog, he slid from the bed, ripped his T-shirt off his head in one movement and kicked off his briefs. Knelt back down and dropped a big kiss right between Maeve's awesome assets. Geez, he loved her breasts.

He slid his hands around her back and unclasped her bra. Sighed as the two gorgeous spheres eased out of the restraining material like big, soft plump peaches. The circular areolas surrounding her nipples were dark peach, highlighted for a tiny baby to find easily, and he skimmed his fingers across in awe while she watched him with a womanly smile as old as the ages.

He swallowed to ease the dryness in his throat. 'They say pregnant women in the third trimester of pregnancy have erotic dreams and surges of erotic desires.'

'That's very true,' she whispered, pulling him closer and tilting her mouth for him to kiss again. When they paused for breath there was no concept of stopping. But he was doing this right, and gently, and he wanted to show her just how beautiful she was in his mind and in his heart. 'Then we'd better take our time.'

CHAPTER EIGHT

Labour and birth

WHEN MAEVE WOKE up Rayne was gone. But the contraction tightenings weren't gone. That darned love hormone.

She did not want to have this baby on Christmas Day. It was okay for baby Jesus. He'd never been materialistic, but Maeve knew how she'd feel about the one day of the year that belonged to everyone, in her corner of her world anyway. But it was her own fault.

Still, she could not regret this afternoon in Rayne's arms. She smiled a long, slow, satisfied smile. Regret definitely wasn't the word that sprang to mind.

Revel, ravish, rolling around with… Scraping the bottom of the barrel there, but *reaaaalllyyy* amazing just about covered it. Her skin flushed at the thought of how wonderful he'd been, so unhurried, showing her a world of gentleness that had brought tears to her eyes. He had paid homage to her body, coveted her belly, and just plain loved her, something she'd missed so badly as her body had changed, and he had banished for ever the idea he wasn't the man for her.

Which was an excellent thing if she was about to have his baby.

Another contraction followed on the thought. That love hormone again.

She glanced at the clock. It was seven-thirty in the evening. Almost sunset. Less than five hours until midnight. 'Hang in there, baby.'

She climbed awkwardly out of bed. Pulled on a robe and gathered something light to wear for the evening. Something comfortable like a sarong. They'd probably sit out the back or go for a leisurely walk along the lake. Another contraction tightened her belly, this time with a little bit of discomfort.

They were still not lasting long but she guessed she wasn't going to go too far from home. At least there was no car journey involved, like there would have been if she lived in the city. Here, they'd just pick up Tara from the room down the hall—she grinned at that, same house—then walk across the road to the birth centre. It was all pretty streamlined, actually. Almost a home birth without the organising of equipment involved.

Rayne would be stressed. Simon would worry. But she would be calm. Could be calm now because she deputised other people to do the worrying and from this moment on she would have faith in her body, in a natural process she was designed to achieve. It was exciting really. And Tara would be there. She giggled. She hoped Tara had digested her lunch by now.

She thought about giggles. That's right. In early labour you apparently felt like giggling. The fact labour had finally arrived after all the waiting. Happy hormones. She grinned in the mirror. Actually, she did feel like giggling. Even the fact that she knew this would pass onto harder and stronger contractions was funny. At the moment, anyway. No doubt she'd change her mind later.

She slipped out of the bedroom door and into the bathroom with a smile on her face. She could hear the rumble of Simon and Rayne's voices coming from the kitchen. The thought made her feel warm. She would not have believed the change in her world in the last day. It was like she'd been released from her own prison. That thought put her feet back on the ground. She shouldn't joke about it. Rayne really had been released from prison.

She hung the robe on the hook at the back of the door, climbed into the shower and relaxed again as she revelled—there was that word again—in the hot water that soothed any tension away from her shoulders. Another contraction started its slow rise in intensity and consciously she sent all the negative thoughts down the drain with the soapy water, and breathed out.

Still ten minutes apart, plenty of time to tell people. She just wanted to hug the excitement and her baby to herself. This was the last day that she and her baby would be together so intimately. A miracle in itself.

She stayed in the shower for a long time.

Until Rayne knocked on the door. 'You okay in there?' A hint of concern in his voice.

She had to wait for the contraction to stop before she could answer. They were getting stronger but that was a good thing. More powerful, not more painful, she reminded herself. A tiny voice inside muttered about that not being true but she ignored it. The pain eased.

'I'm fine.' Wow. Her voice sounded kind of spacy. Endorphins.

'Can I come in?'

'Sure,' she breathed. Then had to repeat it a bit louder. 'Come in.'

Rayne pushed open the door and a cloud of steam billowed out past his head. He waved it away and stepped into the bathroom. 'You've been in here for ages.' He crossed the tiles to the corner shower. Stood outside the curtain. 'Is there something I should know?'

He waited. She didn't answer and he could hear her breathing. Eventually he pulled back the curtain so he could see her. She smiled at him and he thought she looked almost half-asleep. Looked again. Now, that was something you didn't see every day. A glistening wet, very rounded, amazingly breasted, porcelain pregnant lady naked in the shower, with her black hair curling on her shoulders.

She said, 'If we ever live together, you'll need a very large hot-water system.'

He had to smile at that. He assumed Louisa did own one of those if this house could sleep twelve. 'I'm getting that.'

'And also,' she went on in the same distant voice, 'my contractions are about seven minutes apart.'

His heart rate doubled and then he slumped against the wall. Sex fiend. He'd done that. Come on. Pull yourself together. You're a doctor, for crikey's sake.

'Is that a good thing?' he asked cautiously. Who knew what Maeve was thinking? He was trying to be supportive because that was his job, and he'd agreed without coercion when, in fact, he wanted to run screaming to Simon.

'As long as baby waits till after midnight, that's fine.'

Rayne glanced at his watch. Eight o'clock. Four hours until midnight. Of course she'd have her own way and the baby would wait. Four hours of stress.

'Shall I go and tell Simon? Or Tara?'

'No hurry.'

It was all very well to say that, along with some heavy breathing, and he observed, as if from a long way away, that his fingers were white where he was clutching the handrail. 'You sure?'

'Mmm-hmm…' Loud exhalation.

Geez. Rayne prised his fingers off the towel rail and

straightened off the wall. 'Um. Might just mention it to them in case they want to go out.' Though where they would go on Christmas night was a mystery.

Quietly, on an out breath, an answer came from the shower. 'Okay.'

Rayne left and he wasn't quite jogging. He skidded into the kitchen but it was empty. Typical. This house had crawled with people all day and now he couldn't find anyone when he needed them. Even Louisa was missing but he guessed she, out of all of them, deserved a rest.

Poked his head out the back door but the darkening yard, a space that had seen so many Campbells, was deserted.

He went back inside, walked down the hallway, but both Simon and Tara's doors were ajar and he guessed if they were in there they'd have closed the doors. He went out to the front veranda in case they were sitting on that bench, looking at the nodding animals, and he was distracted for a minute by the fairy-lights that had come on with the sunset. Nobody there. He glared at the manger. Mary and Joseph had had their baby in a manger, with animals and wise men, so what was his problem?

He ran his hand distractedly through his hair. Took a deep breath. It was okay. Maeve was calm. Happy even. The hospital was across the road for pity's sake. He could see the porch lights. All he had to do was be a support person.

It would have been nice to have that 'couples' discussion with Tara that he'd had a knee-jerk reaction about today before Maeve had gone into labour. But, *no-o-o*, Maeve had had to have nookie.

What was it he'd learnt in med school? A first-time mum, after a slow start while the contractions got sorted out, dilated about a centimetre an hour. To get to ten centimetres was ten hours. Right? Or maybe she was already six centimetres then it would be four hours. Or less if she'd got there this quickly. His mind was spinning faster than the wheels of the new Christmas push-bike some happy, oblivious-to-the-drama-inside kid was pedalling past too late to be out.

He forced himself to take another breath. Yesterday he would not have believed all this was going to happen. Yesterday he had been wondering if she would see him. Today she was his responsibility.

Well, he'd been in at the beginning so he had to stay for the hard part.

'Rayne?' He spun round and Maeve was leaning on the door to the front veranda. She looked like she'd just stepped off a plane from Fiji, with a hibiscus sarong wrapped around her and not much else. He could see her cleavage from here.

'Why are you staring at the manger?'

He wasn't looking at the manger now. Cleavage. 'Umm. Looking for Tara and Simon.'

She leant her head on the doorframe. 'They're on

the side veranda outside their rooms, watching the stars come out.'

He strode back across the lawn and up the steps to her side. 'Okay. You okay?'

'I'm fine. But I'd sort of like you to stay with me.'

'Yep. Of course.' He was obviously really bad at this support-person caper. Where was the midwife? 'So did you tell Tara?'

'I wanted to find you first.'

Not the choice he would have made. 'Fine. Let's do it now.'

'You said *fine*…'

She leant against his arm and smiled up at him and as if she'd pressed a button he leant down and kissed her lips in an automatic response. Just one day and they had an automatic response?

He stepped back. Must have picked up on some of her endorphins because he could feel his panic settle a little. *Fine.* Yep, he had been feeling freaked out, inse-cure, neurotic and emotional.

His voice softened, lowered, and he gently turned her back towards the house. 'How can you be so calm?'

'I've had nine months to think about this happening. You've had twelve hours.'

Had it only been twelve hours? It felt like twelve days. But, then, that's how things seemed to happen around Maeve and him. Acceleration with the pedal pressed and they were driving off into the future at a hundred miles an hour.

'Do you do anything slowly?' he said as they walked down the hall. He grinned at her. 'Apart from the way you're walking up the hallway now.'

'I put my make-up on slowly.'

'Does that mean if I took you out I'd be one of those guys hanging around waiting for his woman to get ready?'

'I might speed up for you.' Then her face changed and she stopped, closed her eyes as she leant against him. He lifted his hand and rested it on her arm and her shoulder dropped its tension beneath his fingers as if he'd told her to relax, and it startled him.

She sighed out, 'Boy, I can tell these contractions are doing the job.'

That was good. Wasn't it? 'We still waiting for midnight?'

'No choice now. It's all up to baby. You just have to hold my hand for the ride.'

He could do that. Glanced down at her hand, thin and suddenly fragile looking, as they set off again. 'It would be an honour,' he said very quietly. And it would be. She was blowing him away with her strength and serenity.

Simon and Tara, also holding hands again—spare me, he thought—appeared in the hallway and Maeve had a contraction before he could say anything.

Tara let go of Simon's fingers with a smile and went towards them. No need to say anything. So he didn't. Wasn't really his place anyway.

And they didn't ask. Their restraint was amazing and he could only follow their lead.

When the contraction was over, Tara murmured, 'Good job. When did they start?'

'About an hour ago.'

'So what do you feel like doing?' Tara was walking beside Maeve as they drifted down the hallway to the kitchen. Simon smiled at Rayne.

'You should see your face.'

'Shut up.' But there was relief and he felt the smile cross his own face. 'Geez, mate. Yesterday none of this was happening.'

'I know. In that context you're actually doing well. But open your letters next time.'

Rayne gave him a hard look. 'Try being where I was and you might not feel so sure about that.'

The smile fell from Simon's face. 'You're right. But I would never do something as stupidly noble as that. But I should have known you would. I'm sorry I was so quick to believe in your guilt.'

Rayne heard Maeve laugh at something Tara had said and looked at Simon and dropped the whole subject. This wasn't about him. Or Simon. 'How can she laugh?'

They both walked towards the kitchen. 'See, that's why I chose obstetrics over paediatrics.'

Rayne thought about the stress he'd been under already. 'You think giving birth is funny? It's a wonder you haven't been killed.'

Simon laughed again and it felt good to loosen the tension between them. The dynamics were certainly tricky. Especially if he didn't make the grade to stay around for the long haul. But he would worry about that later.

'Rayne?' Maeve's voice.

He quickened his pace and left Simon behind. 'I'm here.'

'I want to go in the bath and Tara thinks it might be easier if I don't have to move from this bath here to the one in the birth centre. So maybe we should go over there fairly soon.'

'Sounds sensible to me.' Sounded amazingly sensible. A hospital, or a birth centre at least with a hospital next door.

Louisa appeared. Caught on very quickly what was happening. 'I'll pack a hamper.'

He looked at her. Felt more tension ease from his shoulders. 'You have a feeding fetish.'

'Must have.' She winked at him. 'I'm too old for any other kind of fetish.'

Simon and the two girls looked at her in comical surprise but Louisa was off to do her stuff.

'I'll see you over there,' Tara said. 'I'll go ahead and run the bath and then come back. We can check baby out when you get there. Take your time, unless you feel you have to hurry.'

What sort of advice was that? Rayne thought with a little flutter of his nervousness coming back. He for one felt like they had to hurry. But Maeve was nodding and doing a go-slow. She didn't even look like making a move.

Simon said he'd leave them to it. Maybe go and see his dad and let him know what was going on.

Rayne watched him go and thought, So the obstetrician leaves? He looked towards Maeve's bedroom. 'Do you have a bag packed?'

'Yep.' She was just standing there with a strange little smile on her face, looking out the window at the Christmas fairy-lights in the back yard. The clock on the wall ticked over a minute. And then another. He felt like ants were crawling all over him.

'Um. You want me to go and get the bag?'

She turned her head and smiled vaguely at him. 'You could.'

So how was he supposed to find it? This must be the kind of stuff normal people talked about when they were planning to have a baby. People who had more than twelve hours' notice they were going to be a support person in a labour. The woman would say, "My bag is in my wardrobe if we need it. My slippers are under the bed." Bathroom kits and baby clothes would have all been discussed. Baby names!

He tamped down his panic again. 'Where is the bag?'

'Behind the door.'

At last. He could do something. He looked at Maeve as if she might explode if he left, and then turned and strode up the hallway for the bag. Was back within seconds.

'Do you need anything else?'

She blinked. Smiled. 'Are you trying to organise me?'

Sprung. 'Uh. Just making sure everything is ready when you want to go.'

'It's really important—' she was speaking slowly as if to a child who wasn't listening '—that the birthing woman is the one who decides when to go to the birth centre. She has to feel like she *needs* to be somewhere else before she leaves the place she feels safe in *now*.'

'So this is what you tell women in antenatal classes? About when they go to the hospital?'

'And the men,' she said with a patronising smile.

They went across to the birthing centre at nine o'clock. Walked across the road, slowly, because Maeve had to stop every few minutes. The stars were out. Christmas night. The air was still warm and Maeve was wearing the sarong.

He had her overnight bag over his shoulder, the hamper from Louisa in one hand and Maeve's elbow in the other.

'It's a beautiful night,' Maeve said after a very long drawn-out breath.

Yes. Yes, beautiful, he thought. *Come on.* 'Yep. You okay?'

She had another contraction and they stopped again.

Tara met them at the door. Nobody else was in labour so they had the place to themselves.

The midwife on duty was over at the hospital but would come across for the birth.

Angus was the doctor on call for obstetrics and would wait outside the door in case they needed him. All these things he found out in the first three minutes because he had requests, too! He really didn't know if he could handle a lifetime of responsibility for Maeve. What if something went wrong?

Tara sent him to make tea because Maeve needed to go to the ladies and he was pacing outside the door.

He was back too quickly.

He could feel Tara's eyes on him and he looked at her.

'Maeve is low risk, Rayne,' Tara said. 'It's her first baby. She's here on the day before the baby is due. Her waters haven't broken. She has no infections. Her blood pressure is normal. She's only been in labour for two hours at the most.' A sympathetic look. 'Why are you worried?'

'It's my first baby too?'

'Sure. I get that.'

He didn't think she did. 'I'm a paediatrician. They only called me for the babies that might need help and I've seen a lot of very sick babies. I guess my idea of normal birth is a bit skewed.' Or more than a bit, and in any case he'd only found out about this baby today.

'I get that too. But Maeve's baby will be fine.'

He wanted to believe that. 'What if it isn't?'

'Then we will manage. It's what we do.' She glanced around the homey birthing room for inspiration, or at least something that would reassure him. 'Why don't you check the equipment? And the resuscitation trolley? All the drugs on the trolley? Check the suckers and oxygen.'

He couldn't help his horror showing in his face. 'You haven't checked those?'

She actually laughed. 'Yes, Dr Walters, I have checked those. But I'm trying to distract you!'

'Oh.' Now he felt dumb. 'Sorry.' He put his finger under the collar of his T-shirt because suddenly it felt tight.

Tara's voice was gentle. 'Maybe doing those things would be helpful if Angus called you in an emergency in the next few weeks.'

He sighed. Get a grip. Thank goodness Tara did have a sense of humour. 'Sorry. It's just been pretty sudden. I'm not normally such a panic merchant.'

She looked at him. 'I have no doubt that's true. I think you've done exceptionally well, considering the scenario you've fallen into. But here's the thing.' Her voice dropped and her face was kind but serious and she glanced at the closed bathroom door. He started to wonder if Maeve and Tara had cooked up this pep talk for him between them.

He guessed he'd never know.

'I need you to be calm. I need you to be Maeve's rock. You don't need to say much—just be here. Agree

with her. She really wanted you to be here. And hold
her hand when she wants you to. Rub her back when
she wants you to. Okay?'

He took a big calming breath. 'Okay.'

'No more panic vibes, please. And in the meantime
you can familiarise yourself with the equipment only
if you need distraction.'

Okay. He got that. The bathroom door opened and
Maeve came out. He sat quietly in the corner of the
room while Tara felt Maeve's abdomen, discussed the
lie of the baby, which was apparently pointing in exactly
the direction and attitude they wanted, and listened to
his baby's heartbeat.

Geez. That was his baby's heartbeat. Cloppety, cloppety, clop. It was fast. He knew foetal hearts were fast.
But was that too fast?

Calm. He needed to be calm. Dissociate. That was
the answer. Pretend it wasn't his baby. Okay. He felt
calmer. In fact, he felt in total control. It was cool. Normal heart rate.

'Rayne?'

'Yes, Maeve.'

'Can you hear our baby's heartbeat?'

'Yes, I can. It seems very fast!'

Tara looked at him with eyebrows raised.

He racked his brains. 'Baby must be as excited as
we are.'

Maeve laughed. 'That is so cute.'

Cute. Geez. He stood up. Might go check the equipment.

* * *

The next hour was traumatic.

Then Maeve decided to get out of the bath and the hour after that was even worse.

But baby was fine. Heart rate perfect, with no slowing after contractions. Rayne's heart rate slowed after the contractions because during the contraction it doubled. And not just because he was rubbing Maeve's back non-stop.

Between contractions Maeve was calm. Rational. Gathering her strength for the next wave. During contractions it was hell.

Noisy. Intense. Painful when she had his hand in hers and dug her nails in.

Tara was the rock. Quiet. Steady. Unflappable. Like the calm in the storm. He'd look across at her when a contraction was at its height and she would be smiling. Gentle and calm. This was Maeve's profession as well. How did these women do this day in, day out?

'I am so going to be at your birth, Tara,' Maeve ground out as the contraction finally eased.

'Good. We'll swap places.'

Rayne shook his head. How could they carry on a normal conversation when two minutes ago she was ready to rip all their heads off?

And then it was time to push. Eleven forty-five p.m. He looked at Maeve. It had been incredibly hard work. Perspiration beaded her brow, and he leant across and wiped it.

'Hey, Rayne,' she said softly. 'You okay?'

How could she possibly care about him when she was going through hell? 'As long as you're okay, I'm okay.'

'I'm fine.'

He smiled. 'I'm *fine* too.'

She smiled back wearily. 'Home straight now.'

There had been a bit of a lull in the contractions after a series of torrid strong ones. 'So why has it stopped?'

'Nature's way of giving us a break before the last stretch.' Then her face changed. 'Oh.'

The next twenty minutes would be forever etched in his mind. Angus was outside the door in case he was needed. He'd checked, but they didn't see him. Simon had arrived as well but was waiting to be invited in afterwards. He'd bet there was some pacing happening out there. As much as he was suffering in here, it would have been a hundred times worse imagining outside the door. Especially with the Maeve soundtrack they had playing.

With each pushing contraction a little more of the baby shifted down. The excitement was building and Maeve was much more focused now she could use the contractions to make things happen. If there was one thing his Maeve could do, it was make things happen.

Maeve was impatient. No surprise there. She moved position several times, kneeling, leaning on a ball, leaning on Rayne. Even sitting on the toilet, but that stressed him out until Tara smiled and put a towel over the toilet seat so he could stop envisaging his baby falling into the toilet bowl. But eventually they were standing beside the bed, and he could actually see the hair on his baby's head.

'You're doing well,' Tara said.

Well? Doing well? She was freaking amazing, incredible. 'Come on, Maeve. You're nearly there, babe.' He saw her glance at the clock and register it was a few minutes after midnight. She'd got what she wanted, and she looked at him.

Triumph, thankfulness and new determination, and he realised it would never be the same between them again. But that was okay. He could admit she was stronger than him. In some ways, anyway. Maeve turned to face him. 'I want to sit back on the bed against the pillows.'

So he lifted her and put her back on the pillows. 'Love that,' she panted, and even in that moment their eyes met and she tempted him. Then she relaxed back against the pillows, hugging her knees, and gave one long outward sigh. And suddenly the crown appeared then a head of black hair, stretched into a face, one shoulder and then the other.

'Want to take it from here, Rayne?' Tara murmured, and he got it instantly. He stepped in and put his hands under his baby's armpits and, gently eased with the pressure Maeve was exerting, his baby entered the world with his own hands around him in a rush of belly, thighs, long legs and feet and a tangle of cord and water—and suddenly in a huge internal shift and crack through the wall of years of keeping emotion at bay, tears were streaming down his face.

Maeve was staring down with surprise and he lifted the squirming buddle of...? He glanced between the legs, grinned. 'It's a boy!' His eyes met hers and for that moment, when she looked at the baby, and then him and then the baby again, he didn't see how anything could ever stand between them.

His son cried. Loudly and lustily, and Maeve gathered him and snuggled him up against her breasts, and the baby's cries quieted instantly.

Boob man. Chip off the old block. He experienced such a swell of emotion his heart felt like it was going to burst.

In shock he saw the second midwife—where had she come from?—lean in to dry the little legs and arms and belly and rub the damp hair before she stepped back and replaced the damp towel with a warm bunny rug over them both until the baby was in a Maeve skin and bunny-rug sandwich.

Tara delivered the placenta and then a big warm hospital blanket covered Maeve's legs and belly and arms until finally her baby was tucked snugly with just his downy cheek against his mother, turned sideways toward Rayne, with big dark eyes and little squashed nose, and deep pink rosebud lips and a gorgeous mouth like Maeve's. And it was done.

His chest felt tight. 'Hello, there, buddy,' Rayne said softly.

He glanced at the clock. Ten past twelve. Boxing Day baby. Eighteen hours after arriving in Lyrebird Lake here he was—a father. New responsibility swamped him.

CHAPTER NINE

Emergency

MAEVE LAY THERE with the weight of her son on her chest, feeling the little wriggles on the outside of her body instead of the inside as he shifted. Could smell the unmistakable scent of new babies, and blood, and almost taste the relief in the room.

Why were they all worried? She had this. She looked at Rayne, who was sinking into the chair beside the bed that Tara had pulled up for him, unnaturally pale. His hand was halfway to the baby and hung suspended in the air as if he didn't know whether to touch or not.

'He's your son,' she whispered. Wishing he would kiss her. As if he'd heard her, he half stood and leaned across and kissed her lips. His hand drifted down and he touched the downy cheek of their child.

'Thank you. He's amazing. You were incredible.' He blinked a couple of times. 'Are you okay?'

'Buzzing,' she said, and grinned at him, and he shook his head and sank back in the chair. Looked like Rayne had aged ten years, she thought to herself. Still, the years sat well on him.

She glanced at Tara, who was taking her blood pressure. Waited until she was finished and then caught her hand. 'Thanks, Tara.'

Tara smiled mistily. 'I'm going to hold you to that promise.'

'Why? Because you know you'll be much quieter than me?'

Tara laughed. 'You always will be more outspoken than I am. You tell it like it is. Fabulous birth. I loved it.'

She glanced back at Rayne, who was looking at them both as if they were mad.

Tara said, 'Can Simon and Angus come in now? Then everyone will go away so you three can get to know each other.'

Maeve looked at Rayne, who left it up to her, so Simon and Angus came in.

After congratulations Tara took Angus aside, and Maeve could distantly hear that they were discussing the labour and birth, the blood loss, which had been a little more than usual but had settled now, and she saw Simon pump Rayne's hand.

'You look ten years younger, Simon.' Maeve teased him, as he leaned in to kiss her.

'I gave them to Rayne. You, sister, dear, are a worry that thankfully is not mine any more.' He slapped Rayne on the back. 'Welcome to parenthood, Rayne. It's never going to be the same again.'

Rayne still looked in shock. For a tough guy that was pretty funny. 'I get that premonition.'

'You look pale,' Simon said.

'I feel pale.' Rayne glanced across at the new baby, a baby with his own huge dark eyes and maybe it was his mouth.

Maeve remembered a new mother telling her once that when her baby had been first born she could see all the familial likenesses but after a couple of hours she'd only been able to see her baby as whole. Maeve tried to imprint the separate features before that happened. She could see his father's stamp as plainly as if there was a big arrow pointing to it. The brows and nose were from her side.

Rayne shook his head and smiled at her and she soaked up like a hungry sponge the amazed awe he was exuding in bucketloads. She must look a mess but for once she didn't care.

Maeve relaxed back in the bed, letting the euphoria wash over her. She'd always loved watching the way new mums seemed to have this sudden surge of energy, and now she was feeling it herself. She did feel that if she needed to, she could pick up her baby and run and save them both. Probably needed a few more clothes on for that, though, or she'd be scaring people.

She'd discarded the sarong hours ago. Clothes had seemed too much of an annoying distraction in the maelstrom of labour. Her baby wriggled and began to suck his fingers on her chest. His head lay between her breasts with his cheek over her heart, and she smiled mistily down at him. Next he would dribble on his fingers then he would start to poke and rub her with his wet hands as his instincts began to take over.

Yep, he was doing that now, she was careful not to distract him as his little head lifted and he glanced around.

Simon and Angus left and she barely noticed as she saw her baby look and sniff for the dark areolas and the nipple he would find a way to arrive at.

'Watch him,' she whispered to Rayne, who leaned closer. 'He'll bob his head and wriggle and find his own way to where he needs to go.'

The baby's hands were kneading the softness of her breast under his tiny fingers, and his pink knees had drawn up under his belly as if he was going to crawl. 'Can't you just move him there?' Rayne said quietly.

'I could, but he needs to do a sequence. He needs to learn to poke out his tongue before he attaches, and he'll get there under his own steam at just the right moment.'

'He's only half an hour old.'

'That's why a baby stays skin to skin on his mother's chest for that first hour. Shouldn't get nursed by anyone else or have needles or get weighed or anything. It gives them the chance to do all this and the breastfeeding rates go through the roof if the baby attaches by himself. You watch.'

Baby was bobbing his head up and down like a little

jack-in-the-box, and Maeve saw him narrow his gaze on the left nipple and lean towards it. Tiny jerking movements, and shoulder leans, and hand scrunching, and slowly his body changed angle, his neck stretched, and incredibly he was almost there. Another wriggle and head bob and stretch, a series of little tongue peeps as he began to edge closer.

'Come on, little guy,' his father whispered, and she had a sudden vision of Rayne on the sideline of a tiny tots soccer game, being the dad yelling, 'Go, son!'

'Do you like Connor as his name?'

Rayne looked at her. Grinned. 'Spelt with two ns.'

'Lord, yes. As much as I like the Irish version of Conor, this child will not go through life having to spell his name, like I did.'

'Or have people say "Rain, as in wet?"'

'I was teasing.'

'Beautifully.' He leaned across and kissed her and in that moment her world was complete. 'I think he looks very much like a Connor.'

'You can choose the second name.' She saw his face shutter. Felt the withdrawal.

'I didn't do enough to warrant that privilege.'

She felt the slap of reality right when she didn't want to. Acknowledged he was feeling inadequate, and maybe even vulnerable at the moment but, hey, she was the one with no clothes and had exposed herself to the world. She narrowed her eyes at him. 'Then try harder.'

She searched in her mind for a way to make him see

that unless he wanted to, they would never lose him. 'Besides, he's going to cost you a fortune.'

He grinned and she saw the tension fall from his shoulders. Saw his look at her and the comprehension of how adroitly she'd manoeuvred him. Given him something he really could do, regardless of his parenting skills. His smile had a touch of the old bad-boy Rayne who'd been missing for the last few hours. 'In that case, how about the middle name of Sunshine?'

She knew he was kidding. She hoped he was kidding. 'Is that Sunshine from Rayne?'

Just then Connor found the nipple, poked out his tongue, opened his mouth wide and swooped. On! And didn't let go. Maeve gasped and smiled. 'That feels really weird.'

Rayne sat back in wonder. Tara leaned in from passing by and nodded. 'Good work, young man.'

'Connor.'

'Nice name. Welcome, Connor.' And she smiled at them both.

'Connor Sunshine.'

'Really?' She grinned at Maeve, who glared briefly at Rayne before looking back at her son. 'Awesome.' Then Tara had a brief feel of Maeve's belly, to check her uterus was contracting, gave it a little rub, then went back to sorting the room and writing the notes.

'You should've seen your face.'

But Maeve had moved on. Was gazing down at her son, whose jaw was working peacefully, his hands each side of his mouth, fingers digging into her breast every now and then. And all the while his big dark eyes stared up into her face. A swell of love came out of nowhere. Like a rush of heat. Her baby. She would protect this tiny scrap of humanity with her last breath.

'He's incredible,' she whispered, and all joking disappeared as they both watched him.

The next fifteen minutes were very peaceful. They didn't talk much, mostly just stared, bemused at the new person who had entered their lives and would change them as people for ever.

Until Maeve felt the first wave of dizziness and realised the wetness beneath her was spreading and she was beginning to feel faint.

Rayne watched the downy jaw go up and down on Maeve's breast and marvelled at the dark eyes watching his mother. He could feel his heart thawing and it wasn't comfortable. Maeve had had his baby.

He thought about the last twenty-four hours. Driving to Lyrebird Lake, not knowing if she would see him. Or knowing if that powerful current between them from the night so long ago had been real or instigated by the events that he'd known would follow.

Then seeing her this morning, pregnant, catching her as she'd fallen, daring to calculate on the slightest chance it could possibly be his child when Maeve should never have conceived. His fierce exultation that had drowned out his shock.

The swell of emotion was almost a physical pain in his chest as he went over the last tumultuous few hours of labour and finally the birth. Now here he was. A father with his son. A helpless newborn with him as a father. At least Connor had a father.

'Take him, Rayne.'

'He's still drinking.' Rayne was glued to the spectacle but something in her voice arrested him.

'Started bleeding,' she said faintly. 'Get Tara.' Her eyes rolled back, and she fainted like she had when he'd first seen her, only this time he caught his son.

Rayne's heart rate doubled. 'Tara!' Hell. He scooped Connor off his mother's chest as Maeve's arms fell slack, wrapped him in the bunny rug that had covered them both under the big blanket and hugged him to his chest as he leaned over Maeve.

Connor bellowed his displeasure at being lifted off his mother and automatically he patted his bottom through the rug.

Tara scooted back to the bed from her little writing table in the corner, lifted the sheet and sucked in a breath at the spreading stain on the sheets that just then flowed down the sides of the bed. 'Hit that red button over there for help and grab the IV trolley. We'll need to insert cannulas.' He saw her slide her hand over Maeve's soft belly, cup the top of her uterus through the abdominal wall and begin to rub strongly in a circular motion as he forced himself to turn away and do what needed to be done.

Once he'd pushed the emergency bell, he strode into

the treatment room he'd cased earlier and grabbed the
IV trolley and pushed it back towards the bed, not as
fast as he'd have liked because it was awkward with his
son tucked like a little football against his chest. Connor had stopped crying and when Rayne glanced down
at him his dark eyes were wide and staring.

Put the cannulas in. That he could do. He glanced
around for somewhere to put Connor. Saw the little
crib and tucked him in quickly. Connor started to cry.

'Sorry, mate.' He could find and secure veins on tiny
infants so he should be able to do it on someone bigger.
Someone he couldn't afford to lose.

'What size cannulas do you want?'

'Sixteen gauge. Two.'

Right. Found the size, the tourniquet, the antiseptic.
Saw the tubes for blood tests. 'Which bloods?'

Another midwife hurried in after him and Tara
glanced up and spoke to her. 'Get Angus back here
first, then lower the bedhead so she's tipped down, give
her oxygen, then draw me up a repeat ten units of syn-
tocinon. Obs we'll get when we get a chance.'

Tara hadn't taken her hand off the uterus and the flow
had slowed to a trickle but the loss from just those few
minutes of a relaxed uterus had astounded Rayne with
its ferocity. At least two litres had pooled in the bed.

She turned to him. 'Purple times two, one orange
and one blue. Coags, full blood count, four units cross-
match.'

'Angus is on his way,' the other midwife said, as
she lowered the bed and slipped the oxygen mask onto

Maeve's white face. 'Just some oxygen, Maeve.' The girl spoke loudly and as he withdrew the blood for the tests he realised Maeve might be able to hear.

'Hang in there, Maeve. Don't be scared. We'll get it sorted.' Incredibly his voice sounded confident and calm. Not how he was feeling on the inside. He wondered if Tara was as calm as she seemed.

Angus hurried in. Took over from Tara down the business end, checking swiftly to see if there was any damage they'd missed, but the sheer volume and speed of the loss indicated a uterus that wasn't clamping down on those powerful arteries that had sustained the pregnancy. Tara began assembling IV lines and drugs. She gave one bag of plain fluids to him and he connected and secured it. Rayne turned the flow rate to full-bore volume replacement until they could get blood.

An orderly arrived and the nursing supervisor who carried the emergency record started writing down times and drugs as she listened to Tara who spoke as she sorted the emergency kit.

The second midwife was writing Maeve's name on the blood-test tubes. When she was finished she wrote out a request form and sent the samples on their way. Then she hooked Maeve up to the monitor and they all glanced across at the rapid heartbeats shooting across the screen in frantic blips. Her blood pressure wasn't too bad yet but he knew birthing women could sustain that until it fell in a sudden plunge. His neck prickled in the first premonition of disaster.

Angus looked up at the second orderly. 'Bring back two units of O-neg blood. We'll give those until we can cross-match.'

'I'm O-neg if you need more.' Blood. She needed blood, Rayne thought, and wondered how often this happened for them all to be so smooth at the procedures. He glanced at Maeve's face as she moaned and began to stir with the increase in blood flowing to her brain from the head-down position change.

He wanted to go to her but Tara handed him the second flask loaded with the drugs to contract the uterus. 'Run it at two hundred and fifty mils an hour,' she murmured, and he nodded, connected it and set the rate. Then stood back out of the way. The whole scene was surreal. One moment he had been soaking in magic and the next terror had been gripping his throat as Maeve's life force had been seeping away.

'Given ergot yet?' Angus was calm.

'No. But it's coming.' Tara was drawing up more drugs. Rayne's legs felt weak and he glanced across at Connor roaring in his cot. He picked him up and the little boy immediately settled. He hugged his son to him.

'You okay?' Angus looked at him.

No, he wasn't, but it wasn't about him. He crossed to sit back in the chair beside Maeve's head so he could talk to her as she stirred. They didn't need him staring like a fool and fainting, with his son in his arms. Couldn't imagine how frightening this would be for her. 'It's okay, sweetheart. Just rest. Angus is here.'

Her eyelids flickered and for a brief moment she looked at him before her eyelids fell again. 'Okay,' she breathed.

He looked at Angus. 'Why is she still bleeding?'

'Might be an extra lobe of placenta she grew that we missed.' Angus was massaging the uterus through Maeve's belly like Tara had been doing. 'Or could just be a lazy uterus. Or could be a tear somewhere. We'll try the drugs but if it doesn't settle, because of the amount of loss, we'll have to take her to Theatre.'

Angus glanced at the nursing supervisor. 'Call Ben and Andy, clue them in, and have operating staff standing by. We can always send them home.'

Nobody mentioned it was early Boxing Day morning. The supervisor nodded and picked up the phone. 'And phone Simon,' Angus said, with a quick glance at Rayne. 'We'll need his consent.'

Consent for what? Operating theatres? He could give that consent. No, he couldn't. He had no legal claim on Maeve or his son. He had nothing except Maeve's permission to be here. He was no one. Shook himself with contempt. It wasn't about him.

And what would they do? But he knew. They would do what they needed to do to save her life. And if Maeve could never have children again? He thought of the powerful woman who had majestically navigated the birth process with gusto. Imagined her distress if the chance would never be hers again.

He imagined Maeve dying and reared back from

the thought. They would get through it. She had to get through it.

'She's started to bleed again,' Angus said to Tara. 'Get me the F2 alpha and I'll inject it into her uterus.' To the other midwife, he said, 'Check the catheter isn't blocked and I'll compress the uterus with my hands until we can get to the OR.'

The next two hours were the worst in Rayne's life. Worse than when they'd come for him in Simon's house and he'd seen Maeve's distress, worse than when he'd been sentenced to prison, worse than when he'd found out his mother had died.

Maeve went in and for a long time nobody came out. Simon sat beside him in the homey little waiting room that was like no other waiting room he'd ever seen.

It had a big stone water cooler and real glasses to drink from. A kettle and little fridge to put real milk in your tea and a big jar of home-made oatmeal biscuits. And a comfortable lounge that he couldn't sit on.

He paced. Connor didn't seem to mind because he slept through it in his bunny rug. Rayne couldn't put him down. Not because Connor cried but because Rayne couldn't bear to have empty arms while he waited for Maeve to come through those doors.

'Do you want me to take Connor?'

'No!' He didn't even think about it. Looked down at his son asleep against his chest. Doing at least something that he knew Maeve would like while he waited. 'What's taking them so long?'

'She'll go to Recovery when they've sorted everything. Then Dad will come through and talk to us. Or maybe Ben or Andy.'

'Are they good?'

'Superb.'

'I feel so useless. I worried about being a good enough father. That's nothing in the big picture.'

'It's not a nothing. But this is bigger. But you'll be fine. She'll be fine.'

Rayne heard the thread of doubt in Simon's voice and stopped. Looked at the man who would become his brother-in-law. Because he would marry Maeve. If she'd have him. He didn't deserve her. Would never have presumed to think she'd have him. But after this fear of losing her he'd take her faith in him and hold it and be the best dad a man could be. And the best husband.

Surely that would be the start of good enough?

He had a sudden vision of waking up in bed beside Maeve for every morning to come for the rest of his life. How the hell would he get out of bed?

But Simon. He'd forgotten that Maeve was the sister Simon was most protective about. How could he forget that in the circumstances? Because he needed to think of other people in his life now. He wasn't alone. He had Maeve, and Connor, and apparently a whole family or two. He glanced down at his son again and then at Simon.

He stopped where Simon was sitting. 'Can you hold him for a sec? My arm's gone to sleep.' It hadn't but he could see Simon needed something to hold as well. Tara was in the operating theatre with Maeve and she couldn't help him.

He watched his friend's face soften as he took the sleeping infant. Saw the tension loosen in the rigid shoulders. He missed the weight of Connor but was glad that Simon had him for the moment. Funny how a tiny helpless baby could help both of them to be stronger.

And then the doors opened and Angus came out. He looked at Simon first and then at Rayne.

'She had a spontaneous tear in her uterus. Probably a weakness in the muscle she was born with. It took a while to find it and she lost a lot of blood. But she's stable now.'

Rayne felt his body sag. Was actually glad that Simon held Connor.

'No more normal births for her. And a Caesarean in a bigger centre next time in case it does it again.'

So they had saved her uterus. Not bad for a tiny country hospital. 'So more blood transfusions?'

'And fresh frozen plasma and cryo. They'll need some of your blood over at the blood bank because we've used nearly all of theirs.'

It was the least he could do.

'Do we need to ship her out to a bigger hospital?' Simon had stood and his father was smiling at him with his nephew in his arms.

'I don't think so. And I would if I thought she needed to go. Would have spirited her there half an hour ago if I could have, but the crisis is past.' He grinned at Simon, who was swaying with the baby. 'Can't you men put that baby down?'

Rayne glanced at his friend. The relief was soaking in slowly. 'We're sharing the comfort. So she'll be fine?'

'She'll have to spend a few more days in hospital than she expected but she'll be spoiled rotten in Maternity.'

Rayne thought of going back to the manse without Maeve and Connor. 'Can I stay there, too? In the room with her and Connor? Help her with the baby?'

Angus raised his brows. 'Can't see any reason why not. Might mean that Tara will hand her over because she's not budging and I think she's nearly out on her feet.' He glanced at his son with a tired smile. 'Tara did a great job, Simon.'

So many amazing people here. So many he had to thank. Rayne stepped up to Angus and shook his hand. How could he ever repay them? 'Thank you. Thank the other guys.'

'We'll call in a favour if we need it.' Angus smiled.

Rayne looked at him. Saw a man who would be ruthless if he needed something for his little country hospital, and understood that. Smiled at it. Got the idea that resources could be hard to come by here when life threw a curve ball but those who had chosen to live here had saved his Maeve. They could have him any time they wanted.

He saw that he'd been accepted and was therefore fair game. He could deal with that. Thought for the first time about where Maeve might want to live and that, for the moment, if it was here he could cope with that.

Ten minutes later Simon took Tara home and Rayne carried Connor back to the room that would be Maeve's. The night midwife, Misty, took him through to the nursery and they finally got around to weighing Connor and giving him his needles, then she ran her hands all over him, checking that everything was fine.

She listened to his heart and handed the stethoscope to Rayne with a smile. 'Tara said you were a paed.'

Rayne listened. His son's heart sounded perfect. No valve murmurs. No clicks. He ran his own hands over him as if he were a baby he had been asked to check. But this wasn't a baby of some other lucky couple. This was his son. His hands stilled. This child depended on him for all the things his own father hadn't given him and he would deliver.

Misty handed him clothes and he looked at the tiny singlet. Thought of Maeve.

'Maeve's missing this. Wish she was here to share it.'

'Have you got your phone?'

He looked at her blankly. It wasn't like he could ring her. It must have shown on is face.

Misty laughed. 'You are tired. I can take photos of you dressing Connor and you can show her later.'

He shook his head. He should have thought of that. Handed her the phone in his pocket and Misty started snapping.

Rayne glanced at the sink as he lifted the singlet to stretch it widely over Connor's head. 'So when do we bath him?'

Misty shook her head. 'Not for twenty-four hours. He still smells like Mum and it helps him bond and feel secure and remember what to do when he goes for his next feed.'

Rayne vaguely remembered that from something Maeve had said, along with the skin to skin with Mum in the first hour.

Connor stared sleepily up at him as he dressed him. 'And what if he gets hungry before Maeve comes back?'

'He'll be fine. Tara said he fed well at birth. That's great. He could sleep up to twelve hours before he wakes up enough to feed again this first day. It's made such a difference letting them have that one long sleep after birth. Breastfed babies feed at least six to ten times a day and he'll catch up later.'

'I should know this stuff.' He shook his head. 'I've been out of it for nearly a year and in the States the doctors don't really discuss breastfeeding issues.'

She laughed. 'Everyone does everything here.'

He captured and pulled Connor's long fingers gently through the sleeve of the sleeping gown. All the experience came back as he turned the little boy over onto his front and tied the cords of his nightgown. Made him feel not so useless. He could do this for Maeve. He folded the gown back carefully so it wouldn't get damp if he wet his nappy. 'Don't you use disposable nappies here?'

'Not until after they do their first wee. Those new disposables are too efficient and it's hard to tell sometimes.'

'Fair enough.' He clicked the pin with satisfaction and tugged the secure nappy. Good job.

Misty nodded approvingly. 'You can even do a cloth and pin nappy without help. Not many dads could do that the first day.' The phone rang and she handed him a clean bunny rug. 'Excuse me.'

She poked her head back into the nursery. 'They're bringing Maeve back now.'

Rayne felt relief sweep over him as he wrapped Connor and put him snugly back into his little wheeled cot. Tucked him under the sheets so he didn't feel abandoned. His eyes were shut. Misty had put nappies and wipes and assorted linen under there in case he needed it in the room overnight and Rayne trundled the cot out the door and down the hallway, where two men were pushing a wheeled bed into the room.

His first sight of Maeve made him draw in his breath. She looked like Snow White, icily beautiful, but deeply asleep and as white as the sheets she lay on with her eyes shut. Her black hair made her look even paler and his heart clutched in shock. Unconsciously his hand went down until he was resting it on Connor's soft hair, as if he needed the touch of his son to stay calm.

She stirred as the bed stopped against the wall of the room. Blinked slowly and then she opened her eyes, focused and saw him. Licked her dry lips. Then softly, barely perceptibly, she murmured, 'Hi, there, Rayne.'

'Hi, there, Princess Maeve.' He pulled the cot up to the side of the bed. 'Your son is beautiful.'

'Our son,' she whispered.

'I love him already.' He didn't know where the words had come from but he realised it was somewhere so deep and definite in him that it resonated with truth and the smile on Maeve's face as she closed her eyes assured him it was the thing she most wanted to hear.

'Then I can leave him to you while I sleep.'

'I'm here. I'm not going anywhere.'

'Thank you.' And she breathed more deeply as she drifted back to sleep.

He watched her chest slowly rise and fall. Glanced at the blood running into a vein in her left arm and mentally thanked the donor who had provided it. Checked the drugs running into a right-arm vein. Watched Misty as she straightened the IV lines, the monitor leads and the automatic blood-pressure machine, set to record every half an hour, until they were all in a position she could glance at every time she came into the room.

Rayne shifted his intended chair slightly so he could see too. Frowned over the fact that Maeve's heart rate was still elevated, her blood pressure still low. But respirations were normal. And even as she slept just a tinge of colour was returning to her face.

He pushed Connor's cot quietly towards the big chair beside the bed and sank back into it. Then pulled the cot halfway between the bed and the chair so that either of them could stretch out their arm and could touch their son. Then he settled down to watch Maeve.

CHAPTER TEN

MAEVE WOKE AND the room was quiet. It was still dark through the windows outside and her belly felt like it was on fire. At first she thought Rayne was asleep but he shifted and sat straighter when he saw she was awake and she wondered vaguely if he'd been awake all this time. Watching over her. It was an incredible thought.

'Hi.' She couldn't keep a frown off her face.

'Pain not good?'

She decided shaking her head would be too much movement. 'Eight out of ten.'

He stood up. 'I'll get Misty.' Left the room in a few long strides and she tried to lessen the tension in her body. What the heck happened to her beautiful natural birth? And how had she ended up being sore both ends? Now, that sucked. Closed her eyes and decided to worry about it tomorrow.

Misty came back in with Rayne and brought some tablets and a bottle of water with a straw.

Rayne slid his arm under her shoulders and eased

her up so slowly and gently that it barely hurt to move. She swallowed the pills and savoured the water as it ran down her throat as he laid her down again.

Misty checked all her observations then Connor's, without rousing him, and then lifted the sheets and checked her wound and her bleeding and nodded with satisfaction at both. 'Looking beautiful.'

She heard Rayne, say, 'You midwives are weird.'

It would hurt to laugh. Misty laughed and left the room and Maeve smiled. She turned her head carefully and looked at Connor. Sleeping like a baby. Hugged that thought to herself then looked at Rayne, who was watching her. There was something different about him.

'You okay?'

He smiled and there was so much caring in the look he gave her that she felt herself become warm. 'I'm okay, as long as you are,' he said.

Meaning? 'Been a pretty torrid day?'

He stood up. Smiled down at her. Took her hand in his and turned it over. Careful of the IV lines, she thought. It was just a hand. Then he kissed her palm and it became a magic hand.

Then he said, 'A first for me as well. You scared the daylights out of me.'

Funnily, she hadn't been scared. 'I wasn't scared. You said not to be. Thank you for being there.'

He shook his head. 'Connor is amazing.' He looked towards the door. 'These people are amazing.' He glanced at her. 'You are beyond amazing.' Then he leaned down. Kissed her dry lips and tucked her in. 'Go back to sleep.'

When she woke in the morning Rayne was still there. His eyes were closed but for some reason she didn't think he was asleep. The drips had stopped feeding blood and had changed to clear fluid, so she guessed that was a good thing.

Connor was still sleeping. She reminded herself that babies could sleep up to ten or twelve hours after the first feed to get over the birth and she didn't need to feel guilty she hadn't fed him again. Remembered he'd probably make her pay for it later by feeding every time she wanted to put him back in his cot. Though she couldn't imagine wanting to put him back in his cot. It felt so long since she'd held him in her arms.

'Good morning.' Rayne's eyes were open. 'How do you feel?'

'I must look like a dishrag.'

'You look beautiful. A little pale and interesting as well.'

'At least I'm interesting.' She winced as she smiled too hard.

'I'll get Misty.' He left and came back with Misty, who was almost ready to hand her over to the morning staff.

So they repeated the whole Rayne lifting her, tablet taking, observation thing, and this time she didn't want to go back to sleep afterwards. She wanted to change out of her horrible gown and get into her nightie. Get up and shower, but she didn't think she'd be able to do it.

Could feel herself getting cross. 'Why don't you go back to the manse and have a sleep?'

Rayne lifted his brows and looked at her. Smiled. 'Later. When you have a wash, and get into your nightie, and have Connor's next feed. I don't know you well but I know you enough to see you want to be fresh, and hold your son, soon.'

He looked at her and shrugged. 'I want to help you, and help the midwife helping you, and I can be the muscle so you don't have to hurt yourself trying to do all those things.'

She looked at him. Flabbergasted. Was this guy for real? 'Aren't you tired?'

'No more than you. I'll sleep later.'

'I can't let you do that.'

Another enigmatic smile. 'You're not running this show, Princess Maeve. I am.'

Ooh. Bossy. She was too weak, and it was hard not to sort of like it. 'Then maybe later, if you're good, you can put me in the shower,' she said with a tired smile.

'I don't think you'll be up to a shower but we'll see.'

But she dug her heels in. 'I'm not being washed in bed like a baby.' They all looked at Rayne for help.

'Fine,' he said.

So they agreed on a compromise before Misty went off. Once Maeve's pain tablets had kicked in and she wasn't too sore, they disconnected her IVs for the few minutes it would take, and Rayne lifted her to the edge of the bed then carried her to the shower chair and the hand-held shower nozzle, and gently hosed her all over, washed her back and her legs, until she began to feel human again. Amazing what some hot water and a change of position could do.

Misty made her bed up with fresh sheets and plumped up her pillows so that when Rayne had helped her dry and dress again she could sink back and relax.

'I'm walking back to the bed under my own steam.' She glared at him. He held up his hands.

'Your call. I'm happy to watch.'

So she eased herself into a standing position, and it wasn't too bad now that she'd loosened up. She tentatively took a few steps, knowing there was no way he would let her fall because his arms were right behind her. Not a bad feeling to have.

She straightened up more and she felt tender, but okay. She could do this. She looked up at Rayne to poke out her tongue, but then a wave of faintness caught up with her.

He must have seen the colour drain from her face because he said, 'No, you don't.' Before it could get too disastrous she found herself back in her bed, with Misty pulling up the sheets and saying, 'Someone needs to tell you about the blood you lost last night.'

When the world stopped turning she looked up to see Rayne frowning darkly at her. She thought vaguely that he was still too damn good looking even when he frowned. 'You're a stubborn woman.'

But Misty smiled at her as she tucked the sheets in. 'Stubborn women are the best kind because they never give in.'

Rayne rolled his eyes. 'Another mad midwife saying.'

Five minutes later Connor made a little snorting noise, and they both turned their heads to see, watched him shift in his cot, blink and then open his eyes.

'He's awake.'

Rayne saw the longing on Maeve's face and was so glad he'd stayed for this.

'Good morning, young man. Your mother has been through a lot while she waited for you to wake up.' He reached down and untucked the sheets and opened the bunny rug. A black tar train wreck lay inside. Was even glad he'd stayed for this. He'd cleaned up enough dirty nappies in his time to make short work of even the biggest mess and it seemed his son had quite a capacity. Go you, son.

Connor grumbled but didn't cry, as if confident of the handling he was receiving.

Rayne looked across at the bed and Maeve was holding her stomach to stop herself laughing, and they grinned at each other in mutual parental pride. Then he pinned up the new nappy efficiently and lifted Connor away from his bunny rug in his hospital clothes so

Maeve could see his long legs and feet as he tucked him carefully in her arms.

Rayne watched her face soften and her mouth curve into such a smile, and the ball in his chest tightened and squeezed. This stuff had turned him into a wimp but he wouldn't have missed it for the world. He tucked a pillow under Maeve's arm so she didn't have to hold Connor's weight and watched as she loosened her neckline to lift out a breast.

Now, there was a sight he'd never tire of as Connor turned his head and poked out his tongue. Rayne put his hand under Connor's shoulders to help Maeve manoeuvre him closer until Connor opened his mouth, had a few practise attempts and then a big wide mouth and onto the breast. Just like that.

Maeve sighed and rested more comfortably back on the pillows, and Rayne sat back with wonder filling him until he thought he would burst.

My God.

How had this happened? Yesterday he had been lost, without purpose or future, a social misfit and almost-pariah, following his instinct towards a woman who so easily could have turned him away.

Now he had a family, Maeve and Connor and him—his family. And this morning he knew there would be battles of will, adjustments to make, discoveries and habits and ideas that might clash, but he could never doubt he had love for this incredible woman he had almost lost as soon as he'd found her, and that love would only grow bigger—probably daily. The future that was theirs stretched before them like a miracle. A Christmas miracle.

Rayne looked with wonder at the big country-style clock on the wall and watched the hand click over to six-thirty a.m. Exactly twenty-four hours since his car had rolled down the street and swerved towards the woman he'd been searching for as she'd walked towards him.

'Rayne?' Maeve's voice was softly concerned. 'You okay?'

He shook his head. The room was blurry. Stood up and stepped in close to the bed, leant down and slid his arm around the two of them and gently rested his cheek on Maeve's hair. He'd just discovered that she made him feel brand new. That he could do anything. And he most certainly was the only man for this job of looking after his family. 'I need to hug the most important two people in my life.'

She rested back into his arms with a contented sigh. 'Feel free any time.'

Over the next day there were a lot of firsts.

Connor's first bath, a joyous occasion where Maeve sat like a princess packed up in pillows and watched while Rayne deftly floated and massaged and swirled his son around like he'd been doing it for years.

'You're so good at that,' Maeve said approvingly. 'Still, I always tell the mums it's nice to shower with your baby. One of the parents undresses and hands baby in to go skin to skin with the person in the shower and the other—that will be you Rayne.' She grinned up at him. 'You lost. You just get to take him back and dry and dress him while I have the fun part.'

Rayne grinned. 'Poor me. I have to watch the naked lady with the awesome breasts in the shower with my baby.' Maeve held her tummy and tried not to laugh.

Then came the visitors with hugs and kisses of relief.

Also along came things for Connor. His first knitted set of bonnet, booties, cardigan and shawl all lovingly created by his step-great-grandmother, Louisa, who also brought food just in case the hospital ran out.

His first pair of tiny jeans and black T-shirt to match his dad's, from Uncle Simon and Tara.

Goodness knew where he'd got it from, because he'd barely left her side, but Rayne produced a bright yellow rubber duck for Connor's bath because his mother loved ducks.

Tiny booties shaped like soccer boots with knitted bumps for spikes from Mia and the girls at morning teatime and a welcome-baby card that had a three-dimensional baby actually swinging in a seat from a tree that the girls had fallen in love with.

But the excitement all took its toll.

'You look exhausted. Enough. I'll go back to the manse and you sleep.' Rayne stood up.

It was lunchtime, and Maeve was ready for a sleep.

Rayne kissed her. 'I'll come back any time you need me. If you want to get out of bed or Connor is unsettled and you want someone to nurse him, I'm the man. Ring me.' He looked at her. 'Promise.'

'Bossy.'

'Please.'

'Okay.' Not a bad back-up plan. She watched him go with a prickle of weak tears in her eyes and sighed into the bed.

'He did well,' Tara said, as she closed the blinds of the room.

'He did amazingly.'

'You did amazingly. But I agree with you and with him. It's time for sleep.' She checked Connor was fast asleep after his feed and quietly backed out.

As the door shut Maeve relaxed back into the bed and glanced at her downy-cheeked son. It had happened. She couldn't tell if he looked like either of them because now he looked like her darling baby Connor.

The whole labour and birth were over. And the next stage was just beginning.

The beginning of shared parenthood with a man she knew she loved. She didn't know if Rayne felt the same, but she was too tired and tender to worry about that now. That he was here was enough.

Rayne's solid support had been a thousand times stronger than she'd dared to hope for, his pre-birth nerves were a precious memory to keep and maybe occasionally tease him about, and she could see that Rayne would take his responsibilities to Connor and to her very seriously.

Lying in Rayne's arms yesterday seemed so far away in time with what had happened since then but as she drifted off to sleep she knew there was so much they could build on. She just needed to be patient, she thought with sleepy smile on her face, and trust in Rayne.

CHAPTER ELEVEN

FOUR DAYS LATER Maeve went home with Connor and Rayne— her family. Home being to the manse and the fabulous cooking of Louisa, who had decided the new mother needed feeding up.

Rayne, being fed three meals a day at least, was chopping wood at an alarming rate to try and keep his weight down from Louisa's cooking.

Simon went back to Sydney for work and planned to return each alternate weekend, and Tara was going to fly down to Sydney on the other weekends until their wedding in four weeks' time.

Selfishly, Maeve was glad that Tara had stayed with them, instead of following Simon to Sydney, and with Rayne booked to do the occasional shift over in the hospital on call, she had ample back-up help with Tara and, of course, Louisa, who was in seventh heaven with a baby in the house.

They'd shifted Connor into Rayne's room with the connecting door open and Rayne bounced out of their bed to change and bring Connor to her through the night.

Life took on a rosy glow of contentment as she and Rayne and Connor grew to be a family. The joy of waking in the morning in Rayne's tender arms, the wonder on his face when he looked at her with Connor, the gradual healing of her body, the steady increase of confidence in breastfeeding, managing Connor's moods and signs of tiredness, and the ability to hand him to his father's outstretched hands all gelled. Life was wonderful.

Her brother's wedding approached and their mother was coming. It was four weeks after the birth of Connor and Maeve was suddenly nervous.

Rayne decided Maeve had been twitchy all morning. Her mother was due to arrive along with Maeve's three older sisters. He'd seen her change her clothes four times and Connor's jumpsuit twice before the expected event.

On arrival her mother kissed Maeve's cheek and an awkward few moments had passed right at the beginning when she looked Rayne over with a sigh and then stepped forward and shook his hand.

'Hello, Rayne. Maeve said you were very good when Connor was born.'

So this was what Maeve would look like when she was older. Stunning, sophisticated and polished, though Desiree was blonde, perhaps not naturally because she had dark eyebrows, but a very successful-looking blonde.

He glanced at Maeve and the woman holding his

son had it all over her mum for warmth. 'It was Maeve who was amazing.'

A cool smile. 'I'm glad she's happy.'

'So am I.' Which left what either of them really meant open to interpretation.

Maeve broke into the conversation. 'You remember my sisters, Ellen, Claire and Stephanie.'

'Ladies.' He smiled at the three women, who were cooing at Connor.

Maeve hung onto his hand and Connor was unusually unsettled, probably receptive to the vibes his mother was giving off.

Luckily Desiree was swept up into the final wedding preparations and they all managed to ease back on the tension for the rest of the afternoon.

The next day Simon and Tara's wedding was held in the little local church and most of the town had come to celebrate with them.

It was a simple and incredibly romantic celebration. The church ladies had excelled themselves with floral decorations. Tara looked like the fairy on top of the cake, thanks to the absolute delight Mia, Simon's stepmother, had taken in spoiling her, and beside him, Simon nearly cried in the church when she entered.

A big lump had come to Rayne's throat when he thought about his friend finding such happiness and he couldn't help his glance past the bride and groom to the chief bridesmaid, his Maeve, who looked incredible in the simple blue gown Tara had chosen for her attendants.

Except for the divine cleavage, nobody would suspect Maeve had recently given birth, because she'd returned to her pre-pregnancy size almost immediately.

As Rayne listened to the words of the priest the certainty inside him grew that he could answer yes to all of it.

By the time Simon and Tara were married all he wanted to do was hold Maeve in his arms and tell her he loved her.

But he would have to wait.

The reception was a huge outdoor picnic, all the speeches a success, and the ecstatically happy couple finally left for their honeymoon in Hawaii and would then fly on to Boston, where Maeve's father waited to meet his stepson's new wife.

Back at the manse after the wedding Rayne needed a beer and a bloke to drink with, because the only sane woman was Louisa, who kept feeding him.

Maeve still hadn't settled, though she seemed to stress more than anything about Connor being even a little upset, which was strange when before she'd sailed along blithely and just enjoyed him. The help from her mother wasn't doing its job.

Rayne decided he would survive until Maeve's mother left. He'd lived with worse people and his lips twitched. Could just imagine Maeve's mother's downturned mouth if she knew he was comparing her to a cellmate.

'There you are, Rayne.' The object of his thoughts appeared and he plastered a smile on his face.

'Connor is crying and Maeve asked for you. Though I can't see what you can do that I can't.'

'Thank you.' Excellent reason to escape. 'The wedding was great but I think everyone is tired now. I'd better go and see.'

When he gently opened the door to their room he found Maeve with tears trickling down her face as Connor screamed and kicked and fought the breast.

'Hey, Connor, what are you doing to your poor mum?'

Maeve looked up tragically and he crossed the room to sit beside her on the bed. He dropped a kiss on her head. 'He won't feed. And Mum keeps telling me to put him on the bottle.'

'Bless her,' Rayne said, tongue-in-cheek and Maeve's eyes flew to his, ready to hotly dispute that, until she saw his smile.

Her own smile, while still watery, gradually appeared. 'She makes me crazy.'

'Really? I hadn't noticed.' He leaned forward, kissed her, remembered again how each day he felt more blessed, and took the unsettled Connor from her. Tucked him over his shoulder and patted his bottom. 'It's been a big day. And you've been busy making sure Tara had a fabulous time so you've run yourself into the ground. Why don't I take Connor for a drive and you can have a rest before tea?'

'No, thanks.'

Maeve looked even sadder and he frowned. 'What?'

'Can't I come with you both?'

He grinned. 'You mean escape? And leave your mother here without us?'

Maeve looked guilty at the disloyal idea. 'She means well.'

'I know. Maybe we could get Louisa to look after her. Your mum's probably tired too. It's a long flight and she only got here yesterday.' He had a vision. One that he'd been building up to for days now but had wanted to leave until after the wedding. 'I'd really like to take Connor to the duck pond. Would you like to come with us for an hour until sunset?'

Maeve nodded, looked brighter already, so he left her to get ready, and sought out Louisa first, begged a favour he promised to repay, then found Maeve's mother.

Gently does it, he warned himself. 'What do you think if I take Connor for a little drive. Just to get him asleep in the car?'

A judicious nod from the dragon. 'That's an excellent idea.'

Now for the smooth part. 'Maeve wants to come but she feels bad about leaving you on your own.' Desiree opened her mouth but before she could invite herself he said, 'But I see Louisa had just made you a lovely afternoon tea and is dying to have a good chat with you. What would you like to do?' Opened his eyes wide.

Desiree slid gracefully into the trap and relief expanded in his gut. 'Oh. Poor Louisa. It would be rude not to stay for that. Of course.' She looked pleased. 'How thoughtful. She really is a lovely woman.'

'One of my favourite people.' And wasn't that true. Then he escaped to his family and bundled them into the car.

Ten minutes later Maeve sat on the bench in front of the lake, holding Connor in the crook of her arm. Their son had decided he preferred to feed alfresco and was very happily feeding. Every now and then Maeve would throw breadcrumbs to the ducks with her free hand.

Rayne stood behind her, gently rubbing her shoulders. They both had smiles on their faces.

Maeve said, 'I don't think I could bear to lose a man who rubs my shoulders like you do.'

Rayne felt the happiness expand inside him. 'Does this mean you want me to stay?'

She twisted her neck to look at him and pretended to consider it judiciously. 'Yes, I think so.'

Rayne had waited for just this opening and unfortunately in the euphoria of successful strategies he rushed it. 'Only if you'll marry me.' The words were out before he could stop them and he cursed his inability to be smooth and romantic when she deserved it all. He'd done everything the wrong way around here.

She opened her mouth to reply and quickly he moved around to face her and held up his finger. 'Wait.'

'So bossy,' she murmured, and he smiled as he went

down on one knee beside her—right there in front of the ducks.

'Please. Wait for me to do it properly.' He took her free hand in his, brushed the crumbs off it and kissed her fingers. Maeve leant back against the bench and Connor ignored them both as he continued with his afternoon tea.

Rayne drew a deep breath and let it go. Let everything go, let the past, the mistakes and the pain and uncertainty all go so they could start fresh and new and perfect. Because the three of them deserved it. 'My darling, gorgeous, sexy…' he paused, smiled at her '…impossible Maeve—'

Before he could finish she'd interrupted. 'Impossible?'

'Shh.' He frowned at her and she closed her mouth. 'Darling Maeve—' and he couldn't keep the smile off his face '—will you do me the honour, please, of becoming my wife and share with me the rest of my life?'

Her face glowed at him, a trace of pink dusting the high cheekbones that were still far too pale. 'Now, that, as a proposal of marriage, was worth waiting for.'

'An answer would be good. Come on.'

She teased him. 'My darling, strong, sexy as all get out Rayne.' Leaned forward and kissed him while he knelt before her. Connor still ignored them both. 'Yes. Please. Pretty please. I would love to be your wife and share your life.'

His relief expanded and he squeezed her hand. 'You won't regret it.'

Her face softened. 'I know I won't. But my mother wants a big wedding.'

He smiled. He could do that. It was a small price to pay for the world he now had. 'I thought she might. As long as Connor is pageboy and you are my bride, I will agree to anything.' He stood up and hugged her gently again and smiled into her hair. 'It's not going to be dull.'

A month later Maeve woke on the morning of her wedding in her parents' house huge in Boston. Down the hall Tara was sleeping without her new husband because Simon had gone to support Rayne on the night before his wedding. She wished she'd been able to stay with Rayne but they would never have got that past her mother.

Connor stirred beside her and she sat up with a warm feeling of relief in her stomach and reached for him. Rayne would be missing Connor and her as much as they missed him.

How could life change so dramatically in just two months? The answer was simple. Rayne loved her. Which was lucky because her mother had put them all through hoops as she married the first of her daughters off in the grand fashion.

There had been family dinners at exclusive restaurants, wedding breakfasts under the marquee in the back garden, and bridal teas with all the local ladies, as well as bridal showers and multiple rehearsals and today, finally, the wedding of the year.

Maeve had always wanted a big wedding, the chance to be the big star, but funnily enough now that it was here she knew she would have been happy with a two-line agreement in front of a celebrant as long as she was married to Rayne.

Her mother wouldn't have been happy, though, and it was good to see Desiree finally pleased with her. But today she would marry Rayne, they would pack up and leave on their honeymoon then head back to Lyrebird Lake, and Maeve couldn't wait.

Her husband-to-be had been amazing. Patient. Comforting when she'd become stressed, loving when she'd least expected it but had secretly needed that reassurance, and always so brilliantly patient and capable with Connor—and her mother.

When she thought about it, Rayne had learnt to be patient with mothers very early in his life and he was showing his skills now.

Her over-achieving sisters were here and she realised she'd finally grown out of worrying that about a hundred relatives were scattered in nearby hotels. She and Rayne and Connor were united in the birth of their family and their future and she couldn't wait.

Eight hours later Rayne stood beside Simon, this time as the groom and Simon the best man, and Rayne's hands were just slightly shaking.

In Boston, their bigger than *Ben Hur* wedding that Maeve's mother had organised had seemed to never get any closer.

But finally, today, it would happen. Their family would officially be joined forever. Maeve was putting so much trust in him he felt humbled, and before God, and before the ceremony even started, he silently vowed he would never let her down.

The music started, the congregation stood, and then she was there. A heartbeat, a shaft of divine light, and she appeared. Standing at the end of that very long, very floral-bouqueted aisle, with her father beside her and a huge church full of people to witness them being bound together.

Maeve's next older sister, the first bridesmaid, was almost up to them, coming closer with stately precision, Connor in her arms in his tiny suit, because that was the only thing Rayne had insisted on.

Then the second sister, and then the third, and then... Maeve. Sweeping down the aisle towards him, way too fast. To hell with the slow walk, he didn't bother to look for her mother's frown at the break in protocol, just grinned at her and held out his hand. He loved this woman so much.

The mass began and he missed most of it as he stared at the vision beside him. Remembered the last two months, the joy he'd found, the deep well of love he hadn't realised he'd had to give.

'Do you take this woman...?'

Hell, yes! He remembered to let the reverend finish. More waiting until finally he could say, 'I will.'

'Do you, Maeve, take this man…?'

The words drifted as he stared again into her eyes. Those eloquent eyes that said he was her hero, always would be, that she believed in him so much and loved him. What more could a man want?

Then she said, 'I will.' That was what he wanted!

'With the power vested in me and before this congregation I now declare you man and wife…' And it was done. Rayne lifted the veil, stared into her tear-filled eyes and kissed his wife with all the love in his heart in the salute.

Maeve clutched her husband's hand and couldn't help the huge smile on her face. The cameras were flashing, she was moving and signing and smiling, and all the time Rayne was beside her. Protecting her, loving her, and finally reaching out to take Connor from her sister so that he carried their son and it was time for the three of them to walk back up the aisle as a family.

Maeve met Rayne's eyes, saw the love and knew this was the start of an incredible life with the man she had always loved. She couldn't wait.

* * * * *

MILLS & BOON®

Exciting new titles
coming next month

With over 100 new titles available every month,
find out what exciting romances
lie ahead next month.

Visit
www.millsandboon.co.uk/comingsoon
to find out more!